Steeped

to

Death

Steeped

to

Death

A WITCHES' BREW MYSTERY

Gretchen Rue

NEW YORK

Published in the United States by Crooked Lane Books, an imprint of The Quick Brown Fox & Company LLC.

Crooked Lane Books and its logo are trademarks of The Quick Brown Fox & Company LLC.

Library of Congress Catalog-in-Publication data available upon request.

ISBN (hardcover): 978-1-63910-164-1
ISBN (ebook): 978-1-63910-165-8

Cover illustration by Mary Ann Lasher

Printed in the United States.

www.crookedlanebooks.com

Crooked Lane Books
34 West 27th St., 10th Floor
New York, NY 10001

First Edition: September 2022

10 9 8 7 6 5 4 3 2 1

To Nutmeg, my soul cat, you make every day a little brighter and better.

Chapter One

The gas gauge on my car was so far past the "E" that it was trembling into the black no man's land beyond the red line. As I pulled up in front of a familiar old Victorian mansion, the car gave a shudder, a sputter, and then died with one final sigh.

"You have arrived at your destination," my GPS assistant announced.

"Yes, thank you. Of course, you said it would only be a two-hour drive, so I planned my gas accordingly. You lied." I pulled my phone off the dash and slipped it into my purse before looking up at the old house.

It was pretty hard to be mad at the GPS when I should have known better myself. After all, it was hardly the first time I'd driven to Raven Creek, but I'd second-guessed myself after being gone for almost ten years, and decided to trust technology over my own memory.

My memory had no problem recalling the big house or the time I'd spent there. It looked ever so slightly worse for wear since my last visit, but it was still a beautiful ode to a time when houses had their own unique personality rather than being cardboard cutouts where every house on a block looked exactly the same but in a different shade of taupe.

The old house was like something a child might have imagined while building a gingerbread mansion, with asymmetrical detailing that saw towers and turrets at its corners and stunning candy-colored stained glass in almost every window. The pale blue paint on the exterior had started to look gray with age, but the house was still as charming and inviting as ever.

I pushed open the wrought iron gate that had a plaque with the letter "B" embossed on it and hauled my suitcase up the walkway.

The mansion was situated on a hill, giving it an incredible view over the town but also leading a lot of local children to believe it was either haunted or owned by a wicked witch.

It definitely wasn't haunted, and I can say with complete certainty my Auntie Eudora wasn't terribly wicked unless she wanted to be. As I hefted my suitcase up the front steps, already out of breath from the incline, a plump orange cat emerged from around the back of the wrap-around porch and settled himself in on top of the welcome mat, blinking up at me with huge green eyes.

"Hello," I greeted him. It had been years since Auntie Eudora had had a cat, and he'd been a skinny black thing that moved around her house like he was made out of shadows. I didn't recognize this handsome fellow, but he seemed to be quite at home. I'd have to ask around later to see if he belonged to one of the neighbors, as he seemed pretty well fed.

"Mrow," he replied, blinking slowly.

"Don't suppose you want to go get one of the bags out of the car for me, do you?"

"Mrow." This sounded decidedly like a no. Go figure.

I fumbled through my coat pocket to find the thick envelope Eudora's lawyer had sent to me. In it was a copy of her will and all the essential information needed to sign over her worldly possessions to me, her brother's only daughter. I had an older brother, Sam, but he and Eudora had never had the same bond she and I did, not to mention he was happily married and living in Colorado, so Eudora must have known which of us needed the house more.

Inside the big envelope, along with paperwork, there was also a smaller envelope with strict instructions—in Eudora's writing—that I was not to open it until I arrived in Raven Creek.

I shook the big envelope, and out slid a heavy, ornate metal key. I made a mental note that as cool as the key was, and as safe as Raven Creek seemed to be, it might be high time to invest in a proper lock system for the old house.

I unlocked the door, and before I could set foot inside myself, the orange cat bolted in ahead of me without a moment's hesitation.

"Hey!"

He did not seem to care that I hadn't invited him.

I dropped my suitcase inside, and before letting myself get sucked into the memories of the place, I made three more trips back to the car to collect everything else I'd brought with me from Seattle. All the little pieces of my life had been few enough to fit in a Nissan Sentra. I wasn't sure if that was sad or a testament to my unintentionally minimalist lifestyle.

If I was a minimalist, then Auntie Eudora was a maximalist. By the time I got the last of my boxes inside and closed the front door, I needed to take a seat on the huge maple staircase in the front foyer, to catch my breath.

As I regretted hitting that fast food drive-thru for an extra-large coffee on my drive here, thanks to the extra anxiety and bonus need to find a restroom, I took in the familiar surroundings of my aunt's home. The walls were all painted in a soft pewter blue, with the original dark wood trim in every room. The lighter walls might have normally helped a room feel larger, but Eudora had covered almost every exposed inch with art. There were old portraits of people we weren't related to, ancient oil paintings of dogs and horses, of cunning black cats stealing food from banquet tables, and of gorgeous Renaissance women weeping in streams. There were animal bones hanging like streamers, loose bouquets of dried flowers, and framed butterflies wherever a gap in the art allowed for them.

Over the fireplace—a real, functional beast that faced into both the sitting room and the kitchen—was a tapestry, a copy of the famous *Unicorn in Captivity* piece. I could recall sitting in front of the fireplace for hours, staring up at the tapestry, imagining what might happen if someone simply opened the unicorn's gate.

The cat trundled into the room and sat down in front of me, his emerald eyes glinting like little jewels in the dim interior light.

"You seem pretty comfortable here, sir."

"Mrow."

I was beginning to suspect that Auntie Eudora might have found herself a new pet in her later years and simply forgotten to mention it. "Well, I'm going to have to figure out what to call you, I guess."

If he *was* her cat, someone had clearly been taking good care of him, because it had been six weeks since Eudora's passing, and he looked healthy and happy. Though there were plenty of mice around the property, and he could have just been feeding himself the whole time. Discovering whether he had been hers—and therefore was now mine—would have to wait a little while. For the present moment, I needed to focus on getting my things unpacked and airing out the house a little. It had developed a musty, unwelcoming scent, having been left empty for six weeks, and I knew Eudora would hate that. Her house always smelled of fresh herbs, cups of hot tea, melting candle wax, and unusual incenses.

Right now, it just smelled like dust.

I did a quick tour of the upper floors, trying to decide where to settle myself. Eudora was the type of person who had spent very little time in her bedroom, seeing sleep as a necessary evil that kept her functioning but wasn't something she enjoyed. Because of that, she had taken one of the house's smallest bedrooms as hers—I wouldn't want to take her space anyway.

The mansion had ten bedrooms in total, though many of them had been converted into spaces that housed all her plants. The houseplants, I noted, were also all in great shape, so someone must have been looking after the place before I got here, though Eudora's lawyer, Mr. Garland, hadn't mentioned anything.

After wandering for a little while, getting reacquainted with rooms I hadn't seen in a decade, I found the bedroom where my parents used to stay when we'd come to visit. It was a big room with a lovely four-post bed and a curving bay window that faced away from the town to overlook the woods, and the creek the town got its name from. I plopped down on the edge of the bed and was pleasantly surprised by how comfortable the mattress felt.

The room was homey and inviting, much like the rest of the house, and it didn't feel wrong to be in it. That was all I needed for a sign from my aunt that this was the right place for me. When I'd been younger, my brother and I used to come here every summer while my parents were busy with work. They couldn't afford to send us to camp, and Eudora had loved the company. We did that every year until I was fourteen, when my dad got a job in Chicago and we'd moved too far away for regular summer visits. Our trips to Raven Creek became few and far between as Eudora opted to come visit us once a year instead. I'd moved back to Washington with my husband, Blaine, shortly after we married, but in spite of how much closer I was to Raven Creek again, I found myself preoccupied with my job, my friends, and my marriage. Eudora made frequent trips into Seattle, so we remained incredibly close, even though it had been a decade since I'd slept in this house.

When I'd spent summers here as a child, I used to love staying in the attic in an old nursery, where I'd unroll a sleeping bag and sprawl my books and toys out all over the huge open space. Eudora would give me old rugs and blankets and help me build insane forts up there. But now, at thirty-five, I was pretty sure my back and hips would protest if I slept on the floor.

I returned to the main floor, collected a couple of my bags, and began the process of getting unpacked. As I hung my clothes up in my new closet, I stared at the small white envelope I had left at the end of the bed. On the outside, in Eudora's crisp writing, it said, *To Phoebe, to be opened on her first night at Lane End House.*

The name Lane End House had always amused me. It was so literal, since the mansion was at the end of the main street in the town. Didn't grand old mansions usually have more interesting or compelling names?

But no, Lane End House it was, and had been since my great-great-great-great-grandfather had built it almost two hundred years earlier. There was something a little grim about the name too. Lane End House, like End of the Road House. As if when you got here, you knew this was going to be your last stop.

I smiled. Eudora would love that macabre thought. She adored it when children would whisper to themselves about the haunted house and the witch who lived there. She loved to be part of a legend, something bigger than herself, even if it meant the local kids thought she was going to turn them into toads, or something.

I finished putting away my clothes, picked up the letter, and headed down to the kitchen. If there was anywhere in the house to read Eudora's last words to me, it was in the kitchen.

Chapter Two

The orange cat followed me into the kitchen, where he found a large pillow on the hearth of the fireplace and settled in quite comfortably, blinking slowly several times before resting his head on his paws and settling into a doze.

Definitely Eudora's cat, then.

An old silver kettle sat on the stovetop as if it was waiting for me, an invitation from my late aunt to make myself a cup of tea. Tea was sort of Eudora's *thing*. She had fallen in love with the different types of tea she had experienced during a year-long trip through Asia, where she'd sampled various blends from India, China, and Japan, and when she got back home to the United States, she was fully and deeply obsessed with tea.

She spent the next decade traveling the world, sampling the best blends available from Europe, Asia, South America, and Africa, deciding what lesser-known teas might be popular locally and which unexpected types she might convince hesitant American clients to buy. She learned more about fruity herbal blends with cutesy gimmicks, like adding crushed candy canes to a peppermint tea, to give it an extra Christmassy punch.

After ten years of travel and education, she'd finally decided she was ready to open The Earl's Study. The local used bookstore in Raven Creek had come up for sale following the death of its long-time owner, and Eudora jumped at the opportunity. She kept the bookstore open, since it was her favorite place in town, and simply converted a cluttered storage space—which turned out to be as big as some of the smaller shops in town—into her tearoom.

That would be my first stop in the morning. The shop had been closed for six weeks since Eudora's death, but thanks to two of her most dedicated employees, Imogen and Daphne, had been running smoothly even as Eudora's health declined. She'd made sure their regular pay continued after she passed, as she must have known things might get messy and wanted to make sure they weren't left in a lurch. Now, technically, the shop—and all its debts or profits—belonged to me. Best to see where we stood, and reopen as soon as possible. Eudora always gave the implication business was profitable, but I had to wonder how well a used-book and tea shop really fared in a small town, even one as popular as Raven Creek.

Of course, being a tea enthusiast meant she needed to try everything out herself, first, and the open shelving in her kitchen was stocked to the rafters with jar after jar of beautiful loose leaf tea choices. There were metal canisters and glass jars, all with black chalkboard paint labels bearing her distinctive writing, explaining what was in each container.

I grabbed the one sitting next to the stove, marked "Lavender Jasmine" and opened the lid, letting the soothing scent of jasmine tea and dried lavender buds waft out at me. The loose tea had a sweet undertone to it, like vanilla, promising a cup that would be calming and the perfect thing to warm me up on a cool October evening.

I filled the kettle from the old country basin sink and set it on the stove to heat, then used a spoon dangling from one of the shelves to fill up a compostable teabag before setting that in a mug—waiting on the counter—to await the boiling water.

Funny, how everything I wanted or needed seemed to be ready for me on the counter, like Eudora had left it all out for me.

Funnier still that the mug seemed fresh and clean in spite of no one being here to drink from it in six weeks.

Once the water was boiled, I filled the cup and brought it over to the small kitchen table where Eudora's letter was waiting for me. Enough procrastination—it was time to see what she had to say. I'd been anticipating and dreading this moment since the lawyer had given me her effects. It wasn't that I was afraid she'd say anything nasty or the letter would upset me, but rather I knew once I read it that would really be it. These were her last words, and once they were read, I wouldn't get any others.

I'd loved my aunt as if she were a second mother. She was older than my father by ten years, making her almost grand-motherly to my young self, but the truth was she was more vivacious and alive than people half her age. A committed bachelorette, she had continued to take long trips around the world all by herself, even as she approached eighty. Now that I was in my thirties and divorced, I could certainly see the appeal in her embracing and glamorizing her spinster lifestyle.

Her loss had hit me hard, even though it hadn't come out of the blue. She'd found out about the tumor with enough time to get in a trip to Brazil before telling her family what was going on. She lived another six months after that, ample time to say goodbye, but not enough time in the least.

I wish I could have had decades more to learn from her—she had so much left to give, and I'd wasted so much time away. I hated that I had spent the last ten years living so close to her but not seizing the opportunity to come here.

I sighed and ripped open the envelope. A folded letter fell onto the table, as well as an old Polaroid photo. I flipped the photo over, and a smile came to my lips just as a tear came to my eye. It was Eudora and I at Disneyland. She'd insisted on taking me by myself—no parents or brother allowed. Sam was too old and too cool for "kid stuff" at that point—and footed the entire bill. We wore matching Minnie ears, posing in front of Sleeping Beauty's castle, grinning like absolute fools.

Touching the photo tenderly I mentally promised to get a frame for it as soon as the opportunity allowed.

The letter was next, and I took a deep breath before flattening it on the table. As I absorbed the words, I could almost hear her speaking them from the other room.

To my dearest Phoebe,

Did I ever tell you what your name means? I'm sure you must have looked it up at some point, what with the internet and all that silliness. But it means "bright" or "radiant one," and I think that's very suiting for you, because knowing you has brought such joy and light into my life. Phoebe was also a Titan, mightier than the gods, who was the grandmother of Artemis and Apollo. I believe you have the capacity for such greatness, though perhaps not birthing gods. We all have our limitations after all.

If you're reading this, then I'm afraid it means my time has come to an end, and while that seems so far from possible as I write this letter, I still know there is a small lump of cells at the base of my brain that has other plans for my life, and I won't be able to sneak my way out of this situation.

I've been very lucky in my life, perhaps too lucky, and that was bound to run out at some point, though I was sure my end would come hiking back up to the Everest Base Camp or trekking through Malawi. I had so many things left I wanted to see and do, but perhaps you may still have time to see and do them for me.

Of course, you know by now that I've left you everything except some money I put aside for Sam. You have always been the most important person in my life (don't tell your father—he'd be crushed), and with no children of my own, it seemed only fitting to give it all to you. The last time we spoke, you seemed at odds, not sure what to do with your future, and I told you that in time you'd get the answers you were looking for. What I didn't tell you then was that I hoped I'd be able to give you those answers, at least for the time being.

If you don't mind me telling you (and you can't be mad at me now that I'm dead—that's just how these things work), that stupid husband of yours never deserved you. Cheating with a waitress—honestly, what a cliché! He was boring and beneath *you on every level, and you're better off without him, if we're both being honest. You might not see it now—fresh wounds and whatnot—but in time you'll see it my way, I think.*

Truly, though, what kind of name was Blaine anyway?

I digress, I suppose. That's what happens when old ladies don't want to talk about death. But the house is yours. I'm sure you'll find plenty of hidden secrets in it that I've long forgotten myself, but don't let the children in town fool you—there aren't millions of dollars under the floorboards. There is a small Picasso in the upstairs bathroom, though, that might fetch a pretty penny if the need ever strikes.

On that end, with the exception of what I gave Sam, I've left you all my money, what there is of it, and the business, which I'm hoping you'll take on, though if you decide you don't want to run it, I'm sure Imogen will be happy to make you an offer. I do hope you will take it over, though, because Imogen would put cabbage flower wallpaper all over the place, and I would have to haunt her from beyond the grave. I don't particularly feel like doing any haunting, thank you.

No pressure.

It has been my greatest joy in life to be your aunt, and I hope that in my death I can make things just a little bit easier for you in what must feel like a difficult time. Trust me when I tell you, my dear one, the answers to everything are in the tea shop, even if you don't know how to ask the questions yet.

And if you stick around town, watch out for Deirdre Miller, that old cow is always up to no good. Would love to stick my undead foot right up her keister.

Much love to you, my darling. Now, always, forever. You've got this.

Eudora
P.S.—Please take good care of Bob, and don't trust him for a minute around a cheeseboard.

I set the letter down on the table, laughing at her last bit of wisdom and wiping tears from my eyes with the heel of my hand. I felt as if she were right next to me, but when I looked up, the table was empty.

Glancing over at the fireplace, I saw the cat lift his chin to observe me.

"I guess it's just you and me, Bob."

Chapter Three

A quick investigation of the kitchen told me that the first stop I made was going to have to be to a grocery store. There was a small bag of dry cat food under the counter, but only a single tin of wet food, and as far as a meal for a human being, well . . . there was the one tin of wet cat food. And a box of stale crackers.

I pulled on my jacket, pocketed the heavy house key, and grabbed my purse off the banister, where I'd left it. I was halfway to my car when I remembered the gas tank was running on fumes. It could probably coast into a gas station, but I wasn't actually sure where the nearest station was and didn't want to risk driving around town until my tank was completely and utterly empty.

It made more sense to walk to the grocery store, which I'd driven past on my way in, and ask them where to find a station. The nice thing about Lane End House was its place rather central to the main strip of shops in town. Everything I'd need on a regular basis—not to mention The Earl's Study—was all conveniently located in a one-mile stretch barely a five-minute walk from my own front door.

I locked the house and zipped up my coat against a growing October chill. The air tasted of campfire, and the cold felt wet. I was used to wet cold, coming from Seattle, but the first real chill of autumn was always an unexpected and rude surprise. I liked the colder months, but that didn't mean I was ever ready for them.

That big fireplace in the kitchen and living room was going to be a real treat when I got home. Mentally I thanked Eudora for leaving me enough wood that I wouldn't need to chop it myself any time soon.

Lost in thought, I'd wandered the handful of blocks from Lane End House to the main drag without passing a single other soul. Everyone else in town was smart enough to be home where it was warm. Glancing at my watch, I saw it was just after five, which meant it was starting to get dark, but also that I might run into whatever counted as an after-work rush in Raven Creek.

The grocery store, still a family-owned place called Lansing's, shone brightly in the growing gloom and, at a quick glance, appeared to be one of only a handful of shops still open on Main Street. If memory served, most places around here shuttered up for the night between five and six. Lansing's was the lone hold-out, staying open until eight on weekdays. Just my luck.

I blinked against the bright overhead lights inside and grabbed a cart, knowing I was going to need a fair number of things. Maybe if I was lucky, they wouldn't mind if I borrowed the cart to get my goods home, so I wouldn't need to try to drag a dozen bags home on each arm.

Soft muzak played a familiar pop song without lyrics, and I hummed along as I slowly moved through the produce section, filling my cart with aspirational fruits and vegetables. A new town meant a new start, and maybe I could pretend to be the kind of woman who liked salads and ate an apple every morning.

Just to be on the safe side, I would also grab some ice cream in the freezer section.

I was perusing a selection of cat food, trying to remember which brand Eudora had for Bob, when I felt the distinct sensation of someone watching me. I looked up from the Feline Frolic in my hand and locked eyes with a woman staring at me from the end of the aisle.

I looked over my shoulder to see if I might be mistaking her intended target, but there was no one else in the aisle with me. She saw me looking back in her direction, seemed to realize she'd been spotted, and hustled away quickly.

She hadn't been carrying a basket or pushing a cart.

A few minutes later my cart was full. Bob had a selection of dry and wet food, and I'd picked up a few new toys and treats to curry favor with my new roommate. As I unloaded the items at the cash register, the same unsettling feeling of being observed made the hair on the back of my neck stand up.

A quick peek over my shoulder confirmed that the same woman was staring at me again. She was in her fifties and tidily—if not fancily—dressed. Her brightly dyed red hair was pulled into a severe bun on the top of her head, and her tortoiseshell cat-eye glasses were about two sizes too big for her small head.

She was a dainty figure in general, maybe five foot two and a hundred pounds soaking wet. Yet the death glare she was giving me made me nervous enough I didn't feel like confronting her. I wasn't a local, but I wasn't sure why someone would have such an immediate distaste for an outsider. This was a tourist town, after all, and the townsfolk weren't unaccustomed to seeing new people on a regular basis.

I paid for my groceries quickly, but the prickly feeling of her gaze on my back never dissipated.

"Do you know where the closest gas station is?" I asked the checkout girl, whose name tag said "Chandra."

She gave me directions to a place barely three blocks away, much to my relief. I'd be able to coast over in the morning and fill up my tank.

"I know this is a weird request, but I didn't bring my car over—you know, no gas—and I'm hoping you won't mind if I borrow the cart?" Upon seeing her uncertain expression, I quickly added, "I just inherited Eudora Black's house. My aunt Eudora."

Chandra's face immediately brightened; then she seemed to think better of her enthusiasm, and she forced a quick frown. "Oh, you must be Phoebe. She talked about you so much. We just loved your aunt. She was in here all the time, of course, what with the shop just being down the street. Are you taking that over too?"

I nodded. "Yeah, I'll be over there tomorrow seeing what needs to be done. It hasn't been closed long, so I should be able to open up again in a day or two."

"Well, my sister Daphne worked there part time for Eudora. She's been helping Imogen, but since the shop closed I know she wasn't too sure if she'd be keeping her job since . . . well, since your aunt died. It was so wonderful of Eudora—and I guess you—to keep paying her while the shop is closed, but she still worries. I know she'd be happy to stay on if you're planning on opening it back up again. She loves working there so much and was really torn up about losing Eudora." Chandra scribbled Daphne's name and number on a Lansing's business card, which I accepted in spite of already having the information in an email from Imogen. "You go ahead and take the cart—just promise you'll bring it back, okay?"

"Of course."

By the time I finished chatting with Chandra, the petite redhead with the death stare was long gone.

Chapter Four

O f course, the moment you assume you can let your guard down is usually the precise moment you shouldn't. That was a universal truth I realized the moment I was a few steps away from the safe glow of Lansing's.

"What do you think you're doing?" a sharp, high voice asked from behind me.

I ignored it, continuing to push the cart up the slightly inclined hill leading back to my house. No need for cardio later because the glutes were going to be plenty worked out by the time I got back.

"I *said*, what are you doing?" the voice chirped again.

"I think what I'm doing is pretty obvious," I wheezed, already huffing from the exertion of the incline. It's easy to forget you live in the mountains until you need to push something uphill. Whoever was following me—and I was pretty sure I had a good idea who it was—didn't seem slowed down at all by the steep slog.

"You can't just *take* that cart."

"I can. I asked."

That seemed to throw her off, because she paused. Briefly, foolishly, I thought she might be done following me, but it appeared I wouldn't be so lucky. A moment passed, and then suddenly there was a tiny, red-headed woman standing in front of my cart, blocking my path. I wasn't sure how she'd moved so quickly or silently, but I was forced to come to a stop or risk running her over.

She gave me a full head-to-toe inspection and clearly didn't like what she saw, her lips forming a thin line and her nose wrinkling.

"Phoebe Black, then," she declared, having established who I was.

"Phoebe Winchester, actually. Black was my maiden name." I had thought about switching back when the divorce was finalized, but I'd been a Winchester for ten years, and I had gotten used to the name.

The woman didn't seem to care too much for these finer details, shrugging off my correction. "I see you're already taking over your aunt's property, and she's barely in the ground."

I bristled at this. I had no idea who this woman was, but she seemed to be accusing me of something, and I was really starting to dislike her tone.

"I'm sorry, who are you?"

"My name is Dierdre Miller. I was a very dear friend of your aunt's."

Upon hearing Dierdre's name, I was immediately reminded of one of the last lines in Auntie Eudora's letter to me: *"Watch out for Deirdre Miller. That old cow is always up to no good."*

Having known Dierdre for all of thirty seconds, I could say with absolute certainty she and Eudora had *not* been very dear friends at all.

Perhaps Auntie Eudora's warning had been more than just an attempt to save me from town gossip or a meddling older woman. The way Dierdre was looking at me right now made every survival instinct in my body come alive. I knew I was bigger and probably stronger than her, but all the same, her fierce stare behind those tortoiseshell frames had me hoping someone else might walk by any time now.

"Do you *need* something, Dierdre?" I asked. I was hoping to keep my tone neutral because she struck me as the kind of person who would ask to speak to the manager of Earth if it was too hot one day, but I was also holding a heavy shopping cart on an incline and didn't want my ice cream to melt while I waited for her to get to the point.

"I'll cut right to the chase, Mrs. Winchester."

"Won't that be a treat." I didn't bother correcting her about the *Mrs.* thing, though it annoyed me.

She ignored me and went on. "I am a woman of quite considerable means, and I know your aunt, in spite of her fancy house, did not have a great deal of money."

"I don't think you could possibly know how much money my aunt had without being her accountant. Are you her accountant?"

Dierdre wrinkled her nose at the mere suggestion of such a plebian job. "I am not. But I have ways of knowing things, and I think you'll come to find, Mrs. Winchester, that there's very little that happens in this town I *don't* know about."

"Cool." It was surprisingly hard to keep the cart in position on the hill's slope, and my arms were starting to vibrate slightly. My goodness, I was out of shape. And I also thought she'd told me she was going to cut to the chase. "And it's *Ms.*, by the way. I'm divorced."

Dierdre Miller made yet another unflattering face, which told me everything I needed to know about her opinions on divorce. She cleared her throat and went on. "I would like to make an offer on your aunt's—on *your* property." She smiled to herself, as if this was some sort of a grand final act in a magic show and I would start the applause any moment.

Instead, I stared at her, not quite processing what she was saying.

"You want to buy Lane End House?"

Her smile immediately faded, and I could tell from her expression she was clearly frustrated with my perceived stupidity.

"Yes, and I'm sure I can pay quite a bit more than it's worth. I know it's in dreadful shape."

I couldn't keep my composure any longer. I felt my features recoil in disgust at her assumptions of my new home, of the place I had spent my summers, and where I would now begin to find a new focus for my life.

Dreadful shape? I'd show her *dreadful shape.*

As soon as I could feel my arms again.

"It's not for sale."

If Dierdre Miller realized the insult she'd caused, she didn't seem at all apologetic about it. She just went right on talking as if I hadn't said a word.

"As a *single* woman with no children, what could you possibly want with a house that big?" I guess she didn't mind my being divorced now that she could use it against me. "Surely the little apartment over the bookshop would suffice handsomely."

I had plans to turn the little apartment into either a rental unit for added income, or potentially a short-term vacation unit I could rent out to tourists. It was small, but palatial compared to my place in Seattle. And yes, Bob and I could live very comfortably there. But why on earth would I want to live in an apartment when I owned a perfectly lovely gothic Victorian mansion with no mortgage on it?

"Dierdre, my answer is no."

"You don't even want to know how much the offer is?"

Why did she want the house so badly? She didn't strike me as someone who wanted to remodel it or live in it herself, which made me wonder what precisely was so important to her about the property. I had a feeling if I knew the answer, it would make me like Dierdre even less.

Instead, I amused myself by imagining she wanted to buy it because she believed the town gossip that Auntie Eudora had millions in gold bars—or old pirate coins, depending who you asked—buried under the floorboards.

"I'm not interested in selling." I started to push the cart, hoping she would get the point and move out of my way. Once she realized I didn't intend to stop, she relented in letting me pass.

"I'm not finished with this conversation. I'll let you think about it and come by later this week with a proper offer letter."

I kept walking, using my newly kindled rage to make the trip a lot easier. Part of me wanted very badly to have the last word and shout something over my shoulder at her, but what little I'd gleaned from our encounter suggested Dierdre Miller was the kind of woman who would not yield on having the final word in every conversation.

As far as I was concerned, that was a battle she was more than welcome to win.

Chapter Five

I woke up the next morning to discover the heat was off but that a large, fur-covered orange boulder was functioning as a space heater under my comforter. Every instinct I had told me not to get out of bed because, based on my frozen nose, there was nothing good to be found out there.

But I had to go start the fire to get the house warmed up, and then figure out why on earth the heat wasn't working. I silently prayed there wouldn't be anything wrong with the furnace because just the thought of replacing the furnace in a big house like this made me want to cry.

Against my better judgment, I climbed out of bed, fumbling for my slippers and the warm robe, which had once been my dad's, that I'd hauled with me from Seattle. It was still dark outside, so I staggered around the unfamiliar room, bumping into furniture, until I found the light switch.

I flipped it, and nothing happened.

Well, that at least explained why the heat wasn't working. The power must have gone off overnight. Wrapping my robe more tightly around me, I made my way to the main floor, clinging to the bannister so I didn't fall in the darkness, and headed right for the kitchen. I'd need to check the fuse box next, but that was in the basement, and I thought it best to get a fire going before I stirred up whatever ghosts and spiders were hanging out down there.

Thankfully, I remembered how to stack kindling and wood in the big double-sided fireplace, and was able to find long matches next to the hearth. With a little newspaper and a lot of luck, the fire started on the first try, casting a warm orange glow over the kitchen. It didn't yet do much to make me actually comfortable, but by the time I checked the box downstairs, it should have started to work its magic.

Bob had followed me down from the bedroom and now settled in like a little ginger loaf on the hearth, blinking happily into the flames.

"Don't burn yourself, buddy."

He made a small chirping noise.

"Don't suppose you want to come downstairs with me? Just to keep me company?" I asked hopefully. Not really sure what protection I thought a big orange tomcat could offer me, but it was probably better than nothing.

Bob lowered his head and closed his eyes, putting an immediate end to my query.

"Go figure."

Using the light from the fire, I was able to find the flashlight Auntie Eudora kept by the kitchen door and whispered my thanks that the batteries still worked as I opened the door to the basement.

The air was even colder down there, and in spite of there being several large basement windows, with no natural light outside this early in the morning, they did nothing to help the dark, spooky atmosphere I descended into.

"Okay, ghosts, I won't bother you if you don't bother me." I held the flashlight out in front of me like a weapon, not really sure what I thought I might need to defend against. I was only half kidding about the ghosts. This house was old, and without a doubt the kind of place a wandering, lonely spirit might want to call home.

My rules with ghosts were, funnily enough, the same as my rules with spiders: you can share my space with me as long as I never have to see you.

I scanned the flashlight beam around the basement, thankfully not seeing spirits *or* arachnids anywhere, and at long last landing on the huge breaker panel on the far wall. I hustled over, quickly found that several of the breakers were off, and flipped them each back on. As soon as I did, the furnace hummed to life and all the lights came back on.

It was a bit odd that more than one breaker would go overnight, but I chocked it up to old house weirdness. There was bound to be plenty more of that over the coming days and weeks as I learned to adjust to the place. Maybe it had gotten used to sitting dormant in the months since Eudora died, and I'd pushed my luck by running multiple electronics last night, and boosting up the heat before I went to bed. This house had a mind of its own, as most houses over a hundred years old did, and I had no doubt Lane End House would be showing me a lot more secrets as she got used to me.

With the lights now on I was able to get a better view of the basement, and my breath caught in my throat. It was absolutely crammed full of a bevy of intriguing things, some of which I remembered from childhood, others that I'd never seen before.

There was so much *stuff* to be seen it was actually impressive I hadn't accidentally tripped over anything on my way to the breaker box.

Several plastic totes against one wall were clearly labelled with different holidays: Easter, Halloween, Christmas, and the ones that were see-through told me they were all likely stuffed to the gills with decorations. I'd mostly spent summers here, but Auntie Eudora had proudly shown me all the work she put in to decorating for various occasions. It had been a really big deal to her.

Actually, decorating was an enormous deal to the entire town. Raven Creek was renowned for the efforts the town put into decorating for each and every major holiday. I'd usually only seen the efforts for Fourth of July, but I knew that every business and almost every home leaned into their holiday themes in a serious way.

It brought a lot of outside attention to the town as people would visit often just to see how the shops and houses were decorated from year-to-year. That, coupled with Raven Creek's advantageous location close, but not too close, to Seattle, to hiking trails, to great birding, and tourist-draw towns like Leavenworth, meant there was no end to tourist traffic throughout the year, though it definitely centered around the summer and the holidays.

I made up my mind, seeing those boxes, that I would decorate the house to the nines for Halloween in her honor. I wasn't particularly gifted with creativity, but she had enough stuff in those boxes I could probably muddle through for my first year.

Behind the boxes and practically hidden in the shadows, was an honest-to-goodness carousel horse up against the wall behind the stairs. Its paint was peeling somewhat, but it was still in pretty great shape. I was about to wonder how the heck she'd managed to get it down the narrow basement stairs when I remembered there was an exterior storm entrance to the basement with big double doors. It was the only logical way for something that size to have gotten in here.

Along the opposite wall were built-in shelves, stacked to the literal rafters with a variety of different jars. At first, I assumed it must be a bunch of canning items—old peaches and pickles down here for heaven knows how long—but as I got closer, I had trouble understanding what I was seeing.

The jars were mostly filled with dried herbs, each meticulously labeled and each label explaining the uses of the herb inside. "Basil, banishes negativity, aids in keeping love," read one. "Spearmint, used in spells of courage," reported another.

I picked up the one labeled "Thyme, repels nightmares."

What on earth?

The shelf next to all the herbs was equally packed, though this one with metal tins, each bearing the name of a different type of tea and noting its country of origin. I doubted Eudora would keep her stock from the store here, it was just too cumbersome to haul back and forth if she didn't need to, so this must have been her private reserve, or blends she was thinking of trying for the shop.

I glanced down at the jar of thyme again. I'd often joked about Eudora being a witch, and knew how common that legend was around town, but I was starting to wonder if maybe there was more than a grain of truth in that particular rumor.

Chapter Six

After feeding Bob and taking a hot shower, I was ready to head back into town and finally see what awaited me at The Earl's Study.

I hadn't been able to get the jars out of my mind. More than the appearance of the carousel horse, dozens of jars of herbs, all labeled with their magical properties, brought up quite a few new questions.

If I let myself dwell on it, it also brought more than a couple of answers as well.

Eudora being a witch would just make sense. She spent so much of her time outside puttering around the garden when she wasn't at the shop, and she never seemed to be sick a day in her life until the tumor that took her from us. All of her closest friends had found lasting, loving relationships, and everyone who crossed paths with her was genuinely the luckier for it.

Then there was me, divorced, newly single, and all alone in a new town. I could have really used some of that patented Auntie Eudora good-vibes luck right about now.

And if she *had been* a witch, had she just been a green, hippie-dippy, earth-loving Wiccan type, or was she, you know, an actual witch? As in, casting spells, talking to cats, or whatever it was "real" witches did.

I shook my head. What was I even talking about? There was no such thing as a "real" witch. Aunt Eudora must have just been interested in new age things like natural healing and whatnot. Still, it left me with some unanswered questions about my aunt that piqued my curiosity.

I'd have to do some more digging around the house if I wanted those questions answered, but for the time being there were larger fish to fry, and one of those was seeing if I had a salvageable business I could open this week.

Eudora had done well at the store, supporting herself and a small group of employees, but now I had to wonder how much of that had been clientele and how much had been . . . magic?

"Stop it, Phoebe, you're being silly," I said aloud, scolding myself. "She didn't use magic to force people to shop at her store, that's just insane."

Bob blinked at me from his place next to the front door, as if to ask, "Are you sure?"

"Don't you start with me, mister."

"Brrow," he replied.

Before I could commit myself to a longer conversation with my aunt's cat, I grabbed my jacket and purse and headed to my car. Fifteen minutes later I had a full tank of gas and was parked behind The Earl's Study in a small lot designated for employees.

The shop was sandwiched between a small bakery and a plant store, the ideal neighbors for a tea-slash-bookstore. Maybe it really was just a good business, no magic necessary. Anyway, I had to hope so because I didn't know the difference between a love spell and a business spell—or any spell at all, for that matter.

Using another set of keys the lawyer had given me, I let myself in through the back door and locked it after me, recalling my unpleasant experience with Dierdre Miller the night before. I had no interest in being surprised by any other helpful townspeople today.

In spite of the shop having been closed for the past six weeks since Eudora died, it was nice and cozy warm inside, a welcome change from the relative chill outdoors. The air had a faintly musty quality to it, much like Lane End House had, but nothing that couldn't be solved by some dusting and a nice scented candle. It didn't feel abandoned—just briefly forgotten.

The shop was divided into two distinct areas, though it was all connected by a big brick arch that led from the bookstore into the tea shop. I'd entered through the bookstore, and it was brightly lit by the huge floor-to-ceiling windows facing out onto the main street. Dozens of bookcases built of dark brown wood were squished together and loaded to capacity with thousands of used books.

Although, ostensibly, the shop carried any type of book, based on the shelving labels the customers here leaned heavily on mysteries, biographies, and romance. Hundreds upon hundreds of brightly colored paperbacks invited passersby to touch, investigate, and read. There was a big fireplace on the far wall—currently unlit—surrounded by a big loveseat and several overstuffed leather chairs that looked like they would envelop you in a hug the moment you sat down.

Everything about the space said, *"Come in, and stay as long as you want."*

Near the window were a handful of wire bins, each loaded with old Harlequin romances, and dime-store noir and fantasy books, most of which looked a little beat up. "One Dollar Each," proclaimed a label on the front, "Or Fill a Bag for Ten Dollars." A little blue recycle bin stuffed with plastic grocery bags was placed in between the two bins. Clever. I'd have to remember to keep an eye on estate and garage sales going forward to help keep the bargain bin stacked, it was probably a pretty popular offer.

I tugged off my jacket and headed into the tearoom through the brick arch. Things on this side were a bit brighter than in the bookstore. No dark wood or leather in here, just soft green paint, white café tables, and a glass-front display at the cash register, where I knew Auntie Eudora had stocked an assortment of baked goods, some from her own kitchen but most ordered special from the shop next door.

She was known for making cookies that contained some of her tea blends—her Earl Grey shortbread was famous—but she left the more difficult stuff to the experts. I'd have to make sure I looked at her records to find out how much her order had been, and get that going again.

On the wall behind the cash register were more of the same metal tins I'd found in the basement, labeled the exact same way with their names and countries of origin on the outside.

Along the counter were smaller glass jars, showing off the blends inside, and these were the ones Eudora custom made.

"Lavender Iced Tea Mix"

"Lemon Meringue Pie"

"Cinnamon Hearts"

I lifted the lid off the "Cinnamon Hearts" jar and was instantly greeted with a blast of cinnamon scent, followed by the aroma of rich black tea. There were actual mini cinnamon hearts mixed in with the tea blend.

She had one she made around Christmas that had broken up bits of candy cane and little mini chocolate chips blended with a peppermint tea base. I had to hope they weren't all just creations of her fantastic mind and that she'd written the recipes down somewhere. Repeat customers would expect those sorts of seasonal favorites, and I hadn't the faintest clue what made Lemon Meringue different from Grapefruit Curd.

I unlocked the office tucked in at the back, where I'd first come in, and left my jacket and purse in there. I'd need to do a more thorough walk-through to make a list of what cleaning and ordering needed to be done, and there was an enormous pile of mail sitting on Eudora's desk awaiting my attention.

Imogen, Eudora's only full-time employee, had been coming into the shop every other day to make sure everything was secure and the place wasn't falling apart, but she'd left it up to me to decide when we would reopen, allowing a grace period after my aunt's death. Since she was still getting her normal full-time wages when we were closed, she made an effort to email me regular updates and make sure everything was in order. She had even offered to run the place while waiting for me to arrive, but I'd needed to see it all for myself first.

Not to mention that all the store's insurance had been under Eudora's name, and the last thing we needed was an employee or customer getting injured while the space was technically in between insurance policies.

Based on what was here and what Imogen had done while I was gone, I felt pretty confident we'd be able to reopen as soon as tomorrow, the day after at the latest.

I took another look at the massive stack of mail and the dusty, old, desktop computer where I'd need to go through the store's records, and decided the first move for the day would be to go next door to Sugarplum Fairy, the bakery, and get us back on their daily delivery schedule, as well as getting myself the biggest coffee they offered.

I left my jacket, took my purse and the shop keys, and headed out the front door, enjoying the little bell that jangled over my head when I entered. Sugarplum Fairy was an Instagrammer's dream come true, with its soft pink facade, adorable little café tables outside—in spite of the chilly, gray October weather—and Parisian canopies over the windows. In the window display nearest me was a stunning wedding cake covered in delicate sugar flowers and positively glittering in spite of the limited sunshine outside.

In fact, the whole of Main Street had a charming European quality, with brightly painted storefronts whose abundant woodwork and fine details gave the impression of their having been dropped here from little Irish or English villages. All the Main Street lights were styled after old gas lamps as well.

Between the picturesque buildings and the town's famed holiday decorating, it was no surprise that people made an effort to stop here.

Much like nearby Leavenworth, or a town like Solvang in California, it gave the illusion of having been transported from somewhere far away or long ago. Raven Creek, however, lacked the uniformity of Leavenworth, which had gone full Bavarian, or Solvang, which was Danish inspired.

The Sugarplum Fairy was distinctly French, while The Earl's Study would have fit nicely into any small English village.

The pink theme of the Sugarplum Fairy continued inside, making me feel as if I'd just stepped into a mound of cotton candy, an illusion that was aided by the smell of caramelized sugar in the air. Glass-front display cases formed an L-shape along two of the walls, with an impressive array of colorful baked goods already inside—everything from rainbow-colored macarons to glistening fruit tarts, to the more commonplace glazed donut; this shop had something for everyone.

Behind the counter was a very expensive-looking espresso machine, which made me sigh with anticipation. Good coffee was only a quick drip away.

A woman who looked to be in her early forties walked out of the back area that I assumed housed the kitchen, wiping her hands on a spotless linen dishrag. She was average height and didn't have a single hard edge to her, as she was all ample curve and wore her weight beautifully.

She reminded me of a Renaissance painter's model, her round cheeks naturally flushed pink. She smiled at me and her whole face lit up, not because she recognized me, but because she just looked genuinely happy to see me.

"Good morning," she said cheerfully. Her voice was high and airy, bringing blonde bombshell Marilyn Monroe to mind. Given that she *was* blonde, her hair worn in a stylish mussed bob, I felt like the voice suited her in the same way her body did.

This was someone who was entirely herself, and it showed. I immediately wanted to be her friend.

"Hi there." I sidled up to the counter, trying not to get too distracted by all the pastries but knowing full well some of them would be coming back to the shop with me shortly. "I'm Phoebe Winchester, my aunt was—"

She didn't let me finish, her hand immediately going to her heart. "Oh, you're Eudora's niece. Of course you are—you look just like her."

This was actually not the first time someone had told Eudora and I how much we looked alike. It was hard to reconcile a younger version with the woman I'd known in her later years, her long, white hair in a braid, and deep-set wrinkles lining her eyes. But in the old photos she had showed me of her and my father when they'd been kids, she and I could have been twins, with matching raven-colored hair and icy-blue eyes.

Haunted was what my ex-husband had called my eyes once when we'd been dating. I still wondered some days why I'd ever thought marrying him was a good idea.

"It's nice to meet you." I offered her my hand, hoping she might tell me her name in return.

She shook my hand with a firm, dry grip. "I'm Amy Beaudry—I own the bakery. I used to have tea with your aunt at least once a week. That Blueberry Apple Crisp tea of hers. My goodness, the best." Amy made a chef's kiss gesture.

"The one with actual dried apple and blueberries in it."

She nodded vigorously. "I keep some stocked over here along with a few other of her popular sweet blends. That's how we arranged things, in case you were wondering. No money exchanged, she just kept my shop in tea and I kept her in daily Danishes and a few other assorted goodies I had in overstock."

I let out a little sigh of relief and thanked whoever it was that invented small towns and the way people did business in them. I was sure I could have afforded to pay Amy whatever her goodies were worth, but knowing she'd be satisfied in trade felt like an unexpected weight off my shoulders. Just one less thing to worry about.

"That's amazing, and I'm more than happy to keep that same agreement or pay you, whatever works best. I'm hoping to reopen the store tomorrow. Would that be too soon for our first order?"

Amy grinned. "Too soon? Sweetie, I have to be here baking all morning anyway—what's a few more Danishes? I'll get Eudora's usual order ready for pickup at seven on the dot. Does that work for you?"

"Better add a standing daily order for an extra-strong coffee, then," I said, smiling. "I'm not exactly accustomed to the seven-in-the-morning lifestyle just yet. Speaking of coffee, I'd absolutely kill for one right about now, to get me through all the mail waiting next door."

"How about our signature chocolate hazelnut latte? On the house."

"Twist my arm, why don't you?"

Amy laughed, a high, bright sound that made me think of the way little girls laugh before they learn to make themselves small and invisible. "Take a look around, pick out some stuff. I can't send you back to drudgery without something delicious to snack on."

By the time I was back outside, I was balancing a hefty pink box of pastry and a sweet-smelling latte topped with whipped cream. I was going to need to start an exercise regimen if I had to work next to Amy all day.

I was just leaving Sugarplum Fairy, my head in the clouds and my mood high as a kite, when I stopped dead in my tracks.

Standing outside The Earl's Study was Dierdre Miller, and with her was a hulking mountain of a man, at least six and a half feet tall and probably about three hundred pounds, his dark hair pulled back in a ponytail.

Dierdre had her face nearly pressed up against the shop's front window, her hand over her eyes to give her a better look inside. I glanced over my shoulder, wondering if I could hide in the bakery until they left, but my curiosity got the better of me. After all, she hadn't said she was interested in buying the store—just Auntie Eudora's house.

Maybe she was on the market for a steamy romance novel, and the giant was her boyfriend.

Besides, I was going to have to perform a balancing act to get the shop keys out of my pocket, and there'd be no way to slip past them without being spotted. I let out a hefty sigh and braced myself, all my former enthusiasm wilting away.

"Good morning, Dierdre."

"Ms. Winchester, just the woman I was hoping to see."

I wish I could say that made two of us.

Chapter Seven

Dierdre stood silently, her gaze darting from me to the door, then back to me.

If this woman honestly thought I was going to invite her and The Incredible Hulk in for tea, she had another think coming. I rebalanced the box of pastries in my hand and took a long, drawn-out sip from my latte—which incidentally tasted like heaven—and made no move toward the door.

I was comfortable enough: I had caffeine and could wait her out.

"I'm assuming you a specific reason why you were looking for me?" I prodded when the silence inched toward the realm of uncomfortable.

She cleared her throat. "It might be easier to discuss inside?"

"The store is closed."

We stared at each other for a long moment. I had a feeling Dierdre Miller was accustomed to getting things the way she wanted them, as most bullies are, and didn't like it one bit that I was pushing back against her requests.

Could I have opened the door to let them in? Absolutely, and my mother would have told me it was the polite thing to do. But the spirit of Auntie Eudora, nestled in the back of my mind like the voice of a little devil on my shoulder, was hooting with laughter that I was pushing all of Dierdre's buttons. Which is precisely how I knew I was doing the right thing.

At last, Dierdre huffed, glowering at the giant man as if perhaps he might be able to convince me to change my mind, but the man was impervious to her sullen stare, and he neither said anything nor moved a muscle in my direction.

"I was hoping that you'd had a chance to reconsider my offer from last night."

I smiled at her, baring all my teeth in what I hoped she would register as a warning but also hospitality, all wrapped up in one sweetly menacing package. "I am going to tell you what I told you last night. The house is not for sale, it will never be for sale, and the more interested you are in it, the more likely I am to add a line in my will that forces the town to turn it into a museum when I die."

I didn't know where the hostility had come from, but I was tired of Dierdre and her inability to take a clear no for an answer. I was honestly hoping that by being mean she might actually realize I was serious and leave me alone.

She gasped, and I wasn't sure if she was acting or if I'd actually managed to offend her, but I wasn't entirely sure I cared. I have almost endless patience for most people and like to consider myself friendly and easy to get along with, but going from cheerful chitchat with Amy to a few minutes in Dierdre's presence was just too much for me to handle on so little sleep and too much stress over the last few weeks.

"Have you even looked at the apartment yet?" she asked. "I'm very certain it would meet the needs of one *single* woman."

She said *single* as if it was the ultimate insult, and not a gift to myself after ten years in a miserable mistake of a marriage.

"Bob and I need space."

"I thought you said you were living alone." Her eyebrows knit together as if she were trying to make sense of this new mystery I'd dumped in her lap.

This also confirmed my belief that she and Eudora hadn't been close at all. If they had been, she wouldn't have been so confused by my mentioning Bob.

"Eudora's cat." The box of pastry in my hand was starting to feel heavy, and the latte was uncomfortably hot to hold but quickly becoming too cold to enjoy drinking. I wanted to ask Dierdre why she wanted Lane End House so badly, as if she might actually tell me the honest reason, but I also had no desire to continue this conversation even a moment longer.

"If you'll excuse me." I elbowed between her and the giant and balanced the latte on top of the pastry box while I fished my keys out of my jacket pocket, managing to unlock the door with only one hand. Points for me.

"This is truly absurd. You're a headstrong, foolish young woman if you won't even listen to what I'm offering you."

I glanced over my shoulder at her, smiling, and said, "Thank you for calling me young."

"Wait! Before you go, this man—"

Then I shut the door in their faces, not wanting to know what kind of insinuation or threat about the silent giant she'd been working on. I locked the door behind me, taking my snacks and coffee back into the office, where I wouldn't need to know if they continued to stand out there all day.

As soon as I was out of sight, I let out a little sigh of relief. Dierdre didn't worry me; in spite of how consistently annoying and pushy she was, I knew she wasn't a threat to my safety.

On her own.

The big guy, though—he concerned me. What was the point of him being with her, and why had she wanted to bring him inside to talk? The part of my mind that watched way too many horror movies, and consumed more true crime podcasts than was healthy, thought perhaps she planned to physically intimidate me into giving up the house.

But it was far more likely he was her boyfriend or maybe even a really poorly aging son or relative. He'd looked to be in his forties, but it was hard to get a read on Dierdre. She had seemed to be fifty-something the first time I'd seen her, but in the light of day she definitely looked older, making it hard to pinpoint what the age gap between them might be.

I just didn't like the vibe he gave off. He was too quiet, too casually menacing to just be there for no reason whatsoever.

And why couldn't she just accept that I didn't want to sell her the stupid house? Auntie Eudora's letter indicated Dierdre was a nuisance, but didn't say anything about a plot to buy her out of her home. Had Dierdre just been waiting for Eudora to keel over before trying to sink her talons into the mansion?

More than anything my curiosity begged me to find out why it mattered so much. Meanwhile, common sense told me to steer clear of her completely. I decided to split the difference and ask either Amy or Imogen about it when I spoke to them next.

In such a small town, I refused to believe someone wouldn't know what Dierdre's plan was and let me know what I was really up against.

Who knew? Maybe she just *really* wanted the carousel horse in the basement.

Chapter Eight

I spent the day buried beneath paperwork, sorting all of the mail into piles. There were book catalogues, notices of upcoming estate sales, bills that were thankfully not yet over-due, and more condolence cards addressed to the shop than I'd anticipated.

Postmarks said they came from as far away as Alaska, and all over the lower forty-eight, all of them telling the staff of the store how much Auntie Eudora had touched them with her gentle spirit, advice, and kindness when they visited. They all offered up stories of how she found them the perfect book, or tea—or even just an unexpected shoulder to lean on when they'd come into the shop—and how they hoped the store would go on without her.

When I was finished going through the mail, I set all the bills in a neat stack to pay as soon as I figured out what accounting software the store used, and I took the cards back out into the bookshop, where I lined them up along the fire-place mantle.

The store staff and myself were not the only ones grieving Eudora's passing, and I thought it might be nice for customers to see how much Eudora had meant to those she'd met, to know others shared in both their grief and their love. It made me feel better, somehow, seeing all those cards. It told me I wasn't alone.

I half expected Dierdre and the bouncer to be outside still, faces pressed against the glass, trying to claw their way in, but the sidewalk was empty except for a young man walking his extraordinarily tiny dog.

I returned to the office long enough to collect Amy's pastry box and take it with me into the café. There, I selected a stunning berry tart—each strawberry, kiwi, and blueberry glazed to a high shine—and put it on a teacup saucer. Then I started the kettle behind the counter and prepared a tea bag for loose leaf tea.

There were a ton of options to choose from, and more unique blends than I remembered her having previously. Yet with all the fun and whimsical options—what on earth was Unicorn Poop?—I had to stick to a tried-and-true favorite and make myself a cup of classic jasmine.

The jasmine blend Eudora had favored was one she'd first tried on a trip to China, where the tea leaves were blended with little bits of dried jasmine flower petals. It made the tea more interesting to look at, I thought, with its pretty white flecks, while still maintaining the subtle floral sweetness that made the tea so popular.

She had a similar blend that also had an enhanced vanilla flavor thanks to vanilla bean–infused sugar mixed right into the loose leaves, but I preferred my teas unsweetened, for the most part.

The kettle whistled and I turned it off, then let it sit for a moment until the temperature dropped below boiling, then poured it over the bag and set the nearby timer for five minutes. People often left their teabags in the cup, which usually resulted in over-steeped, bitter teas. By using the right water temperature and only leaving the bag in a set amount of time, the perfect flavor was able to emerge, and the experience of the tea was infinitely better.

I took the steeped tea and tart into the bookstore and settled into one of the overstuffed armchairs facing out toward the street. I hoped no one would think the store was open if they spotted me, but I was also sick of looking at the same four walls of the office and needed to give myself a better view.

As I sipped the tea and smile crossed my lips. Maybe, just maybe, I'd learned enough from Auntie Eudora I could pull this off. I knew how to recommend books, I knew how to brew a good cup of tea, and if I could figure out how to duplicate her blends, I could probably manage to keep this business going as she had.

Of course, I didn't have the same popularity and appeal with the local crowd and tourists as she did. Eudora was warm and open; she had a great sense of humor and loved to have long chats with strangers and get to know them. I, on the other hand, liked to share polite conversation, but never longer than absolutely necessary. It had been a long time since I'd worked in customer service of any kind, and that would prove to be the most difficult thing that awaited me.

I still hadn't found any of Eudora's recipes in my exploration of her office, and suspected she might have them at the house somewhere, where I hadn't really had an opportunity to dig through everything.

There was one more thing I needed to check here before calling it a day, and that was the apartment upstairs that Dierdre kept telling me I should live in. If I wanted to use it as an extra source of income, I should see what it needed in terms of fixtures, furniture, and even whatever cleaning supplies or odds and ends I might have to purchase to get it ready to go.

The store and the apartment weren't directly connected, so I put my empty cup and plate in the kitchen at the back of the tea shop and headed outside again through the front door, locking it behind me. Directly beside the shop's entrance was a second door, plainly marked with "642," and leading to stairs going up. The mailbox for the apartment and the shop were on top of each other, and it appeared that the apartment box was empty.

Unlocking the door, I headed up to the second floor. The air was surprisingly warm, and I hoped the heat hadn't been running this whole time while the place was vacant. There was a good chance it might just be residual warmth from the shop below, though.

I used another key to unlock the internal door at the top of the stairs and let myself into the apartment. Where, naturally, I walked directly into a man standing on the other side of the door.

Chapter Nine

I screamed.

He screamed.

We both staggered away from each other, which unfortunately meant I backed toward the open door at the top of the stairs. Before I was able to go too far and accidently take a tumble all the way down to the street, the man grabbed my wrist and pulled me back into the room.

I stared at him, my mouth agape.

He was handsome, probably only a few years older than me, with dark, curly hair that was damp. Realizing his hair was wet was also what made me realize he was wearing nothing but a towel, having clearly just gotten out of the shower.

For some reason, him showering made me unexpectedly angry.

This guy was probably squatting here, or had broken in, and he had taken a shower?

"Hey." He snapped his fingers to get my attention. "Are you okay? Do you need medical attention—or food? I don't have any drugs."

I blinked at him. "Excuse me?"

"You broke into my apartment. I don't want to alarm you, and I don't want to call the police if I don't have to—no sense anyone getting in trouble—but you have to go."

"I broke into *your* apartment?" I repeated back to him, not comprehending what he was saying to me.

"Yes. I must have left the door unlocked, but that doesn't make it okay."

He had the most beautiful brown eyes I'd ever seen, with a rich, honey undertone. For a moment I was too busy staring at him to really understand what was happening. "No, this is *my* apartment," I said finally.

As I looked around the room, however, I realized something wasn't adding up. There was a lovely brown leather sectional in the open living room space and a wall-mounted television. Several pairs of boots and shoes were lined up neatly near the door, and down the hall I could see a tidily made bed in the bedroom, with navy blue slacks laid out on it, just waiting for him to get dressed.

If he was a squatter, he'd made himself *very* comfortable.

"*My* apartment," he corrected, pointing to himself like maybe I was a bit stupid. If he believed me to be a burglar, he was being very patient in trying to convince me to leave peacefully.

"Who are you?" I spit out. "This is my aunt's apartment. She owned the shop downstairs, and no one told me anything about a renter. So, who the heck are you?"

Realization slowly dawned across his features and he nodded. "Phoebe."

"Yes. But I already knew that."

"Can you give me a minute to—you know?" He gestured to the towel he had around his waist. Whatever was happening here, this guy probably wasn't breaking and entering, so it seemed like a pretty reasonable request to let him put some clothes on.

"Yes, oh goodness, sorry. Please make yourself less naked." My cheeks flushed furiously as the stupid words left my mouth.

He smiled, and it was one of those crooked grins that made him look briefly like a teenager up to no good. It also tugged at a corner of my memory I couldn't quite reach. My heart fluttered, but I wasn't sure why.

The man went down the hall to his bedroom and closed the door. A moment later he emerged wearing the nicely tailored navy pants and a crisp, white, button-down shirt. He was still doing up the buttons on his cuffs when he returned.

"Let's have a seat in the kitchen?" Without waiting for me to agree, he passed through the living room and into a small, bright white kitchen with new appliances and a few postcards on the fridge, but not much else in the way of personal decoration. There were two stools tucked in under the peninsula counter, so I pulled one out, and he went around the other side, leaning causally against the counter, running his fingers through his damp hair until it held its shape.

He was so handsome it made me mad.

I was supposed to be grilling him on why he was in the apartment, but instead I was just eagerly waiting for him to tell me who he was. I looked at him expectantly, as if I might be able to psychically hurry along his answer.

"We actually know each other. It's been about twenty years since we got too cool to spend summers together, but when we were ten or eleven, we were pretty inseparable. I didn't recognize you right away—guess you grew up."

While this wasn't exactly giving me his name, suddenly the foggy memory that had been roused earlier by his smile came back into sharp focus. I remembered him, that same curly hair an absolute mess in dire need of a cut or a comb, skinned knees, and a smile missing more than one tooth.

"Ricky?" I stared at him, open-mouthed in surprise.

Just like he'd said, Ricky Lofting and I had been absolutely joined at the hip when we'd been kids and I'd visited during summers, but by the time we were teenagers, we couldn't be bothered with each other. I wanted to sit on the porch and read, and he wanted to do—well, whatever Ricky wanted to do, I suppose. We had parted on good terms but hadn't stayed in touch over the years. When you're a teenager and move to a different state, you tend to forget summertime friends pretty quickly.

"It's Rich now." He smiled.

"I can't call you Rich."

He laughed, and it was a grown-up version of a sound I used to know so well. Wow, this was too surreal for words. "You can call me whatever you want."

Why did that make butterflies come to life in my stomach?

"That doesn't explain what you're doing here, though. I can't believe Eudora wouldn't tell me you had moved in over the shop. She actually hadn't mentioned *anyone* living up here. I thought I might be able to rent it out."

"Well, then you're in luck—you already have a tenant."

That hadn't even occurred to me in all of this. I'd considered making it a vacation rental property, but having the guaranteed income of a monthly renter was just as good, if not better. "You didn't answer my question, though."

"I've been here just a little over three months. It wasn't meant to be more than a few weeks at most, and Eudora wouldn't even let me pay her at first, but just before she died, we both realized I wasn't leaving any time soon, and she finally let me start giving her rent. She might not have told you because it wasn't ever supposed to be long term."

"Why so temporary?"

He gave a small shrug and sighed. "I was hoping that it wouldn't really be a divorce, ya know, but it looks like the other guy has already moved in, and the house was a gift from her parents."

"Oh." I could relate. My ex had a live-in girlfriend less than six months after we split. "Sorry. Me too, I guess. Who would have thought we'd both be divorced and back at the shop together now?" I laughed but then realized he might not find it so funny.

"Does that mean you're going to be sticking around?"

"Yeah. Was the town convinced I'd show up, sell the shop, sell the house, and disappear?"

"To hear Dierdre Miller tell it, you were going to sell her the house, for sure."

"Dierdre Miller might be out of her mind."

He snickered. "You wouldn't be the first one to say so. You might even be right."

"She won't stop insisting I sell. I'm not selling."

"Good, I'm sure she'd just tear it down to build condos or something equally terrible. Dierdre always claims to want what's best for the town, but for some reason that always ends up being something that's really just good for her."

We sat in silence for a moment, I wasn't sure what to say. A few minutes ago I'd thought I was walking into an empty apartment. About a minute ago I thought I had found a potentially violent squatter, and now here I was in a nicely outfitted kitchen with the boy who used to be one of my closest friends as a child.

All grown up.

"Ricky Lofting."

He smiled. "Phoebe Black. Or I guess it's Winchester now, isn't it? Eudora told me you'd gotten married. Anyway, Phoebe, I'd offer you a coffee, but I actually need to head out to work. How would you feel about a proper catch-up soon, though?"

"I'd like that."

"Good. I'll call you at your aunt's later this week, or pop into the store, and we'll work out a plan."

He ushered me out with much more grace than I'd entered, and it wasn't until I reached the sidewalk downstairs and he was walking off in the opposite direction that it occurred to me that aside from news of his divorce, he hadn't told me a single thing about who he was now.

Chapter Ten

I called Imogen and asked her to come into the shop for her usual ten-to-six shift the next day. I'd do the early bird shift that Eudora had favored, which would mean showing up a bit before seven to pick up the pastries at the Sugarplum Fairy and opening up the store at eight.

Since we hadn't advertised reopening, I assumed the first few days would be quiet until word spread, which sounded ideal to me. Once we got into the swing of things as a team, I'd take a better look at what Eudora's marketing platform had been. A shop like The Earl's Study would thrive on Instagram, so if she didn't already have a social media presence, it was time to get the ball rolling on that.

My work done for the day, I made the short drive home. Before I could get lazy and distracted, I walked my borrowed shopping cart back to the store, waving at Chandra through the window so she'd know I'd made good on my promise. As I gestured enthusiastically at the returned cart like it was a prized object, she gave me a big thumbs-up from inside.

I could get used to this whole small-town thing.

I managed to make it all the way back to the house without another run in with Dierdre, and as soon as I got through the door was greeted by Bob, who sat primly on the grand staircase, his green eyes fixated on me as he let out one loud, long howl.

"Oh my goodness," I said. "Are you dying? How terrible of me to starve you. What a monster I am." I draped my bag over the banister and hung my coat up on a hook near the door. The house was warm, having spent the whole day being lovingly heated by a functional furnace, and the power appeared to have held steady as well.

Small favors.

"Dinner?" I said to Bob.

He didn't have to be asked twice and bolted for the kitchen. It's funny, but it had only taken me a couple days to become completely adjusted to having the big furry lump in my life. I could see why Eudora had liked him, and why she'd left him for me to take care of.

Having him around made me feel like I wasn't entirely alone, and that was definitely a gift I appreciated, considering how alone I really was here. Sure, Eudora's friends would be kind to me, and I could already see connections I might be able to foster into friendships—Amy, Imogen, and maybe even Ricky . . . no it was Rich now—but it was still just me and this big old house at the end of every day, and having Bob here made it that much easier to handle.

If I was being honest, he made the old place a lot less spooky too.

Visiting when it had been Eudora's home was different because she'd loaned her light and energy to the place. There was still a lot of her within the walls, but at the same time, with her gone, it felt like different kinds of ghosts were working their way to the surface, and I didn't just mean the lingering memory of my divorce.

In the kitchen I emptied a tin of wet food into a dish with Bob's name on it as he wove his body in between my feet, purring loudly. Once his dinner was served, it was time to think of my own. I was halfway tempted to just eat what was left in the box of pastries Amy had given me, but I knew too much sugar at night would just make me wake up with heartburn, and I had no interest in dealing with that.

Thankfully, yesterday-Phoebe had had the good sense to go grocery shopping, so I grabbed one of the premade salad kits I'd bought out of the crisper and began to assemble it, hoping some of the vegetables might offset all the sweets I'd eaten that day. That was how healthy eating worked, right? Lettuce counteracted chocolate?

I'd just keep telling myself that.

I was just about to take my big bowl of Santa Fe salad mix into the living room, to unwind with Netflix, when the house phone started to ring, nearly scaring me out of my socks.

It had been ages since I could remember hearing anything other than a cell phone ring, and mine was always set to vibrate anyway. The sound, so unexpected and late in the evening, immediately set my nerves on edge.

"Hello?" I answered warily.

"Hello, is this Mrs. Winchester?"

"Ms.," I corrected, still not sure if this was a real call or a very, very quick telemarketer to have updated the number with my name.

"Ms. Winchester, this is Officer Crane. I'm sorry to be calling so late, but I'm afraid we're going to need you to come on down to your aunt's store."

I glanced at the clock, which read slightly after eight.

"Is everything all right, Officer?" My mind, racing with possibilities, wondered if something might have happened to the store. A break-in?

"Well. No, ma'am. You see there appears to have been a murder, and we'd really like to have a chat with you."

"I'm sorry, did you say a *murder*?"

Chapter Eleven

When I arrived at The Earl's Study, the wind was blisteringly cold, and in spite of my heavy wool coat, I had a chill, right down to my bones, that I couldn't quite shake.

But once I spotted the flashing red and blue lights and the men in blue uniforms standing outside the shop, I was pretty sure my chill had nothing to do with the weather.

I pulled my car into the back lane and didn't get too far before I was stopped by a uniformed police officer who shone a flashlight in my car window. I rolled the window down, blinking into the sudden blindness of his light, and before he could ask anything, I announced, "I'm Phoebe Winchester. This is my store."

He switched off his flashlight, which was somehow even worse, because all I could see were the cruiser lights and little dots of red, blue, and white in front of my eyes. "A'yup. Crane 'n' the detective are expecting ya." He pointed me toward my own parking space, where a police cruiser and an unmarked car that positively *screamed* "I belong to a cop" were already taking up space.

I parked next to a dumpster across the back lane and got out, the wind clawing at my hair and clothes. The air smelled the way it did when the seasons shifted and the clouds remembered the taste of snow.

There was a tall, balding man in a uniform, standing next to a petite black woman in a nice-looking pantsuit. Given what the other officer had said, I figured the man must be Officer Crane, and the woman was the detective.

Clearing my throat so not to take anyone by surprise as I crossed toward them, I noticed the lights were all on upstairs in Rich's apartment, and my stomach suddenly dropped to my shoes. While I'd been imagining break-ins and dead strangers, I had completely forgotten about my new-slash-old friend who just happened to live *at* the crime scene.

"It wasn't Rich, was it?" I asked breathlessly, forgetting all my manners as the fear stoked higher. "Please tell me it wasn't Rich."

The pair exchanged befuddled glances before the detective spoke. "No, Ms. Winchester. Mr. Lofting is fine. He's upstairs speaking to a few other officers." Again, she looked over to Officer Crane, whose expression gave away nothing. Inscrutable if ever there was a human representation of the word.

"I'm Detective Martin, and this is Officer Crane. I think he's the one who called you down here."

I nodded. It was then I noticed the white sheet lying across the area just behind my back door. The sheet covered an absolutely massive lump, much too big to be Rich.

"Is that—"

"Yes, I'm afraid so. I don't want to upset you, but the victim was found at the back of your store, and based on what he had with him, we have reason to believe his intentions in being here were to break in."

"To . . . break in? To my store?" I must have sounded so stupid, but nothing Detective Martin was saying really made any sense to me. There was a body only fifty feet away from me, and he had died trying to break in?

Martin and Crane waited a moment or two for my brain to catch up with their words, and finally Martin spoke again, her voice low and calm. "If you're feeling up to it, I'd like you to see him, maybe tell me if you recognize him."

My head whipped around at her words; I had been so busy staring at the lump that I almost missed what she said. "Oh."

"Only if you're feeling up to it. We can always show you photos later if you think it would be too much."

I swallowed hard. Before this, I had only ever seen dead bodies in funeral homes. I had a hard time believing this man would look quite so peaceful as my great-uncle Dell.

"No, it's fine—we can do it," I answered. While I hated to admit it, my initial fear and revulsion had been replaced by something that felt an awful lot like my old, familiar friend curiosity. I really *did* want to see who the man was, especially if I knew it wasn't Rich.

Detective Martin guided me over to the body and, allowing me a pause to change my mind, pulled back the white sheet to reveal the dead man underneath. "We don't think he saw his attacker coming. Blunt force trauma to the back of the head," she explained to me. "He was probably unconscious by the time he hit the ground."

He actually did look surprisingly peaceful. I wasn't sure if I'd expected something more bloody and violent, but there wasn't a speck of blood on him that I could see, and he just looked a little surprised.

That made two of us because as soon as his face was revealed, I recognized him immediately.

It was the beefy man Diedre had been dragging around with her earlier when she had stopped by the store to pester me about selling my house. I don't recall if she'd ever said his name, but now, seeing him dead, I was starting to wonder if Dierdre might not be a lot more dangerous than I'd given her credit for.

Chapter Twelve

After I identified the man—or at least was able to point Martin and Crane in the right direction with Dierdre—I invited them to come inside. While they looked around inside the shop, I turned on the kettle and prepared a nice chamomile.

I doubted any of us would be sleeping soon, but the illusion offered by a bedtime tea gave me comfort.

Eudora's signature chamomile had a little bit of valerian root mixed in, as well as dried blueberry, which gave the blend a faintly fruity vibe while the valerian helped with sleep. As I prepared cups for myself and the police, I listened intently to the faint footsteps upstairs.

I hadn't seen any sign of Rich and had to wonder what was keeping the officers up there so long. Surely they didn't think he had something to do with the murder, did they?

My hand went still, with the teabag hovering over one of the cups.

I didn't actually know adult Rich well enough to immediately assume his innocence, did I? While it had been lovely reconnecting with him this afternoon, I didn't know anything about who he was now. Maybe he really was the kind of man who was capable of violence, or even murder.

He was here and would have had easy access. Perhaps he had come upon the man breaking in and just reacted in a panic.

Placing a teabag in each cup, I poured some nearly boiling water over them and let the delicate floral aroma soothe me.

I might not know Rich well, but I'd known Ricky, and I couldn't imagine that sweet boy with missing front teeth ever being capable of something like murder. Plus, I had watched enough detective shows to think if Rich was a suspect in anything, they would be questioning him at the police station, not in the comfort and safety of his own apartment.

When Martin and Crane arrived back on the café side, I set the cups of tea I'd made for them on the counter and nudged the saucers in their general direction. They both looked as if they might protest—drinking tea probably doesn't look very cool for a cop—but both relented and sat on the stools at the counter. Crane's utility belt banged against the metal legs of the chair.

"Do you have any idea what it was he might have been after in here?" Martin asked, sipping her tea politely but then smiling in a more genuine way when she tasted it. "This is really good."

I smiled back. "Thanks. And no. My first thought was that the shop has been unopened for a few weeks while I've been getting my aunt's accounts in order, but that should make someone *less* likely to rob it, not more. There are no recent deposits here—no money. It's not like there are any rare books, worth millions, we have locked away—it's not that kind of store. We have some first editions, but they're only worth a few hundred dollars each, and that's *if* you know where to sell them. We're a bit more frugal here." I pointed in the direction of the dollar book bin to make my point.

"You said earlier that Dierdre Miller has been harassing you?"

"*Harass* might be a bit dramatic of me. Let's just say she continues to make it abundantly clear she wants to buy my aunt's house."

"Has she mentioned why?" Crane asked, and I think it was the first time he'd said a single word since I'd arrived. His voice sounded deeper in person, very commanding, which made it all the more refreshing that he let Martin do all the talking.

Aside from the obvious fact that she was the ranking officer here. I'd had my fair share of situations in life where, no matter how good at something I was or how much seniority I had, there was always a man around, willing to talk over me and tell me how to do my job. It was unfair of me to assume a small-town police officer would be that kind of person, but it was nice to be proven wrong of my assumptions.

Auntie Eudora used to say, *"That's the thing about assumptions: they make you look really dumb."* She knew perfectly well that wasn't the phrase, but I liked her version a lot better.

"She hasn't given me any reason for her interest," I answered at last. "Only several reasons why I should stop saying no." When Martin raised her eyebrow, I realized how my words could be taken, so I waved my hand quickly. "I don't mean to say she threatened me. She just tried to tell me that, as a single person, I didn't need a house that big, and I could live in the apartment upstairs—that sort of thing."

"The apartment where Mr. Lofting lives?"

I nodded. "I don't think she knew Rich was up there. I certainly didn't."

Martin made a note and slowly sipped her tea before asking her next question. "You didn't know someone was living in an apartment you own?"

"I know how that might sound, but I've only been here for two days, and I've just been wrapping up a lot of things related to Eudora's estate, and the store specifically. Rich has been staying there for free up until recently, so it's not a huge surprise that there weren't records of it that sparked my attention. He's an old family friend, and Eudora had been letting him stay during his divorce." I snapped my mouth shut. Maybe I was giving them too much detail. Did the cops really need to know about Rich's failed marriage?

Martin jotted down a few more notes but seemed satisfied. "We'd like you to take a look around tonight, or in the morning, and see if there's anything missing. From what we can tell, the shop wasn't disturbed, and he died before he was able to get inside, but on the off chance you notice anything out of the ordinary, give me a call." She handed me a plain white business card with her name on it: Patricia Martin.

"Thank you, Detective Martin."

"You can call me Patsy," she said with a small smile. "I'm terribly sorry about what's happened here tonight, and I want you to know we'll get to the bottom of this."

Coming from a big city, it was easy to dismiss this, but for some reason her assurances gave me comfort. Maybe that was naive of me, or perhaps this being a small town I believed Martin would care more about finding out who did this. I wasn't sure of the reasons, but I believed her.

I thanked her and Crane profusely, though for some reason it bothered me that Crane hadn't even touched his tea, which now sat cold in its pretty porcelain cup. Martin had managed to drink hers entirely, even though she'd been the one doing most of the talking.

Sure, tea wasn't for everyone, but this was really, really good tea!

After walking them both to the back exit and assuring them several times that I had Patsy's card and wouldn't hesitate to use it, I locked the door behind them and made my way back into the tea shop. I took the cups back to the kitchen behind the tea counter, hidden from customer sight, and rinsed all the dishes, carefully setting them aside to dry.

It was in that mindless, hazy state of barely paying attention and running mostly on autopilot that I noticed a row of glass containers above the sink that I had never really looked at before. One row was dark brown bottles, another dark green, and a third a beautiful teal sea-glass blue.

Each one bore a hand-drawn label that looked like it had come fresh off a feather quill.

"Lover's Walk," one bottle said. "Lady Luck," said another.

I picked up a green bottle labeled "Money Tree" and twisted the lid off the top. It was filled with tea, which shouldn't have surprised me, but inside was also a stack of small papers that had the same writing on them as the label.

Eudora's writing, but fancier.

Steep one heaping spoonful overnight in boiled rainwater, and drink on the night of the full moon. Think of your greatest financial needs and open yourself up to unexpected rewards.

I sniffed the tea and smelled the licorice-rich scent of dried basil, thyme, and something sweeter. I peered into the jar and could make out two distinct white flowers. Chamomile was the easiest to recognize, but I had to pull the other one out and rub it between my fingers before the scent revealed itself to me.

Honeysuckle.

The mixture smelled incredible and made all the hairs on the back of my arms stand up when I sniffed it. This wasn't like any other tea I'd ever encountered before. The ingredients were all things Eudora had mixed into the blends offered out front, but it was impossible not to notice that this was something entirely unique from those.

I put the lid back on the jar, and though I was tempted to go through some of the others to see what kinds of unique ingredients they contained and brewing directions they called for, it was getting late, and I'd have plenty of time to explore them the next day when the shop was open.

But these new discoveries, combined with all the things I'd found in the basement earlier, had the gears in my mind churning again.

Had Auntie Eudora really been a witch? Was this something other people had known about? It seemed likely if she'd had these teas at The Earl's Study—and yet no one had made any accusations of her being an actual witch since I'd been home. It had always just been town gossip, in the grand tradition of tales told about old spinsters who lived alone with their cats. I'd always assumed only children really believed she was a witch, but now I had my doubts.

The idea left me wondering if that had something to do with the reason her home and shop were clearly the target of some unpleasant focus.

Just what had Dierdre and her goon been looking for?

Chapter Thirteen

The next morning came a lot earlier than I would have liked, as my phone's alarm blared at me starting at six o'clock. For a bleary, bewildered moment, I couldn't remember why on earth I would have set such an unfair time for myself—it was still dark outside for goodness sake!—until I remembered I had to pick up my bakery order from Amy by seven.

I was itching to ask someone else if Eudora's more, shall we say, *specialized* blends were common knowledge in town. Did everyone in town think she'd been a witch? I'd certainly teased her about it when I was a kid, because of her old house and penchant for trusting herbal remedies, but I'd also bristled when other children called her the same thing.

It was a lot to wrap my head around.

Bob was curled up at the small of my back, acting like my own personal hot water bottle, and I was loath to leave him given how cozy we both were under the duvet.

The only thing that could tempt me out was the promise of Amy's incredible baking—and maybe one of those chocolate hazelnut lattes she'd made me the day before. I had a full work-day ahead and wasn't entirely sure what that would look like. The shop had been closed for weeks, so either it would be completely quiet, or everyone would want to come in and see if I'd totally changed the place since Eudora died.

I wasn't sure if they'd be relieved or disappointed that I was leaving it exactly the same, but it didn't feel right trying to mess with something that was already pretty perfect in my estimation. I had a quick shower, hoping it would help wake me up, then hurriedly dressed in a pair of dark wash jeans and an off-the-shoulder dove-gray sweater that had a pretty ribbon tie detail on the back.

I called it my off-duty ballerina sweater.

As I was putting on my watch, I noticed something on the dresser I was sure hadn't been there before: a necklace on a long silver chain, with a simple pendant that was a large, dark gray polished stone. When I held it up to the light, it looked either brownish or greenish, depending which way I moved it.

I had absolutely never seen this necklace before in my life, yet it was sitting next to my watch and earrings on the dresser, as if it had always been mine.

At this point in my weird week, I was beyond asking questions. Someone wanted me to have this necklace—be it Eudora, the house, or even Bob the cat—and I was starting to believe every one of those options was possible. There was also the much more realistic possibility that it had been here the whole time, and I'd just overlooked it during the stress of the move. I slipped the necklace over my head and rubbed my thumb over the smooth, cool stone.

It was pretty, and it matched my outfit. Who was I to turn it away?

I curled the ends of my hair and pulled it into a high pony-tail, did a slightly too hasty job of applying some makeup—who knew when I might bump into someone like, say, Rich?—and was out the front door by quarter to seven, having fed Bob at the last minute. I hated leaving him and might ask Imogen if she minded the idea of an in-store cat. If those trendy cat cafés could get away with having animals and drinks in one place, surely there was no reason I couldn't let Bob lounge by the store fireplace all day.

I arrived at the Sugarplum Fairy right before seven, and though the sign on the door said closed, the lights were bright inside, and I could smell fresh bread as soon as I got out of the car. I'd decided to park in front of The Earl's Study rather than behind, just for today, because I still couldn't quite shake the reminder of seeing a dead body the last time I'd been back there.

I shuddered just to think of it again.

After tapping on the glass door, I waited a moment for Amy to appear, and when she did, her smile at seeing me was bright enough that I didn't mind getting up so early. She had the kind of calming aura that my aunt had had, and it chased away a lot of the dark thoughts lingering in my mind from last night.

"Well, good morning," she declared brightly. "Ready to tackle your first big day?"

"I would be a bit more ready if things hadn't gotten off to such a dramatic start last night." I'm not sure why I wanted to tell her so badly, but it seemed likely she would find out sooner or later since news traveled faster than light in this town.

"Oh gosh, what craziness, right?" She started making a latte for me without even being asked. Bless her. "They were still back there, scouring for clues and whatnot, when I got in this morning. Guess they were pretty surprised to see someone show up at three." Amy laughed at this, as if her accidentally showing up at a crime scene wasn't an incredibly upsetting way to start her morning. "They obviously couldn't tell me too much, but from the questions they asked, I guess it sounds like the guy was trying to break into your store?"

The espresso machine hissed loudly as she steamed the milk.

"I wish I knew what he wanted." I briefly explained to her that I'd been able to identify the man and his connection to Deirdre, which really just created more questions than answers. "Do you think my aunt had something in her shop they were after?"

Amy set the latte on the counter in front of me, her face temporarily pensive as she considered my question. I desperately wanted to ask if perhaps something *magical* had been the reason for Deirdre's interest, but I didn't know how to bring that up without sounding totally mad.

"Your aunt didn't exactly have millions stashed away in that store, but she has things in there that I think some people might value more than money." Amy leveled a meaningful stare in my direction, and I wondered if she, too, was trying to say something without exactly saying it.

"Like rare books?"

She laughed. "I think you'll understand what I mean when you find it. Let's just say there's a good reason your aunt's shop was so popular and did so well, and it has nothing to do with the discounted paperbacks."

I bit my tongue, not sure if I wanted to take the plunge and just outright ask the question, because frankly I was pretty sure it was going to make me sound completely and utterly insane if I did, no matter how big the hints Amy was dropping.

"Have you ever bought anything from her?"

Amy smirked at me. "You mean besides all the tea I keep behind the counter?"

I nodded.

"Of course. I think almost everyone in town has, at one point or another. Whether they'll admit it to you or not." She shrugged. "No one wants to say they bought a magic potion or a spell, you know? They want to say they bought some lovely tea; read a piece of paper; and then, on some completely unrelated note, something good happened to them afterward."

"So those *were* special teas," I declared excitedly, almost dropping my latte on the floor from sheer enthusiasm and relief. I stopped myself short of using the "W"-word, because I really wasn't ready to make that mental leap just yet, but it was getting a bit hard to ignore the big neon signs pointing me in that direction.

Amy laughed brightly. "Is that a surprise to you? All the time you spent at her house? All the cups of tea she ever made you? Surely you must have been a little curious about some of her concoctions or the incredibly specific way she insisted certain blends be made?"

I thought back, trying to remember my youth and all the bitter blends I had been expected to swallow. Once, it had been sitting on a back porch, exactly at sunset, after I'd skinned a knee. Other times she would send me sachets of rose tea when

I was in college, but insist I leave a rose quartz crystal in the cup when I drank it.

I had thought her instructions were whimsical or just a funny old lady being a funny old lady at the time. Heck, half the women in my yoga classes in Seattle talked about charging their crystals, thanks to some article or another they'd read on a lifestyle blog. The stuff Eudora did had been weird, but I'd never really put the pieces together, to think she might be an actual witch.

I still didn't believe she was a *witch*—not a broom-flying, cauldron-stirring Halloween staple—but it was pretty evident she fit the bill of a new age, hippie-dippy Wiccan, at the very least.

"It makes so much more sense now that I actually know. Wow." I sipped my latte, which was still much too hot, then added, "Didn't it bother her, the way all the kids in town would call her that like it was a bad thing? Especially since it seemed like her goal was just to help people."

"Oh, she thought that was hilarious. You've seen how she would decorate her house for Halloween. All the while I'm sure she was casting some spell or another to make sure those same kids all got home safe and didn't get any cavities. That's just who she was."

I ignored her comment about protection spells but appreciated that Amy seemed to be totally fine with whatever Eudora had been doing in her spare time. I was itching to ask Amy what kind of a tea she had requested from Eudora, especially after seeing so many different kinds in the back room, but I decided that was private information, and if she wanted me to know—well, she'd have to come buy some more.

Then something else Amy had said took root in my mind. "Do you think this has anything to do with Deirdre and the dead guy? When you say there's valuable things in the shop, you mean her special teas or other things she concocted? Could that have been what he was trying to break in and find?"

Amy set two boxes of pastry on the counter in front of me and locked eyes on mine with a meaningful stare. "All I'm saying is that when someone learns these things can be real, they will go pretty far out of their way to try using it to their own advantage."

I stared at her, processing the dark tone of her words and thinking of the manic way Dierdre had followed me down the street on the first night I'd met her.

Chills ran down my spine.

Just what was Dierdre after, and did she have something to do with the dead man behind my shop?

Chapter Fourteen

I had never met Imogen Prater in person before and had only heard her mentioned in my weekly calls with Eudora, but the second I saw the statuesque black woman with icy-blonde strands woven through her dark braids, standing in front of The Earl's Study, I knew exactly who she was.

When I exited Amy's café, Imogen spotted me right away, rubbing her bare hands together for warmth before coming to help me with the boxes.

"You didn't waste any time getting the pastry order set up again, I see." She beamed brightly, probably as excited as I was to see what beautiful treats Amy had in the white boxes for us.

I noticed that she didn't confirm who I was or even introduce herself right away. I think anywhere else I might have found it rude, but here it was like picking up a conversation that had been left lingering with an old friend. We'd also been chatting via email for several weeks, so in a way it was like we *did* already know each other.

Imogen was younger than I'd expected. The way Eudora had described her to me in the past had always made me picture someone more Eudora's age, or maybe Amy's. But one glance at Imogen's flawless skin, and I was pretty sure she was even younger than I was.

Good. The store could use as much youthful energy as possible if we were going to stay fresh and relevant. It's hard to sell tea and musty old books to a younger crowd, so having input from Imogen on how to increase our presence in the digital world would be good. I had thought of Instagram, but was too out of the loop on things like TikTok to know how to use them to our advantage.

But maybe that was putting too much pressure on Imogen. She looked like she was thirty at the oldest, but even that might be too old to be in the know with what was trending with the new generation. I might need to rely more on Daphne for the youth angle. Eudora's description of her made me think she was probably twenty, tops. That was more the age to know what was cool, right?

Heaven help us, I remembered being cool once.

"Thanks," I managed, as she took the box. "I just couldn't leave that dessert case empty. It would have been tragic."

"You're telling me!"

She used her key to open the front door and held it open for me so I wouldn't need to balance my own box plus the latte I was holding.

"Not that I'm not grateful to see you, and to finally put a face to the name—hello, by the way—but I thought your shift wasn't until ten." Had I already forgotten what was on the schedule board? The shop really didn't need many employees, so if I opened it up at eight, she and I would overlap for the midday rush crowd, and then she would be there to close up at six, when Main Street shuttered for the night.

"I know, but it's our first day back in six weeks, and I have a pretty good feeling the early crowd is just going to be the nosy old gossip fiends. *Especially* now that there's been a murder." Her eyes widened as she said it. "Is it true you found the body?"

I almost spit out the mouthful of latte I was sipping, which would have been a terrible waste of chocolate hazelnut.

"Where on earth did you hear that?"

"Word travels pretty fast around here."

"Well, word got that one a bit wrong. I didn't *find* the body, but I did come last night in time to see it." A frown pulled down the corners of my mouth. I'd really been hoping I might be able to avoid talking about the dead body and all that went along with it, but between Amy and Imogen, it was pretty clear that the murder would be the only thing anyone wanted to talk about.

Imogen went around the back of the tea counter, and I handed her the second box of pastries. She pulled several white ceramic platters out from under the cash register, gave them a quick dusting, as they hadn't been touched in a few weeks, and started placing on them the treats from Amy.

I was momentarily distracted by the shiny finish on the strawberry tarts and how utterly delectable the cannoli looked. I was hoping there might be something left at the end of my shift I could swipe, but once people looked at the offerings, I doubted we'd keep them stocked for long.

On my schedule for the morning was our own baking. Eudora was famous for her Earl Grey shortbread, and it was a recipe she had thankfully taught me when I was young. I had also had the unusual idea of using one of her specialty teas to make up scones—perhaps a love potion scone or a prosperity scone. There were some pretty specific directions that went with the actual teas, so if Eudora's magic *was* real, which I was beginning to suspect it might be, then just using the tea without the spell components might give a less potent version of the intended effect.

A voice at the back of my head told me I probably shouldn't be messing with witchy stuff I didn't understand, but at the same time I couldn't shake the feeling that it was Eudora herself suggesting I do this.

"You know this town better than I do," I said to Imogen. "Do you think it would be incredibly tacky of us to put up a display of some old Agatha Christies and Ellory Queens on the front stand?" There was a round, three-tiered table just inside the front entrance. Right now, it was displaying some six-week-old new releases—Imogen had unpacked all our more recent deliveries but hadn't put anything out—and was in dire need of a makeover.

I immediately felt terrible for suggesting it. After all, someone had been killed behind the store last night. But before I could withdraw the suggestion, Imogen began to laugh. "What an incredible idea. If they're going to be in here putting their noses in your business, maybe we can get them to buy a couple of books while they're at it."

I let out a sigh of relief. If the murdered man from last night had been a beloved member of the community, I obviously would never have even considered the idea, but since he'd been attempting to steal from me, and no one seemed to have the slightest idea who he was, there didn't appear to be much harm in capitalizing on our newfound—if macabre—fame.

If Imogen and Amy were any indication, it seemed like this little town might have a sense of humor. Perhaps that was what had made Eudora so beloved here. It would certainly make sense: she was the queen of dark humor and sarcasm in my experience. She would have been the first person to put up a murder mystery display after a literal murder mystery took place behind her store.

"Do you mind tackling that? I need to get the shortbread dough chilling for a bit before we bake the cookies, and I have a new scone recipe that came to me last night."

"You sound just like your aunt," Imogen said with a smile. "She was always coming in here with these breathless ideas for new tea blends, or some kind of crazy matcha-infused dessert. Matcha panna cotta was an enormous hit, by the way, but she never wrote the recipe down, so if she sends you that one in a dream, the town would be grateful."

I couldn't tell if she was kidding or if she actually thought Eudora was sending me recipes in my dreams.

At this point, I couldn't be sure either.

Imogen had already taken the rolling library cart out of the office and into the bookstore, where she was busy loading it up with vintage paperback whodunits, so I took the opportunity to make myself at home in the little kitchen area behind the tea shelves.

It was about the size of a decent apartment kitchen, with open design shelving so I could see all the trays and tins for baked goods. Nothing here was designed to cook a full meal, but any baking whim I might have seemed ready to be catered to.

Since the shortbread had to chill for at least thirty minutes before baking, I started there. Eudora's recipe was sinfully simple, but the reason it was so popular was the quality of the tea. I took out a coffee grinder from under the cupboard, preheated my oven, and dumped two teaspoons of the shop's famous Strawberry Fields Earl Grey into the grinder.

The key for the recipe was to use the best possible loose leaf tea and grind it just enough so you wouldn't be picking tea leaves out of your teeth later.

I'd seen versions of these kinds of cookies online that suggested steeping tea, and others that made a syrup of the tea, but in my experience, after eating these cookies my whole life, you simply had to use the dry tea itself, specifically, the delightful strawberry version of the tea, which had freeze-dried strawberry bits in it. When drunk as a tea, they gave a tartness to the first sip that mellowed into the classic bergamot after. As an edible treat, it meant there were adorable flecks of bright red strawberry in the cookie.

Once the tea was refined, I pulled out the pale blue stand mixer and added flour, sugar, butter, vanilla extract, and salt. That was another sneaky secret of Eudora's recipe: tea salt. She had a variety of different homemade salt blends that she mixed with loose leaf tea, adding that extra little bit of unique flavor.

When everything was combined together, with beautiful flecks of color throughout, I laid the batter out on a sheet of plastic wrap, rolled it into a tight log, and put the finished logs in the fridge. In half an hour I'd take them out, slice them into perfect rounds, and bake them until they were golden brown on the edges.

Absolutely perfect when served alongside a hot cup of tea. Next up was the scones.

While we ordered standard scones from Amy for the less adventurous crowd, Eudora also had created her own unique version at The Earl's Study, which had a sourdough base. Most traditional British scones used heavy cream or buttermilk, and a mix of dry ingredients, but Eudora used sourdough discard in hers. It gave the scones a delicious, tart flavor, but surprisingly didn't interfere with the rise, meaning they looked like a normal scone but with a surprise, fun, sourdough taste.

I pulled out the starter from the fridge, grateful Imogen had been keeping up with its regular feedings. Sourdough was somewhere in between a houseplant and a pet in terms of care and maintenance. It could be left unattended in the fridge for lengthy periods, but it was best to feed it at least once a week.

Now that we were open again, I'd leave the starter on the counter and feed it at the beginning and end of each day, to keep it active and bubbly.

These scones didn't need active starter, though—just the discard I would need to throw away anyway before feeding it, which made them a perfect option to reduce kitchen waste.

I would be using heavy cream in these as well, as a way of getting my tea into them. I set a pot on the stove and poured cream into it, then paused in front of the shelf of Eudora's "special" tea blends. I'd initially thought a love spell tea might be a fun way to try this new recipe out, but the more I thought about it, the more that seemed like a literal recipe for trouble. Too strong and it could really mess with people's emotions, which I didn't want to do.

Then I spotted the perfect thing in a brown jar on the top row.

"Truth Be Told."

I picked it up and looked at the label. It was a mint-based tea with evening primrose, honesty seed, and bluebell blossoms. It smelled interesting, slightly sweet but with the vaguest hint of mustard, which was probably from the honesty seed. The directions inside suggested adding several drops of evening primrose oil to someone's cup and having them drink it at midnight the day before you wanted to ask them an important question. It suggested two tablespoons to a cup, which was a lot for one cup of tea, so it clearly needed to be potent. If I mixed two tablespoons into the cream, divided between the scones it would likely result in a less potent version of the spell.

If anything happened at all.

I put the loose tea into a metal tea ball and dropped it into the cream, turning the heat to medium to let it slowly steep. Then I mixed the sourdough discard with the butter and other dry ingredients. I sprinkled a tiny bit of the loose tea blend into the dough, just for aesthetics, and then fed the starter while I waited for the cream to be ready.

After all the ingredients were mixed—by hand, because scones like the personal touch—I dropped the dough onto the work counter and rolled it out so it was even but still thick, then used a cookie cutter to create perfect rounds. I brushed the tops with the leftover cream and put them in the oven.

As they baked, I cleaned up the kitchen and clipped the timer to my apron so I wouldn't miss it going off, then headed out into the shop to check on Imogen's progress.

Chapter Fifteen

The front table display looked adorable, with piles of old pulp paperbacks from the great mystery masters that I loved, like Christie, Queen, and Dorothy L. Sayers. I noticed that Imogen had put the female writers on the front side and relegated the men to the back. Arthur Conan Doyle, John Dickson Carr, and Raymond Chandler were heavily featured on the backside.

I smirked, knowing it would probably drive old Arthur batty to know his female contemporaries were getting more attention than him, but give me Poirot over Holmes any day.

"It looks awesome," I enthused. "I can't believe you got it done so quickly."

"I picked over the bargain baskets pretty heavily, but the bonus is if we sell them for a bit of a markup, we can afford to hit up a few more estate sales, right?" She was holding a whiteboard like a baby in the crook of her arm, drawing on it with dry-erase markers. "What do you think about a buy-two-get-one-free deal?"

The books were all well-worn, spine-cracked paperbacks. Some of the more vintage titles might have value in mint condition, but as it was, they were more for personal enjoyment than anything. We could definitely afford to give some away, especially since we were already marking them up over the bargain bin pricing.

"Great idea."

She finished what she was drawing, smiling smugly to herself, then turned the whiteboard around so I could see her masterpiece. All around the edge of the board, she'd drawn little footprints; a magnifying glass; Poirot's traditional bowler hat, with his iconic mustache underneath; and a cup of tea with a bottle of poison next to it. In pristine script she'd written, *Murder Most Foul*, and underneath it said, *Paperback Mysteries: Buy Two, Get One Free.*

"Wow, I love it."

"Thank you. It's starting to smell great in here. Are those your new scones?"

I nodded. "A little something extra in them. I can't decide if Eudora would be proud or appalled." When Imogen raised a questioning eyebrow, I added. "I might have used some of the . . . uh . . . special blends?"

Imogen burst out in a laugh. "Oh, proud. She'd definitely be proud." Then her expression clouded for a moment. "Actually wait—what did you use? Because once Eudora overdid it a little with the love tea at Valentine's in these little chocolates she made, and—*oh my god*—Theo, the delivery guy from the plant shop next door, followed me around for weeks. Literally weeks. I never got so many flowers in my life before."

"That doesn't sound so bad."

"You come back to me when your whole apartment is filled with roses and you can barely breathe because the smell is so intense. Also Theo, lovely as he is, is a seventy-year-old widower, so definitely not my type."

"Oh no. Okay well, note to self, no love tea truffles."

"What *did* you make?" she asked again.

"I figured if people were going to come snooping in our business, we might as well see if they know anything. So, I made some Truth Be Told scones."

Imogen looked up from her display, an amused glint in her eye. "You made lie detector pastry?"

I shrugged just as the timer on my waist began to beep. "It's a pretty diluted version of the tea, so I don't have much hope of it working, but I'm also not a witch, so I didn't want to try something too dramatic my first time out of the gate, you know?" In the back of my mind, I was already trying to figure out how I might get one to Dierdre and start asking her some questions about the man she'd been with yesterday.

At the same time, I wasn't really sure I wanted to have a run-in with someone who could potentially be a killer, or at least be the reason someone had been trying to break into the shop last night.

Which brought me full circle, back to wondering what it was Dierdre or the man had been after in here. There really wasn't anything of value hiding inside the shop besides some vintage first editions in a cupboard on the bookstore side of the shop. You'd have to be pretty desperate to try to steal those because I'm sure the market for fencing old leather-bound books was a pretty niche one and a difficult way to make a quick buck.

I came back to what Amy had said earlier about a taste for magic and power, and wondered if Dierdre knew something about Eudora and the shop—or my house—that even I didn't.

It was clear there was something she wanted, and it was right under my nose. I just couldn't quite figure out what it was.

In the kitchen, I took the scones out of the oven and put them on a rack to cool. Once they were cooled, I'd do a very basic lemon icing drizzle over the top, both for a touch of sweetness and so I could suggest pairing it with the Lemon Meringue Pie tea. I took the rolls of shortbread out of the fridge and made quick work of slicing them in into little silver-dollar-size circles before putting them on trays and popping those into the oven.

In about thirty minutes, just as it was time to open the doors, I was sliding trays of perfectly baked cookies and scones into the front display cabinet, feeling fairly pleased with myself for how things looked on my first official day running the store.

Imogen, seeing that I was ready to go, unlocked the door and flipped the light switch for the sign in front to read "Open."

Not two minutes later, Dierdre Miller came swooping through the entrance.

Chapter Sixteen

M y breath caught in my throat at the sight of her fiery red hair and equally heated expression. She looked downright furious, her hands clutched into fists at her side and her skin an almost ashy gray.

My original plan to try to give her one of the scones vanished, and now all I wanted was for her to leave the store.

Imogen had wandered off into the bookstore after we opened, but I could see her braids over the top of the bookshelves, and I spotted her peering over to see who had entered. As soon as she registered who it was, she turned around and pretended to be dusting something.

I didn't doubt for one second she was already on high alert to listen to every word Dierdre said. I just wished I didn't have to be at the front, in the line of fire.

"Good morning, Dierdre." I tried to keep my tone light and calm, but I was struggling.

"Good *morning*?" she parroted back. "I don't know where you come from, missy, but here in Raven Creek, we open our stores promptly at eight o'clock sharp."

Looking over at the clock on the wall, I saw it said 8:05. Which meant we'd opened maybe a minute or two late, and she had come in right after. She definitely hadn't been standing outside when Imogen had turned the sign—I knew that much.

Instead of feeding into her obvious attempts to rile me up, I just shrugged. "Can I get you something? Was there a hot copy of the new Stephen King you were desperate to get your hands on before nine in the morning?" Maybe I should have kept sarcasm out of it, but I was only human, and sometimes, in spite of myself, it just snuck in there. Got me into trouble more often than not—just ask my divorce lawyer.

Dierdre suddenly seemed to remember where she was, casting a withering glance at the stacked shelves of books before seeing the display we'd set up at the front. Her lip curled in revulsion.

"Is that supposed to be *funny*?"

If she was acknowledging the murder, that meant she knew about it. According to Imogen, everyone in town did, but clearly Dierdre's response told me she felt differently about it than the other town gossips did.

"I suppose that means you've heard about the dead man we found trying to break into my store last night." I decided to forego niceties and just jump in with both feet. Dierdre didn't strike me as someone you could subtly needle information out of. I suspected she was more the type to accidentally say more than she intended to when she got too worked up. She was clearly well on her way there, so I might as well poke the dragon a little more.

She wouldn't do anything to me with Imogen in the store.

I hoped.

Honestly, I had no idea what this woman was capable of, as everything she'd done since the moment I'd met her only continued to deepen my belief that she was totally off her rocker. Maybe antagonizing a potential killer wasn't my best move, but here we were.

Her face had already been white to begin with, but now it was so ashen and waxy that it was almost clear. Clearly my words had struck a nerve, but I wasn't sure what nerve it was.

"You are *just* like your aunt," she spat finally. "Insolent and bullheaded to the very end. People loved Eudora for some reason that's perfectly beyond my comprehension. But they don't know you, and if I have my way, not a soul among them will care for you one bit. This store will be shuttered by Christmas."

Now it was my turn to feel angry, but instead of rising to her level of hostility, I replied with as calm a voice as possible, "Well now, I'm confused Dierdre. If the store closes, how can I live in the apartment overhead and sell you Eudora's house? Come to think of it, if you and Eudora were such *good friends*, I'm not sure you'd be in here calling her names. Why don't you just tell me what it is in here you and your buddy were after last night?"

Whatever she'd been expecting when she came in the shop, it clearly hadn't been for someone to give back as good as Dierdre dished it out. She sputtered, fumed, but the words just didn't seem to want to come out. I glanced across the store to where Imogen was pretending to dust, but it was obvious she was watching us with rapt attention.

"My buddy? Are you *accusing* me of something?" Dierdre snapped.

"Let's just say I think it's pretty convenient that you were here yesterday, peeking in my windows with the very man who showed up dead on my doorstep later that same night."

"So *you're* the reason that detective was knocking on my door at all hours. What did you tell her?"

I was getting sick of Dierdre and of her ongoing presence in my life, but I still wanted to see if I could potentially annoy her into giving up more information that she meant to. "I told her this irritating woman I'd just met kept insisting I sell her my house, and then was poking around my store the next day."

"Well, I *never*."

"That's exactly what happened, though, Dierdre. You've been awfully interested in Eudora's house and shop ever since she died, and if your buddy was trying to break in last night, there was probably something he was looking to find." I shrugged and pulled out one of the Truth Be Told scones and put it on a plate, then put the plate on the counter for Dierdre. Over in the bookstore, Imogen audibly let out a snort. Dierdre either didn't hear her or didn't care, because she made no indication of responding.

"I don't think I like what you're implying." Her gaze drifted to the scone, suspicious but curious.

"I wasn't really implying."

"If you're suggesting I'm interested in stealing something from you, that's balderdash. And as for the man yesterday, he told me he was an old friend of your aunt and asked me to show him the way to the store. Since I wanted to come speak to you anyway, I didn't see the harm in him tagging along. He's no one I know personally."

The way she said it was almost convincing, and had it come from anyone else at all, I might have believed her, but since it was Dierdre and I had zero reason to trust a single word out of her mouth, I assumed this was just one more lie or misdirection on her part.

"Sure. Did this friend have a name?"

"Calvin? Carlton? Something like that. You simply can't expect me to remember the name of every vagabond claiming to be your aunt's friend and looking for her store. He looked familiar, but I don't associate with *that* kind of person—unlike that aunt of yours." She waved her hand airily around her, some of the color coming back to her cheeks now that she'd settled herself into a narrative. Her anger seemed to have dissipated down to three on a scale of ten, instead of a twelve, and I couldn't tell if that was good or bad for me in terms of finding out what I needed to know.

"So, this Calvin or Carlton character wasn't *with* you yesterday—you just happened to be showing him the closed store. And then figured you'd invite him in to have a chat with me?"

"I did no such thing. *I* wanted to have a chat with you. Whatever he wanted with the store is his business, and based on what happened last night, it sounds like his intentions were not altogether honorable."

"No kidding."

Since she was evidently in a chatty, open mood now, I held the plate with the scone out to her. "Did you want to try today's special? It's a lemon-glazed scone."

She waited for a moment, then came over to the counter. "I suppose it's the very least you could do, considering how dreadful you've been to me since we first met." She crossed over to the counter and took the scone from the plate, jamming half of it into her mouth and chewing loudly.

Dierdre frowned ever so slightly, wiping crumbs from the front of her dress. For a moment I thought she was going to be sick, and then she said, "You know, it would serve that terrible aunt of yours right, getting robbed. She never wanted to share a darned thing with anyone else who needed it."

My gaze jerked across the store, and I locked eyes with an equally stunned Imogen.

Dierdre might be pretty forthright at the best of times, but either she was feeling *extra* open right now, or the Truth Be Told tea might have been a bit stronger than I had given it credit for.

Chapter Seventeen

Dierdre seemed to realize her own words a moment too late and clapped her hand over her mouth. "Oh. That was an awful thing for me to say. I mean, it's true—I couldn't stand Eudora, but I certainly never meant to say that out loud."

Once again, she became aware slowly that she was putting all her internal thoughts out into the world with zero filter. Her eyes went wide, then lowered to the scone in her hand, as if she immediately recognized the moment things had begun to take a terrible turn for her.

"Did you poison this?" she asked.

"No. It's just a scone."

She put it back on the plate. "I should have known better than to eat something from this dirty witch's shop. Should have known you'd be just like her."

As angry as she was making me by speaking her personal truth about Eudora, I knew I'd never have another chance like this. She had basically taken a powerful herbal truth serum, and I'd only have one chance to hear her honestly answer the most important question I could ask.

"Did you have something to do with that man dying behind my store last night?"

I'd never seen anyone do a full-body sneer before, but Dierdre managed it somehow, and it was a withering sight to behold. "Like there's anything in this dinky little shop I would want to steal. No, your aunt probably owed him money. I'd never seen him before yesterday afternoon. Now if you'll excuse me, I need to go report you and *those* to the sheriff's office." She threw what was left of her scone on the floor. "You can't simply run around drugging your customers with . . . with . . . *narcotics*."

She stomped out of the store, the bell jingling behind her, leaving a faint whirlwind of dust and old book smell in her wake.

After we were sure she was gone, Imogen reentered the tea shop, her unused dust rag in hand, and crossed her arms over her chest, staring with bewilderment at the front door.

"I think you might need to adjust the strength of those scones a little before we serve them to anyone else." She bent down, plucking up Dierdre's leftovers with her towel.

I was already pulling the tray out of the glass display case so I could stash it in the kitchen. "I thought for sure the tea would be so diluted it would barely have any impact at all." If I was being honest myself, I hadn't expected them to actually work in the first place, let alone work *so* well. "Dierdre isn't very shy with her opinions on a good day, so maybe she was just more open to being honest, but you're right: if I give these to our customers, people will be sharing all sorts of things they don't want to, and that can't be good for business."

"Wrap one of those up for me, though. I'm meeting my ex-boyfriend for drinks later tonight, and I'd *love* to find out if there were some things he was being shady about."

I put the tray in the kitchen, not wanting to waste the scones by throwing them out, but also not sure what to do with concentrated truth bombs. Day one of playing with magic, and I couldn't tell if I was a natural or an abject failure.

At least I knew the shortbread wouldn't make anyone spill their guts to anyone they came into the shop with, and I wouldn't need to feel responsible for any breakups or fights among family members for the rest of the day.

The doorbell jangled again, and I took a steadying breath. My first day on the job wasn't shaping up to be quite what I had expected when I'd arrived at the shop this morning. I'd figured it would be a few book sales, some folks curious about the store now that Eudora was gone, and maybe a few true crime junkies who wanted to see the place where there'd been a recent murder.

Instead, it had been confrontation, yelling, and some accidentally potent witchcraft.

In the main alcove there was an older man with a full head of white hair and equally bright white teeth, which he was using to smile broadly at Imogen. Imogen was smiling back politely, but it didn't take a body-language expert to see that she was keeping herself distanced from him and had crossed her arms over her chest in a defensive posture. Her jaw was tight in spite of the smile.

"Hello." I kept my tone casual, but not too friendly. He couldn't have been in the shop for too long, so it was unlikely I'd interrupted anything, but I wanted them both to know I was here.

The man's smile broadened, to almost comical effect, and he quickly lost interest in Imogen and came over to me, extending a large hand. I put his age at probably late sixties, but he was in good shape, and his handshake was firm. His irises were bright blue, but the warmth of his smile didn't go as far as his eyes.

"You must be Eudora's niece. Penelope, right?"

"Phoebe," I corrected.

"Oh, of course, of course. My mistake. She talked about you an awful lot."

Not often enough for him to remember the right name, apparently. I shrugged off my annoyance. He was an older man and probably didn't see much point in memorizing the name of someone he never planned to meet. It was a fair thing to forgive him for, so I let it go.

"My name is Owen Talbot, I'm your neighbor."

Thinking he meant Lane End House, I said, "I don't exactly have any neighbors."

Imogen let out a small laugh sound and quickly covered her mouth. Owen, on the other hand, dropped his friendly expression, and for just the smallest flash of a second he looked really annoyed with me. It had the effect of being in a high school classroom and seeing a glimpse of real human anger on the face of a teacher.

It made me very uneasy.

"I own the shoe shop, Talbot and Son, just one door down, next door to The Green Thumb." He glanced down at my shoes, a well-worn pair of brown leather knee-high boots. He schooled his expression enough not to show how he really felt about them, but I was guessing they weren't quite what he typically sold. "We sell new and repair old. If you're ever . . . in need."

It took positively every nerve in me not to sneer right in his face when he said it.

"That's lovely. I appreciate you stopping by to welcome me."

"Of course, of course." He glanced around the room, as if trying to find something in particular, and I doubted it was a copy of the new John Grisham. "Heard you had quite a scare last night. I was surprised to see all the police tape when I arrived this morning. Is everything all right? Nothing damaged or stolen, I hope."

Given what Imogen had told me about the Raven Creek gossip mill, there was no way Owen hadn't heard what went down last night. Best I could tell, they must have some sort of phone tree or group text in town that shared all the latest big news in one swoop. Owen struck me as the kind of guy who liked to keep in the know.

Before I could answer, he added, "Dierdre Miller just stopped by my store and seemed quite out of sorts. She all but said that the two of you had a bit of a run-in and that you were accusing her of murder." His mouth formed a thin line, and he shook his head. "My dear, I know your aunt was a beloved fixture in this town, and I know you come from a big city, but I hope you understand that here in Raven Creek we are all family. We'd like to make you a part of that family, but you can't just run around accusing people of murder." He said it like he was reading from Emily Post's Guide to Murder Accusations.

I sighed. I'd been ready to be friendly with everyone, and I wanted to do my part to fit in here, because as far as I was concerned, this was supposed to be the big restart to the second chapter of my life. But so far, the second chapter wasn't reading quite the way I had hoped.

"I didn't accuse her of murder. I asked how she knew the man who *had* been murdered, because I saw the two of them together outside my store yesterday." There. Plain, simple, true. I had no interest in giving him any information about the attempted break in. The fewer people who thought there was something worth stealing in here, the better.

"Well, she was very upset."

"Imagine how I felt seeing a dead body on my steps last night."

Owen assessed me quietly. I'd obviously caught him without a quick, pithy retort. I would be proud of myself, but honestly, I was just tired, and it wasn't even nine in the morning.

"It was lovely to meet you, Miss Winchester. I trust that you're doing your part to keep our block safe. The last thing we want is lax ownership inviting undesirables in and driving up crime."

There was no way I could reply to that without saying anything nasty, so I simply smiled. Owen took the hint and showed himself to the door, evidently satisfied he'd gotten the last word.

Once he was gone, I glanced over to Imogen and let out the breath I'd been holding in.

"I don't mean to be rude, but this town's Welcome Wagon leaves a lot to be desired."

Chapter Eighteen

The rest of the day flew by without further drama. My shift was supposed to end at four, and Imogen was meant to take the last few hours on her own, but we both ended up staying until closing time at six. I wanted to get a sense of how she usually shut down the store, and even though she'd arrived early, she wanted to stay through the day to make sure I was comfortable.

After Owen had left, the remaining visitors to the shop that day had all been precisely what I originally expected. Some wanted to say hello and meet the new owner of The Earl's Study. They were all gracious enough to tell me how much they loved and missed Eudora, and all of them told me if there was anything I needed in town, I shouldn't hesitate to reach out.

A few others were absolutely only interested in getting the latest news about the murder, and they all seemed fairly disappointed when neither Imogen nor I had anything especially tantalizing to tell them.

On the plus side, we managed to sell a good thirty percent of the marked-down detective novels we'd put on the front display table, and not one person thought it was in bad taste (thank goodness). A few even snapped photos to share on Instagram, and I politely begged them to tag the store in their posts.

In the last few minutes before we closed up shop, Imogen took the library cart back into the bookstore to try to find more used whodunits to load the table up for the next day. We had a pretty impressive selection to choose from, which made me wonder how many residents of this town were secretly wannabe closet sleuths.

I completed an initial cash-out of the till but was not quite ready to run the final numbers, in case we had any last-minute shoppers, and was pleasantly surprised with our daily sales.

Secretly, I'd worried taking on Eudora's shop was going to be an effort in futility, and I'd be lucky to make it last through the winter. Who wanted tea and used books these days? But our sales for the day were much better than I'd anticipated. I'd been filling up paper bags of loose tea consistently all afternoon, and the tea counter had sold out of all but a handful of pastries— enough that I was going to have to hunt down Eudora's Lemon Meringue Pie tea recipe and make more tonight.

The bookshop had done steady sales all day as well. Since it seemed used books were a more popular buy than new ones, we weren't getting quite as impressive an amount per book, but with used copies people tended to buy multiple books instead of just one at a time.

I remembered I hadn't had a chance to unpack the new release stock sitting in the office, and made a mental note to update that shelf in the morning before we opened.

All in all, it had been an excellent first day. I was grateful that the initial wave of frustration and bad vibes had been worked through in the first hour of the day, leaving the remaining hours to be smooth sailing and a generally positive introduction to the town and its people.

On the pad next to the cash register, I made a few notes of things I'd have to tackle in my first hour in the morning, but if I could make the loose tea blend at home tonight, using the stock in Eudora's basement, that would be one less thing to worry about.

The moment the clock hit six, Imogen locked the front door and turned off the "Open" sign.

"You survived your first day. How do you feel?"

"Like I've definitely earned a glass of wine and a nice long bath." I wasn't kidding. My feet weren't accustomed to a day spent standing. If I was going to be moving around nonstop for eight or nine hours a day, then as much as I'd hate to do it, I might need to go visit Owen later this week to find something a little bit more comfortable than these boots. My former life with a desk job had not prepared me for the harsh realities of retail ownership.

"You did great. I think you were a hit, especially with the Knit and Sip crew."

"The . . . what?"

Imogen laughed. "Oh, sorry. I guess that was more of an in-joke with Eudora. I thought maybe she'd told you about them. All those little blue-haired ladies who offered to bring you casseroles and bought up all our Ellory Queen—Eudora and I liked to call them the Knit and Sip crew. You'll see them in action, no doubt, because on Friday every week they come in here around two in the afternoon and stay until eight, because it's our late hours. They'll order enough tea to satisfy half of England, and they settle themselves in by the fire and chat about whatever book they've all been reading. Usually book talk becomes grandkid talk, becomes town gossip, becomes full-on arguing about politics by the time we close, but they love it."

"I can't decide if I'm looking forward to it or if I'm terrified."

"Both—definitely both. Lucky for you I close on Fridays, so you don't need to risk life and limb when it comes time to kick them out."

I laughed and bagged up the garbage at the front counter, then combined it with the big bag from the kitchen. The scones from earlier were still sitting there, waiting for me to decide what to do with them. I'd put one aside for Imogen, as promised, but I still didn't feel right throwing these out, even though they were a bit dry now. A quick warm-through, and they'd be fine.

Grabbing a bag from the cupboard, I loaded them all in and put them in the freezer, deciding I could deal with them later, when I had a better grasp of the magic I'd worked.

For now, I wanted to focus on things I understood, like taking out the garbage.

I ducked out the back door and ran almost directly into Rich, who had been crouched down near the ground, so hidden I hadn't noticed him at first. Dropping the garbage bag, I almost fell, but in a swift motion, Rich caught me in his arms before I completely lost my balance.

"Whoa, gotcha."

I waited, held close to him, briefly caught up in his fresh linen and bergamot smell, like he'd just gotten out of the shower and everything around him was extra clean. His eyes glinted like amber jewels in the low light from the streetlight overhead, and when he smiled, my heart did a stupid little flip-flop. I felt like a teenager.

Realizing I couldn't just stand like we were in an old Hollywood dip, I righted myself and stepped away from his embrace, feeling the chill of the night air even more than I had when I left the building.

I glanced around, realizing the crime scene tape was gone, and my parking space—and Rich's—were now ours to use again. I also noticed a shiny silver Mercedes parked behind what must have been Owen's shop. Guess the shoe business in Raven Creek did pretty well.

"You okay?" Rich asked, bringing my attention back to the man standing in front of me.

"Yeah, sorry—you kind of took me by surprise."

"I have a bad habit of doing that to you." He smiled at me, resting his hand on my arm still, as if he was worried I might still be on the verge of falling, even though we were both firmly planted on our own two feet. "Have a good night, Phoebe."

"You too." I watched him as he took the narrow alley between my store and The Green Thumb, heading for the entrance to his apartment.

It wasn't until he was gone that I realized he'd been kneeling exactly where the dead body had been last night.

Chapter Nineteen

My heart had been in my throat the entire drive home.
Even as I entered the house and was greeted by Bob's loud, demanding meow, all I could think about was Rich, crouched near the ground, doing heaven knows what to the now-open crime scene.

For all I knew he could have been tying his shoes, but that seemed just too much of a coincidence for me to let it go that easily. Someone had been dead on that same spot the night before, and while the police had surely found all the important evidence, it was still awfully strange for me to find Rich in the *exact* same spot when I came out the back door.

I didn't want to believe that my childhood friend might have something to do with the murder last night, but the more I thought about it, the more there were things I couldn't entirely account for when it came to Rich.

He did *live* at the crime scene, after all, and the police had been busy questioning him in his apartment when I'd arrived at the shop the previous evening. Then a stark and unsettling thought struck me.

What if the dead man hadn't been trying to get into the store at all? What if he had been there looking for Rich, and something happened between the two of them that had resulted in the bigger man's death.

I'd known Rich when we were just children, which made me inclined to want to believe he wasn't the kind of person capable of murder. But I had no idea who he was as an adult. Charming? Yes. Handsome? Obviously. But all he'd needed to do to win my trust was tell me his name and that Auntie Eudora had invited him to live in the apartment.

I realized I knew very little about the man Rich had become, and that meant I couldn't necessarily say I fully, completely, one hundred percent believed that he wasn't capable of killing anyone. Heck, I didn't even know what he did for a living. He could be a hired assassin for all I knew.

I swallowed hard and tried to shake off the thought because it was just a hair on the side of absurdity.

One thing was certain: I had absolutely no intention of letting a murderer live in my aunt's apartment, spending time above *my* store.

Bob meowed at me again, weaving his big body between my legs and distracting me from my macabre reverie. If I didn't pay attention to him, he was bound to trip me, so it would be a wise move for me to give my ginger roommate what he wanted most: food.

We went to the kitchen together, him leading the way like a tabby orange dart as soon as he knew where we were going.

Once inside, I set my bag on the kitchen table and put the almost empty canister of Lemon Meringue Pie tea mix on the counter. Whatever else happened tonight, I couldn't just spend the entire time thinking about Rich and his connection to the murder. I had tea to make.

I tried to tell myself I was getting carried away and looking for potential killers where there weren't any. Owen's rather cold warning from the morning echoed in my mind: *"We don't go accusing people of murder."* He was right, as much as it pained me to admit it. I couldn't just run around town assuming anyone that came near the store over the past two days could be a potential killer.

If I did that, I'd have to add Imogen and Amy to the list, not to mention every single person who owned a shop on Main Street, and any number of the customers who regularly frequented those businesses.

Certainly, if I was being honest, from an outside perspective *I* probably made a pretty compelling suspect. I was new in town, no one really knew me that well, and I'd been at the shop most recently when the murder happened. Of course, I knew I had nothing to do with it, but I could see how my profile might stack up against those of the other potential killers I was accusing in my head.

As I cracked open a tin of wet cat food and filled Bob's dish, I promised myself I would stay out of this case. There were police officers with more training and knowledge than me who were perfectly capable of solving this murder and didn't need my help.

All the same, those officers didn't spend day in and day out at the scene of the crime. And neither of those officers had accidentally made a delicious batch of honesty scones. I set Bob's dish on the floor, and he purred enthusiastically while chowing down on his special dinner. I made sure his dry food was filled as well and cleaned out his water dish to refill it with fresh. All the while I was thinking about the scones.

Maybe I'd imagined Dierdre's reaction to them, but then again, Imogen had been there as well and seemed just as impressed with what she'd seen.

It was time for me to stop pretending I could explain away the magic with logic. That tea had done something to Dierdre Miller, and enough people had told me that my aunt was a witch that it was time for me to start believing it.

Not just a new age Wiccan, but an actual honest-to-goodness *witch*. Whatever that meant, I didn't know, but this wasn't just herbs and crystals. This was magic.

Casting a glance at the tea canister on the counter, I picked it up and steeled myself at the top of the basement stairs.

My aunt had been a witch. I had been able to do something that looked an awful lot like magic today, with no training whatsoever. I wasn't mentally prepared to draw the line between point A and point B quite yet, but I knew I had to find whatever else Eudora had left me in this house, and I was going to start from the bottom.

Chapter Twenty

The basement was exactly as I had left it the day before, but now with the dark shades of evening, the overhead lighting gave the carousel horse an unsettling, almost menacing visage. Ignoring it for the time being, I made my way over to the shelves where Eudora had stored all her surplus teas.

They were shelved in alphabetical order, blessedly, and sure enough there was a big tin of Lemon Meringue Pie in between Juicy Berry and Licorice Twist. Freeze-dried fruit like strawberries and raspberries were the bonus ingredient in the former, while bits of Good & Plenty candy and fennel gave the latter its signature black licorice taste. I hated that tea, but then again, they weren't all going to be for me.

I took the big tin of Lemon Meringue Pie to a nearby table and set it beside the almost empty one from the store. Inside, Eudora's stash was pretty full, but once I took some for the store, even it would need to be replenished. Since most of the raw ingredients for her tea seemed to be down here in the basement, I decided it was high time I learned the family business.

Of course, she'd shown me dozens of times how she made her teas, even when I was a child. But watching her make them was very different from being here without her, doing it myself.

Luckily for me, and for all of her die-hard customers, inside the home canister was a five-by-seven laminated card that contained Eudora's handwritten instructions for creating the tea.

Eudora's Lemon Meringue Pie tea used a rooibos base. The bristly-looking red tea was native to South Africa originally and was a common base for herbal teas. It meant the finished result had a reddish hue to it—which I know had initially bothered Eudora—but the version she'd tried with a green tea base had been a bit too grassy for her tastes.

I followed her directions, mixing the rooibos base with dried lemon peel, which she had peeled into beautiful long ribbons. There was a big jar of them sitting with the other tea supplies, and I remember being so in awe of the peeler she used to get those perfect long curls instead of a finely grated yellow dust. I then added some dried marigold petals, a bit of Eudora's homemade vanilla sugar, and the secret final ingredient: mini white chocolate chips.

No one would expect something so artificial in an otherwise very natural tea blend, but as the chips melted, they added sweetness and even a little extra creaminess to the blend, making it something delicious and entirely different from similar blends online.

When all the ingredients were combined into a big glass bowl, I used wooden salad mixers, shaped like claws, to blend everything together until the contents looked like they were spread out evenly. I glanced into the canister from Eudora's shelf and sniffed, then looked at my own. I might have put in too many marigold petals, but otherwise I thought the two looked almost identical. They certainly smelled the same.

I used Eudora's reserves to fill the canister from the store, then added what was left into my mixing bowl, and combined hers with mine. When it was all blended together, I refilled the reserve container and put it back in its place on the shelf.

What I hadn't expected when I'd come downstairs was finding such a peaceful outlet for my anxiety. But making the tea and being reminded of all the things Eudora had shown me when I was a child made me feel more at peace and safer than I had in a very long time. It was as if the house itself and all its contents were giving me the comfort Eudora no longer could.

I couldn't exactly hug the house to thank it, but I patted one of the nearby walls tenderly, as if greeting a giant, friendly dog. As I finished tidying up, my stomach gave a loud rumble, reminding me I had a box of leftover pastries upstairs, but also that I should probably eat some real food before I indulged in an éclair.

I was almost back in the kitchen when I heard a loud pounding noise.

At first my brain registered it as the house, perhaps rejecting my kindness entirely, and planning to collapse in on itself now that my aunt was gone. But as I came back to reality, I recognized that no, it was actually someone knocking insistently on the front door.

I was reaching for the knob to open it, when the pounding stopped, and the resulting silence rang in my ears unexpectedly. My pulse kicked up several notches as it occurred to me I had absolutely no idea who might be outside the door because no one had ever bothered to install a peephole.

There were small windows on either side of the big double doors, but the embarrassed part of me didn't want to be that weirdo who stared out windows before opening doors. Raven Creek might not be a leave-your-doors-unlocked-at-night kind of town anymore, but it was definitely still an open-your-door-to-neighbors kind of town.

Still, I was reasonably on edge, considering everything that had happened over the last twenty-four hours, so it took me a few moments to psych myself up, then unlock and open the door, holding my breath almost the entire time.

My breath came out in a whoosh when I saw that my front porch was completely empty.

No one was there.

Chapter
Twenty-One

With the hesitancy of a groundhog in February, I slowly peeked my head out the door, looking left and right to see if my would-be visitor had just wandered off briefly while waiting for me to answer.

But no, it appeared I was entirely alone, and what's more there was no sign of anyone nearby. If it had been a door-to-door salesman or someone offering to paint my house, surely I'd be able to see them walking away. Lane End House was literally at the end of the road, after all.

Yet there was no one.

A chill crept up my spine, and the voice in the back of my mind whispered, *Go back inside.*

I didn't need to be told twice. I closed the door and locked it, then double-checked the lock immediately, just to be sure I'd done it right the first time.

That had been very weird, and on top of all of the other things going on this week, it set my nerves on edge all over again. Living in a small town was supposed to be quiet and relaxing, but in my short time here I'd been accosted, yelled at, proxy to a murder, and generally spooked out of my wits more than I would like to admit.

I don't care what people say about big cities, because frankly small towns could take the cake in terms of being unsettling to the max. I waited by the door for a good five minutes, half expecting my mystery guest to knock again the moment I stepped away from it, and I wanted to be ready to catch them in the act.

"Probably just teenagers playing a joke," I mumbled, reminding myself Lane End House had its own mythology in Raven Creek, and I was going to have to get used to the local kids using it as a way to frighten each other and test their fortitude.

In Eudora's life, it had been the witch's house, and now that she was gone, they probably shared stories about it being haunted by her ghost. In both cases, I couldn't decide how close the rumors were to reality. As it turned out Eudora really *had* been a witch. And with more and more frequency I'd begun to wonder if her spirit was still lingering around the place.

When I finally decided that no one was planning to knock on the door again, Bob and I returned to the kitchen to focus on my rumbling stomach. Props to the fat cat for following me to the door, though I wasn't sure if it was to offer protection or just the curious desire to see a stranger murder me.

Bob was still something of a mystery to me, but I was fairly certain that if I kept feeding him wet food on a semi-regular basis and gave him a warm roof over his head, he probably wouldn't eat me in my sleep.

Probably.

I didn't have a lot of energy to cook something fancy and was incredibly grateful to my past self for planning ahead in terms of grocery shopping. It had all been worth it to haul that shopping cart up the hill on my first night here.

Very few things in life served to comfort me quite the way that carbs did, so I set a pot of water on to boil, then added a healthy dose of salt to it. Once the bubbles were rolling, I added linguine into the pot—I always preferred linguine to spaghetti because of its nice broad noodles—and dug a jar of pasta sauce out of the pantry.

Normally I might pretend to make it a healthy well-balanced meal by adding a side salad, but I couldn't be bothered to fake it tonight. Who was I going to impress—the cat? I poured the jarred sauce directly onto the strained pasta, and the extent of my fancy life choices were some nice, petal-shaved parmesan flakes and fresh basil leaves from the little pot Eudora kept in her kitchen window.

Add some fresh ground black pepper and *voila*, a lazy meal that could almost pass for rustic gourmet if you squinted at it long enough.

I dumped the whole thing into a big pasta bowl and with a glass of wine in tow, Bob and I made our way to the living room.

In spite of the mostly antique wares in the house, Eudora had an incredibly modern entertainment setup in the living room. About a year before she died, she had splurged on one of those fancy TV sets that looked like framed art, so when I walked into the room, it was set to John William Waterhouse's *The Lady of Shalott*, the iconic, sad portrait of a heartsick women in her boat, headed to heaven knows where.

Eudora had loved the real painting and had a few other Waterhouse prints stashed around the place, including *The*

Magic Circle, which was so damned witchy it was a wonder I hadn't figured out the truth about my aunt a lot sooner.

Honestly, I must have known all along, but I think I'd assumed she was one of those hippie "witches" who charged their crystals under a full moon and thought burning some palo santo sticks was the height of enlightenment. Never in a million years had I thought she was a *witch* witch, who was capable of genuine influence over others.

Instead of thinking too much about what that made me, and whether I should be upset about not getting my letter to Hogwarts as a child, I plopped down on Eudora's overstuffed crimson velvet sofa and turned on the big TV.

There would be plenty of time to worry about my potential latent magical powers or question whether my new crush might be a murderer.

For now, there was *Bob's Burgers* and pasta.

Chapter
Twenty-Two

That night I dreamed I was caught in a spider's web.

I was small, the size of a fly, or maybe the web was as big as my house—it was impossible to tell within the confines of the dream. First, I noticed a sticky feeling under my hands, but as I lifted them to see what I had touched, they wouldn't budge.

Then as I struggled to get my hand free, my arm became stuck, and the more I moved and thrashed, desperate to get free, the more the web kept me tightly in place. I tried to scream, but my voice was useless and empty. Nothing came out, and there was no one here to help me anyway. I was alone in a void of blackness.

As it became abundantly clear I would not be able to wrench myself free, the web began to vibrate and hum. At first, I thought it was just from my struggling, but soon the sensation began to move closer, and it reminded me of the way you could touch railroad tracks sometimes and feel the movement of a train that was still a long way off.

Something was coming toward me, and it was incredibly big.

I swallowed hard, my heart pounding so loudly the throb of my pulse was the only thing I could hear. The creature came closer and closer, the web beginning to bob and shudder, and then just as the spider was about to emerge from the darkness, I was suddenly standing in the middle of a sidewalk. I could tell I was on a block in Raven Creek, but there were no houses or stores on either side of the sidewalk, just the same inky blackness.

The sound of footsteps on concrete echoed from the darkness, getting louder as they grew nearer. I didn't know where I was or which way might get me to safety, nor could I tell where the footfalls were coming from.

Without a doubt, I knew that whoever was running toward me was the person who had killed the man behind my store, and if I could just see through the darkness, I would know who it was, once and for all.

Instead of dread, I squinted, urging it to come closer, come closer. An unfamiliar tingling sensation tickled my fingertips, and there was a buzzing sensation at the base of my brain, like I was trying to remember a word or a gesture that might help me part the shadows.

I felt so close to what I needed—if I could just reach out a little further, see a little better, remember the missing words.

Then, from the dark under me, Eudora's voice said, *You're not ready for this just yet.*

* * *

I sat bolt upright in bed, panting from the adrenaline of the nightmare and swatting at my arms as if there might be little spiders all over me even now. Spiders freaked me out at the best of times, and it had taken almost my entire adult life to be able to deal with them without the help of a parent or my ex-husband.

Now I was probably going to need therapy before I ever looked at one again.

Yikes.

Talk about a messed-up dream. The eight-legged monster had been a spider, yes, but then it had become something else. At first I thought it had also been the killer, like I knew the answer to the puzzle, and all I'd needed was that last little piece, the glimpse of the monster's face. But then I heard Eudora's voice, and it made me wonder if maybe it *wasn't* the killer, but rather something else my mind wanted to reveal to me.

All of this was crazy, of course. A *dream* couldn't tell me who had killed my would-be thief. That remained a job for the police in spite of my complete and utter lack of willingness to let it go. And a dream couldn't tell me secrets about myself either.

Could it?

I glanced at the alarm clock on my bedside table, which told me it was shortly after five. I could try to go back to bed for an hour before getting myself ready for the morning pastry pickup, but after that dream I wasn't really sure I ever wanted to close my eyes again, thank you very much.

Sighing loudly, I kicked off my duvet, regretting it instantly when the cold wall of early morning October air hit me. At least it wasn't so cold that it suggested the furnace was off again. No, this was just the usual late autumn reminder that I was better off in bed.

I decided the best thing for my nerves and my restless mind would be a good run. I'd been neglecting my fitness routine throughout the course of my move, which meant I'd done little more than pack boxes for the past six weeks. Now that I was settled, it seemed like as good a time as any to get back into my normal rhythm, which usually consisted of a nice three-mile run every morning, followed by a scalding-hot shower and a good cup of coffee.

Every part of that sounded ideal to me right about now.

I rifled through my drawers, trying to remember where I'd stashed my workout apparel, then slipped into some running gear that would protect me from the chill of the morning air but that I wouldn't melt in. With my shoes on and my earbuds tucked into my ears, I gave a still-sleepy Bob a farewell pat and locked the front door, tucking the key into the zipper on my sleeve.

The sun wasn't up by the time I hit the sidewalk, but the horizon was turning the light purple hazy shade that indicated sunrise wasn't far off. Since I wasn't used to running in Raven Creek yet, I decided to just stick to the nearby residential areas and loop back to Main Street before heading home. I was sure there were some great running trails nearby that would get me into the wilderness, but for now I wanted to stay where I could easily find my way back to the house.

Even though it had been weeks since I'd last been running, I soon found my stride—perhaps a little slower than I was accustomed to—and turned the volume up on my music to keep me motivated on my pace. Daft Punk was my favorite for runs because it was such a consistent drive that I never wanted to slow down.

Fifteen minutes into the run I started to turn toward Main, knowing I probably only had about another fifteen minutes more to go to hit my three-mile goal, and I wanted to be back home when I did. As I turned down Mockingbird, running past all the dark houses, only one or two lights on to indicate other people in town might be starting their day, the hairs on the back of my neck stood on end.

Someone was standing in the middle of the sidewalk.

It was still dark enough out that I couldn't make out their face, and they wore a large hat and bulky coat, making it completely impossible to even tell if it was a man or a woman, whether they were fat or thin. The figure was at the end of the block, outside the light of the nearest streetlamp.

I stopped running.

At a different time, in a different place, and with one fewer murders, I might not have even noticed them. I might have assumed it was someone walking to work or taking their dog for a morning potty break.

But not today.

The figure didn't move, but just stood there in the middle of the sidewalk. They weren't exactly blocking me, and they weren't close enough to be actively threatening, but all the same, I was terrified and had no interest in getting any closer to this person.

As I glanced over my shoulder, trying to decide the best direction to run to get away from them while also heading to a more populated area, they started walking toward me. They weren't running, but the strides were fast and purposeful. I didn't want to lead this person to where I lived, but turning back and running toward home seemed like the only logical plan, since they were blocking my way to Main Street.

I turned off my music, the stupid, polite-neighbor part of my brain wondering if maybe they were trying to get my attention.

No, they weren't saying anything; they were just moving toward me quickly enough that I knew I ought to get the heck out of there.

I ran.

I ran without looking back or thinking about anything beyond putting one foot in front of the other and setting a new personal best for getting myself to the safety of my home. Even though I couldn't hear them behind me, I continued to run at practically my top speed until Lane End House appeared around the bend.

Slowing down just enough that I could recover my key without dropping it, I took the stairs two at a time, unlocked my front door, and threw myself inside, hurriedly locking it behind me.

It was only when I was safely inside and the adrenaline began to fade that the shock and fear really hit. I slumped to the floor in front of the door, pulling my knees against my chest, and took some slow, steadying breaths to try and regain my composure.

Once again, the logical part of my brain tried to tell me I was making too big of a deal out of this, and that there was a good chance one of my new neighbors now thought I was a crazy person for running away from them when they were just going to say hi.

But the part of me who had seen one too many scary movies knew it hadn't been crazy to run away, and that sticking around to be polite was how well-meaning people got themselves killed.

At the end of the day, someone had been murdered, and I didn't feel like being the next person on the list.

Chapter
Twenty-Three

"You look like you've seen a ghost," Amy announced when I dragged myself into her café an hour later.

Evidently the hot shower and a layer of my most expensive makeup had done nothing to keep me from looking like a shell-shocked scaredy cat. Oh well.

"Whatever the special is today, better make mine a double."

She smiled, though the concern she'd shown when I walked in hadn't left her eyes. It seemed like she wanted to ask me more about it, but instead she set to work filling up a paper cup for me.

The café smelled like cinnamon and fresh bread, and just being so close to so many incredible smells was doing wonders to steady my frayed nerves. My two big pastry boxes were already waiting for me on the counter, a large smiley face drawn on the top in black marker.

"I heard that Dierdre came into the shop yesterday and caused quite a scene. I really hope you're not letting her get to you. She's a lot of huff and puff, that one, but she won't actually blow your house down."

I leaned against the counter with one hip, crossing my arms over my chest and wrapping my thick cardigan around me as I did. Between the oversized sweater and the scents floating around the café, I could almost transmute myself back into being okay.

"I don't know about her," I confessed. "Folks make a lot of excuses for people like Dierdre Miller, and then suddenly those same friendly neighbors are being interviewed on the news, saying things like *She was always so quiet and reserved, none of us ever thought she'd secretly be an axe murderer.*"

Amy laughed as she poured steamed milk over my drink. "We might say a lot of things about Dierdre, but *quiet* and *reserved* will never be among them. You don't actually think she had something to do with the murder, do you?"

"Are you going to give me the same lecture that Shoe Store Owen did yesterday?"

Amy set the drink down in front of me. It smelled chocolatey and delightfully full of sugar and coffee. Heaven. I resisted picking it up and sipping it immediately because I didn't feel like burning my mouth, and also because Amy looked like she might have something to say.

"Owen Talbot?"

"Yeah, are there a lot of Shoe Store Owens running around?"

"No, just the one. What did he say to you?" She seemed genuinely curious, but a little more curious than my comment perhaps warranted.

"He gave me a bit of a lecture on how people in this town are good to each other, and we don't run around accusing each other of murder—something along those lines."

"Hmm."

"Hmm?"

"It's just funny that Owen would come in at all. I think he's still pretty mad about what Eudora's estate lawyer said to him."

Now this tidbit was news to me. I hadn't heard anything about Owen before meeting him yesterday. What could he have possibly wanted from Eudora's lawyer? Did he think he was supposed to be in the will?

Oh goodness, had he and Eudora been . . . an item?

I somehow couldn't picture her smooching Owen, even if he was pretty handsome for his age. He was a little too *much* to be someone I could imagine Eudora with. Their personalities would have clashed from day one.

"When your aunt died, two people were *very* interested in picking up her lease on the shop, to close it up and start something new. One of them was Dierdre."

"So, she wanted the house *and* the shop. Wow, she didn't waste much time circling the grave, did she?"

Amy gave me a soft smile and continued. "It didn't matter. I'm sure the lawyer explained this to you, but maybe the importance didn't sink in at the time. I imagine you were dealing with a lot when you inherited the estate. But Eudora must have added your name to the shop's lease before she died. The way Main Street leasing agreements work is that the shops can be owned by families in perpetuity for as long as someone in the same family is listed on the lease.

Dierdre probably thought that because Eudora had no children, the lease had restored to the landlord after Eudora died, and she was *very* interested in getting her hands on the location. It's a pretty prime space, as I'm sure you can imagine."

"I can see why." I hadn't realized Eudora had done that for me. It showed how much faith she had that I would uproot my life and come run her beloved store. I was a bit surprised she hadn't explained it in her letter, but Amy was right: the lawyer had probably said something when I hadn't been paying complete attention. "What does that have to do with Owen?"

"Well, Dierdre wasn't the only person who wanted to get the lease on that shop. The other person was Owen Talbot."

Chapter
Twenty-Four

Entering my shop in a daze, I wished Imogen were there to open with me so I could talk to her about what I'd just learned.

Since it seemed like everyone in this town was enmeshed in all the business and personal dealings of those around them, I was willing to bet she already knew about the attempts to undermine Eudora's lease. Heck, since she'd been the one holding down the fort here since my aunt died, I wouldn't have been surprised if she had been on the front lines of fending off the commercial vultures.

The more I thought about it, the more it made sense that Owen had wanted to try to lease this unit. He had a business practically next door, and his shop was a heck of a lot smaller than ours. Eudora effectively owned two stores' worth of space and had made the most of it. Any other retailer on the block would covet having so much room to work with.

I hadn't loved my interaction with Owen, but I could definitely understand why he might be a little prickly toward me since I had denied him the opportunity to expand his business into a bigger space. Amy made it sound like he bore a bit of a grudge, which definitely showed in his attitude, but aside from being a bit gruff, it wasn't like he'd threatened to run me out of town or anything.

Maybe I would take a little time this week to stop in at his shop and ask him about the lease request to see what he had to say about it.

Dierdre wanting the shop was more mystifying. I had to admit that in spite of all my chatter about her and all our interactions, I still had no idea what Dierdre *did* for a living. She struck me as an independently wealthy type who flaunted her money around but didn't actually do much for her community or hold down a regular job.

That might have been unfair of me, but I had seen her numerous times, in the middle of a workday, just waltzing around downtown like she had nothing but time on her hands. If she had a job, she didn't seem to be there much, so what did she need a large storefront for?

I set the boxes of pastry on the counter, busying myself with putting them out onto clean platters and filling up the display cabinet. I returned the newly filled canister of Lemon Meringue Pie tea to the shelf and tried to push all these intrusive thoughts out of my mind.

I told myself that when Imogen arrived, I would call Detective Martin and let her know what I'd learned about Dierdre's connection to the case. I still couldn't quite decide what to make of her confession session the day before, but if the man had been claiming to know my aunt, the police should know about that so they could look for potential connections.

But what about Rich?

It was so suspicious that he'd been outside looking at the crime scene, but maybe that was my mind playing tricks on me, making him look guilty of something when he hadn't actually been doing anything wrong.

I would decide when I called whether or not I'd mention Rich, or my little morning run-in with the figure in the overcoat. If I told the detective too much, she was going to start thinking I was inserting myself into the case. Any true crime fan knows that's a sure-fire way to have the police think you're suspicious. Sloppy criminals, desperate for attention, love to get involved by offering the police tips or assistance.

Didn't those same rules also tell me that killers loved to return to the scene of the crime?

Which meant whoever had killed that man might show up at my store any time.

"Stop it," I scolded myself out loud. I was about an hour away from turning into a tinfoil hat–wearing conspiracy theorist at this point, where I might start believing the whole town was in on it just to scare me into leaving, and *that* was as crazy an idea as I could come up with.

I was being silly, and I was trying to solve a crime that I didn't have the knowledge or skill set to solve on my own. I told myself that as soon as I reported what I'd learned about Dierdre to Detective Martin, I was done getting involved with the case and would leave it to the experts to solve.

When the front display cabinet was loaded with goodies, I headed back into the kitchen to put away the dishes I had cleaned last night, prep the daily batch of shortbread, and make a preferably non-magical bread option.

I got the shortbread mixed and packed into its tight rolls, then popped it in the fridge to chill. The scones yesterday had been lovely, and I was betting a batch of the same, but slightly less truth inducing, would be a hit today. I opted for Eudora's Lemon Lavender blend, knowing the combo of bright lemon rind and floral lavender would taste incredible with a light lemon glaze and partner beautifully with any of our citrus or creamier tea blends.

I got to work mixing the sourdough batter together and decided that while I was at it, I might prep a few proper sourdough loaves for tomorrow. Sourdough bread is definitely a plan-ahead thing to bake, since the dough needs to go through several lengthy rises. I could do the initial rise during work today, then beat it down and let it rise again overnight before baking it in the morning.

We didn't often sell full loaves here, but I suspected some folks would like the broad slices of bread with honey, or even an avocado toast lunch special if the grocery store had decently ripe avocados. I'd have to check after work.

Filled with absolute delight over the idea of lunch specials *tomorrow*, I almost forgot to keep an eye on the clock today. The scones were fresh out of the oven, and I had enough time to put the shortbread in and start tackling the new release wall.

It would be a job that would probably take me a few hours, but because the wall was situated right between the tea shop and the bookstore, it was an easy enough chore to work on while we were open.

First thing, though, I needed a blank canvas, which meant finding a home for the almost two-month-old collection of books already on display. I went into the bookstore side of The Earl's Study, grabbed the handy-dandy library cart, and proceeded to empty six long front-facing shelves of the newest and best . . . from August.

Some of the titles that I'd seen listed in the most recent *New York Times* bestseller list I moved to a "New and Noteworthy" table that was a few feet in front of the wall, but the wall itself—according to Eudora—was strictly new releases of any conceivable genre.

If a book was coming out in a given week, whether it was romance, sci-fi, literary fiction, or a long-awaited cookbook from a celebrity chef, it would find its home on this shelf. Eudora didn't believe in marginalizing genre fiction because she thought it gave readers a reason to put the "guilty" in "guilty pleasure." In Eudora's opinion, and mine, there should be no such thing as a guilty pleasure, only things you liked.

In some stores the new release wall could look like a competition for literary awards or display only highly touted biographies, but ours was a bit more eclectic. Since nothing was technically in its long-term home, we could mix and match which titles went where, with no need to stick to author naming or title conventions.

I thought today it might be fun to put them in a rainbow pattern.

Once the older titles were off the front shelves, I pushed the cart back over to the bookstore side, where I hoped Imogen might help me find long-term living arrangements for them. She had been consistent with unpacking the weekly deliveries in my absence, but since we hadn't been open, she hadn't bothered to change over the wall, which was fine by me.

It meant I only had this week's new books to unload, rather than over a month of backstock. It was still a good half-dozen large, heavy boxes that would need to be sorted through, but I liked the idea of a task to keep my hands busy and my mind occupied.

The timer clipped to my apron beeped at me, to let me know the cookies were now ready to come out of the oven, which was also a sure sign it was time to open the front door. I loaded up trays with the non-magical but still delicious goodies I had prepared and added them to the display case alongside the decadent treats from Amy's.

With everything in its right place and all my boxes stacked by the new release wall, ready for me to get creative, I switched on the "Open" sign and unlocked the front door. A wave of anxiety hit me the moment I turned the bolt, as I half expected Dierdre to barge in, or perhaps to come face to face with the eerie figured I'd seen that morning during my run.

Instead, everything remained quiet.

We were one of only a handful of businesses that opened as early as eight, so I guessed the first day had been a bit of an anomaly, with so many guests eager to see things—or lecture me—that they'd been early risers. Being open early made sense for us, though, especially with Amy being open early next door.

What went better with a latte than browsing a bookstore?

Of course, I was partial to tea with my books but couldn't deny that a good bit of caffeine in the morning was usually just what the doctor ordered. I remembered, then, my own delicious latte, which was surely now cold, but I couldn't let it go to waste.

I recovered the cup from the kitchen and took a long drink. This brew wasn't her usual chocolate hazelnut blend. The chocolate base was still present, but the flavor was rich and spicy with notes of cinnamon and . . . was that chili powder?

The latte was indeed cold by this point, but it was still incredible, and I finished it in a few quick gulps, the espresso hitting my system all at once. Riding the high from my latte superpowers, I got the new release wall unpacked in about two hours and met a few more curious townspeople who were either interested in seeing me, or interested in asking about the murder.

Unfortunately, that meant I couldn't fully forget about it, so by the time Imogen arrived at ten, I knew I had to make a call to the detective.

Chapter
Twenty-Five

I said a polite hello to Imogen when she arrived, then begged off, saying, "I just need to make a quick call, okay?"

She didn't ask any questions and instead immediately grabbed the loaded library cart and set to work finding space for the new books. I'd ask her what her expert opinion on my wall was as soon as I got off the phone with Detective Martin.

I considered taking the call in my office, which would have been private, but decided I needed a bit of fresh air and a break from the store, so I ducked out the back with my cell phone, Martin's card stowed safely in my apron pocket.

My initial plan had been to sit on the back stoop, but as soon as I was outside, all I could see was the spot where the dead man's body had been lying, and I couldn't bring myself to sit there. It just felt weird at this point. I wasn't sure I'd ever be able to walk past that place and *not* see a body.

I dialed Martin's number and wandered out into the empty lot behind my parking spot, where the dumpsters sat, as well as a fair bit of unattended garbage.

"Detective Martin." Her voice was cool and calm, even over the phone.

"Hello, Detective. It's Phoebe Winchester. Um, from the . . . uh, crime scene?"

Idiot.

"Of course, Ms. Winchester, what can I do for you?"

I explained to her what I'd learned over the past day, trying to avoid any implication that I'd been sticking my nose where it didn't belong. I emphasized both Dierdre's claim that she hadn't known the dead man and also her apparent interest in getting access to the shop's lease.

"We also spoke to Ms. Miller."

"Oh yeah, I guess you would have."

"She failed to mention to us that she had interest in leasing the shop after your aunt died, though. That's very interesting. Was there anything else you happened to learn?" The way she said *learn* made it pretty clear she knew I was being a grade-A busybody. Oh well.

I glanced up at the building, to where Rich's apartment windows faced the back lane. I half expected him to be standing there, watching me. But the blinds were drawn, and the lights appeared to be off.

It didn't sit right, him being out here last night, but the police had talked to him and clearly hadn't found a reason to arrest him. Maybe they knew more than I did, and I had to accept that.

I also briefly considered telling Detective Martin about my encounter with the person on my run that morning, but I wasn't sure what I could say that wouldn't sound insane. *I'm pretty sure a weirdo wearing a coat was following me this morning.* I shook my head, deciding some things were just better left unsaid. If I saw the creep again, maybe I'd bring it up, but for now there were any number of explanations that could account for what I'd seen.

"We don't go around accusing our neighbors of murder."

"Ms. Winchester?" Detective Martin interrupted my daydream.

"No, nothing else."

She made a small *mmm* noise like she didn't entirely believe me, which is fair because I'm an absolutely dreadful liar, but she didn't push it. "I appreciate you calling. If you learn anything new or remember anything, you know where to find me."

I remembered a question before she was able to hang up. "Oh, Detective Martin?"

"Yes?"

"What was his name, do you know?"

"The victim?"

"Yeah."

She hesitated. "I suppose that's not top secret. We've identified him from his fingerprints, his name was Carl 'Ox' Bullock."

"Ox?"

"Mm-hmm."

"Fitting."

"You have a good day, Ms. Winchester." She hung up before I could distract her any longer.

I pocketed my phone and stared at the place where they'd found Carl. Ox. Between the beefy nickname, and her casual mention of finding his identity from his fingerprints, I had to assume Ox had a criminal past. That wouldn't be too unexpected given that they thought he'd been breaking in when he died.

Still, a criminal past—or even criminal intent—didn't mean the guy had deserved to die. I played with the necklace Eudora had given me, wishing she'd been considerate enough to leave me a working crystal ball too.

I just wanted to know who in this town was capable of murder.

Chapter
Twenty-Six

Imogen and I were kept busy for the rest of the day, with the lemon lavender scones being a big hit and our mystery book table a popular draw for the second day in a row. At four, things were slowing down enough that I thought it might be safe to leave Imogen on her own for the last two hours.

"I can stay," I offered for about the twelfth time.

Imogen practically pushed me out the front door, shaking her head. "You're as bad as Eudora, I swear. There's life outside the shop, Phoebe. Go explore your new town, try out a new restaurant. Do *something*."

I wanted to argue that work was doing something, but before I could, a deep, smoke-and-honey voice interjected from behind me. "I can think of a couple good places to eat. If you're hungry, that is."

I didn't even need to turn around, the way my heart had started pounding at the first syllable was the only clue I needed to tell me who was standing there.

"Yes," Imogen said, clapping her hands together gladly. "Let Rich show you around—he's the perfect person." I was pretty sure anyone that would get me out of her hair for the last two hours of her shift would be the "perfect person," but I slowly turned around, a nervous smile on my face, and looked into Rich's beautiful amber eyes.

Ugh, why did he have to be so *pretty*?

"You want to go?" he asked me directly.

No. Yes. No. Maybe? *Argh.* "Sure." I couldn't say no just because I thought there was something fishy going on. And maybe if we were sitting down together, I could get him to open up a bit, and he might spill something he didn't intend to. It was a bit of a long shot, but if he was involved in Ox's death, I needed to know one way or another.

We waved goodbye to Imogen and headed down the block, past The Green Thumb, a plant store, and then Owen's shop, which were both still brightly lit but didn't appear to have anyone inside. Seeing Owen's place reminded me I still needed to get myself some comfier shoes and perhaps chat with him about his interest in my shop, but this probably wasn't the best moment for a detour.

"How are you liking the town so far?" Rich asked.

I snorted out a laugh.

"I suppose that might be a bit of an unfair question given how your first week has been going."

"Yeah, maybe ask me again in a couple of months." I silently added an *if I'm still here.* I couldn't picture myself leaving, because I had nowhere else to go, if I was being honest, but to say things were off to a rocky start here was quite possibly the understatement of the year.

We walked down Main, which was already fairly quiet in the early evening, and he used a hand at the small of my back to indicate we would be taking a left turn at the next corner. Once again, I was surprised by how comforting and familiar his closeness felt, and scolded myself that I was letting my potential feelings for Rich blind me to any of his possible super-problematic flaws.

But if I was making a habit of trusting my gut, which generally seemed to be a good idea on most days, then maybe I should trust that I liked Rich for a good reason and that my gut was smart enough to not let me fall for a killer.

Your gut also let you marry your ex, I reminded myself. This wasn't altogether true, though. Even as I'd headed down the aisle with Blaine, something had been telling me loudly that it was a big mistake. And lo and behold, it most definitely had been.

See? Gut check.

I appreciated that Rich let me have my extended moment of internal contemplation, because it must have looked to him like I was quietly off in my own world. Most people got bored with waiting for me to come back on my own when I got lost in thought, either nudging me or repeating their last question, but he seemed content to let me get there on my own.

Three blocks off Main was another stretch of shops, these ones feeling slightly cozier and more laid back than the highly trafficked ones on the main drag. The Earl's Study would have felt perfectly at home between the yarn shop called Knittin' Pearl and the charming, witchy, new age shop called New Moon.

I'd had no idea there was a new age shop in town, and part of me wanted to go in and start grilling them about Eudora and whether I was a witch too, and how I could potentially use magic to solve crimes, but I put a hold button on that.

For one thing, the people who ran the shop were very likely not witches, or at least not the same kind of witch that Eudora had been, and I would probably freak them out if I went in demanding too much info.

The other thing was that Rich pointed toward the most enchanting little diner I'd ever seen. A big neon sign on the front read "Sweet Peach's," and though it was still early for dinner, not even five, quite a few cars were parked out front.

"Why did I think you'd be taking me to, like, a fancy Italian place or something? I figured you would try to impress me," I teased.

"Trust me, I *am* trying to impress you, and if I can't do that with Peach's milkshakes and a press burger, then I'm afraid you've seen all my tricks."

We went up the stairs, and the girl behind the counter, in a cute teal uniform, waved us toward a bank of empty booths. "Sit wherever you want—be with you in a sec." She smiled warmly, but it was obvious she was busy.

Five other tables were filled, mostly with folks I would classify as "seniors," but also one couple with young kids, probably hoping they could sneak in an early bedtime once everyone was stuffed with burgers.

Rich guided me to a booth with a window that faced the street we'd just come from, so we could see the comings and goings of people at the nearby stores, as well as anyone coming into the diner.

He didn't bother to pick up a menu, but I wasn't a regular and needed a bit more time. "What do you recommend?" I asked.

"You can't go wrong with anything you choose; I have to admit, even their salads are good. But if you come to Peach's and order a salad, you're living your life wrong. Cheeseburger. Fries. Milkshake."

"That sounds like something a teenage boy would order before a football game."

"No, no. It sounds like what a sensible person who likes good food would order so they can enjoy their evening. And their company." He smiled at me, and my insides melted like ice cream on a hot sidewalk.

"Well, all right then, consider my arm twisted."

Our waitress appeared shortly, a pretty Asian girl whose name tag said "Lyla."

"You guys have a chance to look at the menu?" She glanced over at Rich and rolled her eyes, but in a friendly way. "Not that I even need to ask you, Rich."

"I'll have the usual, Lyla."

"Of course you will." She didn't bother writing anything down, and I had to wonder just how often he came here that the staff knew his precise order.

"How about you, hon?" Lyla was probably a good ten years younger than me, but she still gave off the comforting cozy vibe of an old-timey diner waitress, so her calling me "hon" didn't feel forced or weird. I kind of loved it.

"I'll get the cheeseburger, add caramelized onions, hold the relish, side fries, and a strawberry shake."

"Comin' right up." Lyla wrote my substitutions down and left the table.

"Strawberry?" Rich said.

"Yup, there's absolutely no better milkshake flavor on earth—I don't care how fancy the options are. Why? What did you get?"

"Oh, I'm a purist. Vanilla all the way."

"And you're making fun of *me* for ordering strawberry?"

"What can I say, I'm a man of refined tastes."

I snorted, unable to help myself. I was being extra-elegant on this . . . was this a date? I wasn't sure what to call it. It was certainly two old friends connecting, but if I had still been a teenager, I would definitely have assumed that milkshakes with a cute boy was a real date.

Of course, I was thirty-five, not fourteen, like I was when I'd last been friends with Rich, so things got a little more nuanced the older we got.

Lyla returned with our milkshakes, and as I was making room in front of me for mine, my elbow knocked my glass of water off the edge of the table.

I panicked, reaching for it reflexively, and everything seemed to move in slow motion. But as I resigned myself to knowing I wouldn't be fast enough to catch the glass, something unusual happened. For a moment I was so fixated on the glass that I barely realized it, but things didn't just *seem* to be going in slow motion: they were actually frozen.

I got hold of the glass, a splash of water frozen in place over the lip like a little mini wave, and I replaced it on the table, letting out a little whoosh of relief.

Then I noticed Lyla was literally immobile, her face locked in an expression of surprise as she watched the glass fall. Rich, too, was frozen where he'd been when I knocked the water over, half out of his seat, like he thought he might be able to catch the glass from there. Around the restaurant, all the diners were motionless, burgers halfway to their mouths, or stuck mid-sentence in whatever they'd been saying.

Outside, a car on the street was paused in the middle of the road, just . . . not moving. It wasn't parked; it had simply stopped moving.

I released my hand from the glass and let out a long breath to steady myself. As I withdrew my hand, the world around me started to move again, going from frozen to live action, just as it had been before. It only took a second or two, but it was wild to see the change happening. The noise returned, and Lyla's reaction shifted from surprise to confusion, as did Rich's.

"I thought . . ." He didn't finish his sentence, just looked from the floor to the table, and realized the glass was sitting there safely.

"Wow, those are some good reflexes," Lyla said once she regained her composure.

I stared at the glass and at my hand, still trying to process what had happened.

Had I just accidentally stopped time?

Chapter Twenty-Seven

Since I couldn't exactly run screaming from the restaurant after my frozen-time moment, nor could I ask Rich or Lyla if they had seen what I had—because neither of them seemed especially keen to suggest they had—I continued through the rest of dinner like nothing had happened.

Rich must have sensed the shift in my mood, though, because I had definitely stopped making jokes or poorly flirting with him. I'd even stopped wondering if every other thing he said was an indication he was secretly a killer and that I should *stop* flirting with him immediately. He soon stopped asking so many questions, and the meal took on a more rigid and formal feel.

I ate and enjoyed my burger, but nothing was the same. I felt like I was in a waking dream where none of this was real, and I couldn't understand what was happening. First there were the Truth Be Told scones, which I'd been willing to write off as a fluke and to think that perhaps Dierdre had just decided to overshare a little that day.

But there was no easy way to explain what had just happened to me without magic being real. Either magic was real, and I might be a witch, or else I was going nuts, and I didn't really like option B. Option A was a hard enough pill to swallow, but at least then a lot of the stuff I'd been experiencing since arriving in Raven Creek would make a bit more sense.

Emphasis on *a bit* because not a heck of a lot was making sense here in general.

"Hey, are you okay?" Rich asked finally. "I thought we were having a pretty good time at first, but now I feel like you want to be anywhere else but here. Did I say something?"

I blinked at him a few times, as if I'd forgotten he was here at all, I'd been so lost in thought and worry over my potential newfound powers.

"No, you've been great—I'm so sorry." I struggled to find an explanation for my behavior that wouldn't send him running for the hills or get me locked up in an institution. "I'm just feeling a little off. I keep thinking about what happened at the shop." This wasn't entirely a lie but also wasn't even remotely the whole truth.

"I know what you mean."

This gave me an unprecedented opportunity to ask him a bit more about the murder, which hadn't been my intent, but I wasn't about to hold back and not ask a few questions. I didn't *want* Rich to be the killer, but I couldn't just let him off the hook because I thought he was cute. I sort of wished I'd brought one of those Truth Be Told scones along with me to see if they worked on everyone or if Dierdre had just been a special case.

"Were you home when it happened?" I asked.

He shook his head. "I work weird hours, so I probably got home not long before the police called you." He must have registered a question on my face that I hadn't asked out loud, because he added, "You showed up about fifteen minutes after I did. I could hear you talking to the detective from upstairs."

I let his words process for a moment while taking another bite of my burger. Now that I'd distracted myself, I could actually really taste the flavor, and it was incredible. "I don't think I ever asked you what it is you do. I know the first time we bumped into each other, you were leaving for work as I was finishing at the shop. Do you have an overnight shift somewhere?" He'd been pretty nicely dressed at the time, as he was now, in a button-down white shirt and nicely tailored pants.

Rich gave a half-hearted smile. "I get the feeling if I tell you now, it's just going to lead to more questions."

At that remark, my brow rose in uncertainty. Why should he be worried about *more* questions? "It's not illegal is it?"

He'd been taking a sip of his milkshake when I asked, and almost choked on it as he started to laugh. "No. Well, not usually anyway."

Red flags popped up all around him in my mind. "I hope you don't think you can answer the question like that and then *not* elaborate."

Rich sighed. "I'm a private investigator." He stole a fry off my plate and popped it in his mouth. "It's a hard job to explain because the second I tell people what I do, they either think I'm Sam Spade from *The Maltese Falcon* or the dad from *Veronica Mars*."

"You could have just said 'Veronica' if you wanted to be cooler."

"I am many things, Phoebe, but I think we can agree I am definitely not cool."

I would probably argue otherwise, especially now that I knew he was a private detective. "Is that why you were poking around in the back alley when I bumped into you the other day?"

"To be fair, that's where I park my car. But yes, I was trying to see if there might be anything lying around the police had missed. It's not every day someone gets killed right outside your house, you know?"

"Or right outside your store."

"So, you can understand, then, why I might have a bit of an extra interest in it? That and it's second nature to me at this point. I was a cop for about ten years before I decided to go solo. You seem to be mighty interested in the case yourself, for a civilian. I heard you basically told Dierdre Miller she had done it?"

I scoffed. "Did you hear that from Owen?"

"No, I heard it from Dierdre and pretty much everyone Dierdre saw that day. Guess you aren't in too much of a hurry to make friends around here." He laughed, but the words stung a little. Between him and Owen, I was feeling guilty, but anyone with the tiniest bit of common sense would have thought Dierdre was connected. I still wasn't ready to say she was innocent, frankly. Her behavior toward me since I'd gotten into town had been suspicious, to put it mildly.

"She said she'd never met him before—the victim, that is. But they were together in front of my store the day he died, so I'm not really sure how I can believe her."

"Did she have an explanation for that?"

"She claims Ox—that's the victim—"

"I know."

"You know?"

He nodded. "Yeah one of the officers mentioned they figured out his name. I know some of the guys from the local PD pretty well from my time working in a neighboring precinct."

"Oh. Well, she said he was an old friend of Eudora's and had been asking about the shop. She claims he was interested in seeing it, and she just showed him the way."

"And you don't believe her?"

"I knew my aunt pretty well, and I have a hard time imagining her with a BFF who's a former con named Ox—you know what I mean?"

Rich shrugged. "I don't think you give your aunt enough credit. She did a lot for the people around her, especially those who might have a hard time lifting themselves up. She actually made it a pretty common habit to give jobs to people whose criminal records could impede them from getting work elsewhere. The guys don't normally stick around too long, but Eudora had more than one former inmate help her stock the shelves at The Earl's Study over the years."

This news hit like a ton of bricks being dropped on my head. I had made an assumption that Ox was there to break in, but if he had been a former employee of Eudora's or knew of her through someone else who had worked there, then there was a chance he was there for help.

Which meant I now had to wonder if a truly innocent man had been killed behind my shop.

"You'd never seen him before, though? Not while you were living over the shop?"

Rich shook his head. "No, Eudora hadn't had any former cons working for her in the last couple of years, not after her health started to fail. I don't recall her ever mentioning Ox, or Carl, specifically, but there's a chance she might have known him personally, or he heard of her from one of the other guys she helped. The cops I talked to said there was no local address for Ox, and when they showed his picture around to local businesses, a few people mentioned that he looked familiar, but no one recognized him or knew him by name. I expect he was just passing through, and maybe when Eudora wasn't there to help him, he decided to help himself."

Most of what Rich said mirrored my own thoughts, except his conclusion wasn't as generous as mine had been. He thought being turned away had driven Ox to try breaking in, while I had to wonder if Ox had just been at the wrong place at the wrong time.

All of which made me wonder: Why would someone want a former convict dead?

Just who had Ox been, and what had he *really* wanted from The Earl's Study?

Chapter Twenty-Eight

I had plenty to think about when Rich and I walked out of the restaurant, and a huge part of me wanted to go home, brew up a pot of Eudora's Slumber Party, a chamomile blend with valerian in the mix to help send you off to dreamland. But as we left the diner, I notice the little new age shop down the block still had its open sign lit.

"I appreciate the dinner and your giving me a little food for thought as well," I said.

"Puns. Oh, Phoebe, I was really starting to have a little crush on you until you used a pun."

I arched a brow at him, trying very hard not to giggle like a fourteen-year-old at his use of the word *crush*. "I'm sorry, if you can't appreciate a good pun—and that one was actually entirely unintentional—but if you're anti-pun, this thing between us would never work out."

Rich smirked. "I'm sure I could learn to like a little word play."

He stared at me, and a warm breeze shifted my hair. He reached out and pushed one of the long dark strands back behind my ear, and for a moment I was absolutely sure he was going to kiss me. My pulse hammered and I considered making a run for it, but then he let his hand drop and stepped back a few inches.

I was equal parts disappointed and relieved. I hadn't kissed anyone, or even thought about kissing anyone, since my divorce, and I wasn't sure I should start with someone I had recently believed might literally be capable of murder. I also hadn't kissed anyone *but* Blaine in a decade and honestly wasn't sure I'd be very good at it anymore.

"Do you want me to walk you home?" Rich asked.

"My car is at the store, still."

"Then do you want to walk *me* home?"

My gaze darted to the new age shop, New Moon. I had no way to know if they were real witches or if they could answer any questions about what had happened to me earlier, but if there was even the slightest chance they could help me, I didn't want to wait another minute longer.

"I think I'm actually going to go check out that shop over there. I've been working late every day to get the Earl opened, and I haven't seen any of the other stores in town yet."

"You need some crystals and incense at six?" A smirk played at the corner of his mouth.

"Maybe they have some sage so I can do a little cleansing ritual of all the bad vibes around the shop."

He held his hand over his heart, pretending to be wounded. "Ouch."

"Hey, if you hear *bad vibes* and immediately assume I'm talking about you, that sounds like a *you* problem," I countered.

"Fair play, fair play. Well at least let me walk you over there."

I wanted to argue that it was only a hundred feet away, but if I protested too much, we'd bypass flirting and go right into rejection, and I really didn't want to do that. I liked him, and I wanted to know more about him. I *needed* to know more about him if I was going to be able to trust him.

He walked me to the door of the shop, and once again we had a moment, a long, lingering stare that felt like the weight of every expectation was hanging on it. I wanted to grab him by the jacket and kiss him, but I wasn't sure I was ready for that yet. I let out a little sigh, and the moment broke.

"I had a really nice time tonight," I said instead of kissing him. And that, at least, was mostly true.

"Me too. I'll see you around?"

"I'm pretty unavoidable. You'll owe me rent in a couple weeks."

Rich laughed and headed back in the direction of Main Street. Meanwhile, I turned my attention toward New Moon, making sure they weren't about to close, as it was almost six o'clock. The hours on their door proclaimed they were open until seven, alleviating any of my guilt about going inside.

Maybe I was looking for an excuse not to.

My heart raced as I pushed open the door and like at The Earl's Study a little bell overhead announced my arrival to whoever was working. The interior of the shop was dimly lit, but that gave the space a welcoming, homey feel. The scent of incense was heavy in the air and reminded me a lot of Eudora's house, though in a much smaller space, which made everything more concentrated and intense.

The little shop was crammed wall to wall with display cases and heavily laden tables showing off their various wares. Little bowls of crystals were everywhere, their polished beauty shown in their best light, with black velvet tablecloths. In the locked glass display cases were more crystals, but these were much bigger and glittered impressively under overhead lights. A giant amethyst caught my eye. Its beautiful colored interior seemed to have a hundred different shades of purple trapped in each jagged facet.

I wasn't sure what was responsible for the change, but now that I was inside the shop, my nerves seemed to be vanishing with each passing second. My anxiety felt like a distant memory. I had never put a lot of faith into crystals as being capable of any real healing, and certainly I'd never charged them in moonlight or anything, but if something in here was able to chase off my very real anxiety, I would buy twelve of it.

"Hello."

I almost jumped out of my skin, completely forgetting that someone else would have to be in an open store with me.

I turned around to see that a young woman, probably younger than me even, was standing behind the glass and wood display counter. She definitely hadn't been there when I walked in. She was beautiful, with light brown skin and an Afro clipped short to her head and dyed an almost white blonde. A smattering of freckles covered her cheeks and nose, and the gold hoop earrings she wore were so large they almost touched her shoulders.

"You're Eudora's niece, aren't you?" she said.

I started, wondering if she was psychic. "H-how did you know that?" I asked, hating the nervous stammer in my voice.

The woman smiled. "Because I knew Eudora very well, and you look exactly like her if she had been able to age in reverse." Her voice was melodic, like she was constantly on the verge of a light, breezy laugh. "Phoebe, right?"

I nodded, still not completely convinced she wasn't psychic. Being so new to town, it was hard for me to believe that everyone always knew who I was, and I was also at a constant disadvantage not knowing who any of them were. Sure, the names rang a bell from Eudora's calls and letters, and I'd likely met some of them when I was a child, but at the same time, so many of the people in Eudora's life seemed to be total strangers to me but acted like I was an old friend of theirs.

"I'm Honey," she said.

Without realizing it, I must have made a face, because this time she actually did laugh, and the sound was like a light breeze through wind chimes. "Don't worry—I get that reaction all the time. My parents decided well after the hippie movement that they were going to live in a planned off-the-grid community, and so, you guessed it, they were hippies, just without all the free love and drugs of the seventies." She made a little peace sign with her fingers. "And I got saddled with Honey Moonbeam Westcott as a name." She shrugged. "Guess no one was really surprised when I opened a place like this."

She gestured around the room, to the various herbs hanging from the ceiling and elaborate crystal chimes. The way the shop's dim light filtered through all the different colored gems made it seem like we were standing inside a secret rainbow world. I wondered what this place must look like in the bright light of daytime.

"Honey is cute, at least. Try having the name Winchester as a clueless married adult when the popularity of *Supernatural* reached its highest point." I shuddered. "It's even worse because I have a brother named Sam. Though his last name is Black. Winchester is my married name. Still didn't help."

"Oof." She faked a shudder. "I never did ask Eudora if your husband's family was related to the same Winchesters who built that bonkers house in San Jose."

"Winchester Mystery House? No. I mean, they might have some common relatives in the tree way back down the line, but he was definitely not in line to inherit any of that rifle heiress money. My divorce lawyer would know, believe me."

I couldn't believe how at ease I felt around Honey. I hadn't known her more than five minutes and already felt like we were fast friends. It was very much the same as it had been when I'd met Amy. Eudora couldn't have possibly known I would find my way to all these people, but at the same time it really felt like she had left me new friends along the way so I wouldn't feel so lonely in my new town.

I felt safe here, the same way I had when I'd first entered The Earl's Study.

In spite of everything that was going on—with the murder, with my less than stellar introduction to some of the other people in town—I was starting to believe that there might just be a place for me here after all.

"So," Honey said, breaking up my internal reverie, "have you accidentally discovered your magic powers yet?"

Chapter
Twenty-Nine

H oney could have run me over with a semi-truck, and I would have been less surprised than I was by her completely calm and casual question.

"Ex-excuse me?" I sputtered.

Her smile faltered into a frown for the briefest fraction of a second, and then she shook it off and resumed smirking sweetly at me. "No, you can't play dumb on this one, I know something had to happen to bring you here. That's what Eudora said would go down. No one who has zero interest in magic just wanders into a witch shop."

"I was having dinner next door," I protested.

"You could have just as easily decided to kill time at the knitting store, pick up some yarn, start a new hobby." Honey shook her head. "You can keep pretending like you're not here to ask me questions, but Eudora told me you'd be coming not long after you got to town, and here you are. So, you can play dumb, or you can ask what you came to ask. I know what I would recommend, and you don't look dumb to me."

"Thank you?"

"Come on then—what was it?" She leaned onto the counter and propped her chin on her folded hands. In the light I could see that her eyes were an unusual shade of brown, almost orange. I'd never seen eyes that color on a person before.

It only took a few seconds for the story to come tumbling out of my mouth. "First, I made these scones that made people tell the truth."

Honey chewed on the corner of one of her nails and lifted one shoulder in a half shrug. "I'm assuming you used some of Eudora's blends for that?"

"Yeah."

"That's only partially on you, then. The reason those teas work so well is twofold. One, whoever uses them needs to channel their intentions into the brewing process. She includes a lot of steps about that in her instructions for those teas, but honestly ninety percent of what makes herbal magic work is to infuse your spells with the right *intention*. So, if someone believes in achieving what they want badly enough, then it works. It's just basic manifestation. But Eudora's teas work so well because she puts *her* intention into them. When she makes a love tea, she thinks about the people drinking it finding their soul mate; she thinks of weddings, of first dates, and she puts everything she can into the tea as she puts it together. Combine that with the intention of the user, and lo and behold: magic tea. So, you must have been pretty dead set on people telling you the truth when you made those scones. Her magic and your magic combined." She knit her fingers together.

I nodded, but I only really processed half of what she was saying, she talked so fast.

"Why don't you believe that's why I came in?"

"Because as interesting and unique as it is to cast your first spell with baking, you had to believe there was a chance it would work, or you wouldn't have tried it. No, I think what brought you in here was a lot weirder, because Eudora said you had no idea you were a witch. Something else had to make the lightbulb go off."

"You know I'm a witch? She knew I was a witch?" I paused, then asked probably the most important iteration of the same question: *"I'm a witch?"*

Honey smiled. "That's an awful lot of questions, but I'm going to answer them all at once. Yes. Now before you start freaking out—because you look like you might freak out—answer *my* question. What happened that made you come in here tonight?"

I was still reeling from her telling me I was a witch. It confirmed a lot of what I'd been thinking but still seemed too surreal to be believed. "I stopped time."

For the first time, Honey's expression shifted to something that wasn't quite fear, but also wasn't the same casual friendliness I'd seen since entering her shop.

"Can you run that by me one more time?"

"At the diner, during dinner, I tried to catch a glass of water, and I stopped time by accident."

"Do me a favor, will you?"

"Sure?"

"Lock the door."

A little chill raced down my spine, but for some reason I did as I was told and locked the shop's door. Out of habit I even turned off the "Open" sign. Honey still looked slightly perturbed, so whatever it was she'd been expecting me to tell her, clearly the answer I'd given hadn't been on her short list of possibilities.

"Did I do something wrong?" I asked. I was the tiniest bit afraid now, all my calm completely erased by being locked in the shop with a young witch I didn't know all that well.

"Are you absolutely sure you stopped time?" Honey came around the counter and was standing in front of me now. She had a distinct smell to her, like vanilla and lavender, but also earthier. "Walk me through it."

I explained what had happened at the diner, from the moment I knocked the glass over to the moment things started going again. Honey listened to me with hyper-focused attention, nodding periodically as I recounted the event.

Once I was finished, she said nothing but beckoned me to follow her as she pushed aside a curtain at the far end of the counter and went through. I hesitated. I could leave right now, pretend none of this had happened, and go on living my life in peace.

But she had known what I was before I set foot in this shop, and Eudora had known but never told me. I wanted to know why. I wanted to know what made her ask so many questions about had had happened in the diner, and more than anything I wanted to know what it meant that I was just now discovering I was a witch, thirty-five years into my life.

I followed her.

Chapter Thirty

The curtain opened to a narrow flight of stairs, which I followed upward, and at the top an open wood door let me into a charming, if small, apartment.

The hardwood floors were covered in layered rugs, and the walls were adorned with art that, like Eudora, seemed to heavily focus on magical women. Witches, warriors, priestesses, goddesses—you name it, and Honey had something depicting it, though her art had a distinctly more African influence than the stuff in Eudora's house that was primarily made by dead white men.

An overstuffed armchair sat in one corner near a window that overlooked the street, and a well-worn loveseat draped in blankets faced the TV set on the opposite wall. With the exception of a bathroom and bedroom, it seemed like all the living spaces were combined into the one small main room. The kitchen was against a back wall and divided from the main room by an island with two stools tucked under the counter, which served as the closest thing to a dining room the apartment had.

More herbs hung from the ceiling over the island, and the room had a sweet basil and thyme fragrance to it.

Honey was standing behind the island. "Do you want a water? Tea? Wine? I'm definitely having wine."

"Sure?" I wasn't sure I loved that she needed to get wine immediately after I told her my story. That didn't seem like a positive response.

She filled two glasses with a currant-colored wine and handed one to me. I pulled out one of the stools and took a seat, so we were facing each other. Once she'd taken a sip—or more accurately swallowed half the glass in a single gulp—she let out a long sigh and appeared to brace herself.

"Don't take this the wrong way, but I'm going to assume you don't know much about witches, am I right?"

I nodded. There was no hiding my ignorance, so I didn't bother.

"Okay. I think when most people imagine witches, they think of Wiccans, modern practitioners who read tarot cards, collect crystals, and have nice gardens, but no real *magic*. They work in manifestation and intent, like we were talking about with the tea."

I recalled the more dismissive way I'd thought of women like that and nodded again.

"Those people are definitely witches, but in a much more new world sense. Witches, *real* witches, don't take anything away from them—their practice is generally very positive and doesn't hurt anyone. But there are other kinds of witches out there, Phoebe. They have real magical powers, though their strength can vary. Some can do some very basic control of elements, others can heal, and some can even help makes wishes come true. Eudora excelled in helping with wish fulfillment. It was definitely her greatest power, and it's why her teas were so popular and effective."

"I guess that makes sense. So you're saying that real witches have different levels of power, and some are naturally better at magic than others?"

"Yes, or better at certain kinds of magic. Think of it like high school classes. You'll have a certain level of ability at all the subjects, but in some you'll be an A student, whereas in others you'll barely scrape by, and in some you're so bad you're looking for a fake doctor's note to get you out of magical gym class." She smiled at me. "Take me, for example. I'm not great at healing or wish fulfillment, but I'm great with influence. I can make people want to do things. And before you get weird about it, I can't *create* the desire to do something. I more or less just have the power to compel indecisive people to make up their minds."

"Do you help them make up their minds to buy things?"

A glint of mischief flashed in her eyes. "Like I said. I can't make anyone do anything they didn't already want to do."

That made me smile and helped break the tension in the room, getting me back to the easier feeling I'd had when we were downstairs.

Honey went on. "No one is limited to one skill, but like I said, we're all better with some gifts than others. I'm pretty good with dream magic and also location magic, which is helping find missing things. My mom is unbelievable at wish magic, just like Eudora was. But some things are a lot more difficult to master, or accomplish in the first place. There are some skills that even the oldest and strongest witches can't use." She gave me a meaningful look.

"I'm guessing the kind of magic that happened in the diner is pretty rare." I swallowed hard, because the last thing I wanted was to learn I was a freak, even by witchy standards.

Honey shook her head and took another sip of wine. "Eudora was never sure what kind of gifts you'd have. When you were younger, she told me she tried to teach you about tea, I think hoping you'd share her gift. She wanted so badly for your powers to manifest before she passed, but I guess that never ended up happening. I know she wanted to guide you, and she tried to lay the groundwork when you were a child, but a witch has to come into her powers on her own. It usually happens a lot earlier in life, normally around puberty. For a long time, she wasn't even sure you'd have magic, but it had bypassed your father and Eudora had no children. The power travels through families and typically shows up in the next generation's daughters. It's not unheard of for there to be male witches, but it's a lot less common. Because it manifested in her, she strongly believed you would come into your power. But she waited and waited, and nothing."

Look at me, a late-blooming disappointment of a witch. Just one more thing to add to the list of things I didn't excel at.

"I had no idea. I wish she'd said something."

"It's hard to believe it until you experience it for yourself. It looks like she did her best to help even after she was gone, though. She told me to expect you, and she left you something." Honey reached across the counter and picked up the crystal pendant hanging from my neck. "This is smoky moonstone. It's for protection, but it also aids in manifestation. I think she was really trying to give you that extra little push. In your case, though, I think I understand now why the power stayed dormant for so long. You wouldn't have been ready for it as a teenager. Heck, I'm not sure most people would be ready for it as an adult."

"What do you mean?"

"Phoebe, the magic you did in the diner tonight is something we call probability magic."

"I don't know what that means."

"It's incredibly rare," Honey explained. "I've only heard it mentioned in passing, and I think it's been so long since we've seen someone do it that most witches don't really believe that the gift ever existed. But if you did what you say you did tonight, I have no doubt at all. Probability magic is the ability to change the world around you, literally. You can't adjust the past, but you have the option to change the present, which in effect can change the future."

"Sorry to *well, actually* this, but can't anyone change the present?"

Honey shook her head. "I don't mean in terms of your actions. I mean you can stop things *as* they happen. The way you stopped time today is an example. A normal person couldn't have kept that glass from breaking. And if it had broken, then maybe someone would have slipped on the spilled water. Or perhaps the waitress might have cut herself on the broken glass. So many things could have had a negative outcome because of one dropped glass of water. But you stopped it. That's just the tiniest taste of what you can do if you learn to use your power."

I still wasn't sure I understood what she was telling me, especially since I still wasn't totally convinced I believed I was a witch.

There was just a lot of data to parse through, and my brain wasn't wired to handle things that dealt with magic and fantasy.

"I can see this is a lot to process," Honey said. "It's always hard when you find out for the first time. I remember being so mad my mom didn't tell me ahead of time. But nothing can really prepare you for your powers awakening. It's something you need to evolve with. Eventually, you learn to do it as naturally as breathing."

"Do I need a wand or something?"

Honey smirked. "No, no wand, no robes, no Hogwarts sorting hat. Your powers are all within you, and we can manifest our powers at will. It just takes time and lots of practice, but soon you can do it without evening thinking about it; it just becomes muscle memory."

This was just too bizarre.

"So you're saying eventually I'll just be able to grant wishes or stop time at will?"

"Yes and no." She finished off the last of her wine. "Your gift is so unique. It needs to be triggered. Stopping time is a big deal, and so is tweaking the course of events. From everything I've read, probability witches only really activate their powers in times of dire need. I know a falling glass doesn't seem like much of an inciting incident, but I think I know why it happened. Your body and your powers were looking for an excuse to show you the magic you had in a way that was safe and low stakes, and so when that glass fell and you felt the need to catch it, you did. Again, probability magic is rare, but from what I've read it's not something you command so much as something that is there for you when you really need it."

"It's a power of necessity, then." Now that I was opening myself up to believing her, understanding began to flood in, and my brain started to assemble her explanation into a full picture of what I was capable of. "So if I saw someone about to step in front of a bus, I could probably stop them."

"More than likely."

"But I can't wiggle my nose and make dinner appear, like in *Bewitched*?"

"Alas, no. We have a lot of cool gifts, but most of them are manipulation of our natural environment. We can't just make things appear out of thin air—or make them disappear, for that matter. And another *vital* thing to remember is that you must only ever use your powers for good. If a witch tries to use her power for ill gain or injury to others, it twists. The power starts to feed on her energy, and more often than not those witches, um . . . well, they don't live long, healthy lives—I'll just say that. But for most witches, the desire to do good is innate. You *want* to use your gift to help others."

I thought about what Rich had told me, about the ex-cons Eudora helped in her shop and how they never seemed to stick around long. I wondered if she'd used her powers to help them go on to lead happier, fuller lives by granting whatever wishes were closest to their hearts.

Again, I speculated about what had brought Ox to her backdoor that night.

Maybe it wasn't an expensive or fancy *thing* he'd been looking for. Maybe what he'd really been trying to find that night was hope.

And death found him instead.

Thinking about death and about my aunt, I thought of something else Honey might be able to help me with. I raised my hand to the necklace around my throat and squeezed the cold stone. "Can I ask you something a bit strange?"

"Sweetie, we're talking about magic and stopping time. If you think you can get weirder, I welcome it."

"I think Eudora might be haunting me?"

Honey sipped her wine and waited for me to say more. When I didn't immediately, she said, "No."

"No? Just no?"

"Well, hon, I could pretend like witches are just one group in an all-star lineup of Monster Mash favorites, but I hate to tell you: ghosts aren't real. Not in a *haunting* way, at least. I think what people often believe are ghosts are just lingering memories. And please, don't think I'm dismissing you. Those memories can often be so strong and tangible that for sensitive people it can feel like a real person being in the room with them. But your aunt isn't haunting you. Everything you're feeling in that big old house of hers is just decades of memories and energy. Not a spirit."

"You're sure? I swear I can hear her sometimes. And my power went out. And this necklace just came out of nowhere. Oh. *Oh.* And I heard someone knocking on my door, but no one was there."

To this last one, Honey snort-laughed into her glass, and needed to wipe a few drops of wine from her cheeks.

"Let me tackle those all in order, because the last one is my favorite. First, you can hear her because you're immersed in everything that was once hers. I promise you, Phoebe, it's memory, not magic. Not ghosts. Your power went out because that house is ancient and sat unused for almost two months. Three, the necklace? Well, that probably *is* magic. Eudora might have cast a spell to shield it. It was probably sitting right in front of your face, but you couldn't see it until you were ready."

"That's possible?"

"Lots of things are possible with magic."

"What about the knocking?"

At this, Honey grinned at me. "No ghosts. No magic. Next time it happens, run to the back door instead."

"Why?"

"Because the kids in the neighborhood still *love* to challenge each other to knock on the witch's door, and I'm sure most of them are whispering ghost stories about her now too. Eudora figured it out years ago after one too many knocks on her front door in the middle of the night. They don't run back toward town, they run around the back of the house and into the woods where all their little friends are waiting." She chuckled. "Little terrors."

I recalled how scared I had been that night when I opened the door and no one was there, and now I felt so incredibly foolish.

"Just kids?"

"Not everything is supernatural, Phoebe. Usually just the good stuff."

Chapter
Thirty-One

The breeze had taken on a colder feel by the time I made my way back to Main Street. I'd barely touched the wine Honey had offered me, but all the same, my head was buzzing, and I felt like the world around me had taken on a surreal, gauzy quality. I could barely focus.

A lot of my questions had been answered tonight, and I had Honey's number in my phone if, and inevitably when, more came up, but I was just as flummoxed as ever about the murder and what exactly had driven Ox to try so desperately to get inside Eudora's shop. All this time I'd assumed he'd been looking for something valuable to steal, but now I wasn't so sure.

I returned to the shop, which was now closed for the night, Imogen probably long gone, and rather than unlocking it just to pass through, I ducked into the small alley between Rich's apartment entrance and the plant store. It was a lot easier to get to the back lane this way, instead of going all the way to the end of the block and back.

I was lazy and a good shortcut was never a bad idea.

As I neared the end of the alley, I heard voices and came up short. It wasn't even eight o'clock yet, definitely not too late for people to be out and about, but I was still surprised to hear a conversation happening so close to my parking spot. It was also dark enough now that I couldn't quite make out the faces of the people who were talking.

Politeness told me the right thing to do would be to pop out now and show myself to those who were standing near my car, but once again the not-so-quiet voice of Eudora in the back of my head cautioned me not to move.

My eyes adjusted to the uneven light in the back lane. There was an overhead streetlight near the vacant lot behind my shop, but its light didn't quite fill the space, so the people who were talking remained in the shadows.

"We have to do something about this, and soon," a woman's voice declared. I'd know it anywhere, even though I hadn't known the speaker long. Dierdre. There was no mistaking her high-pitched intensity.

"I don't know what you expect me to do now—there's too much attention on the place." This was spoken by a man, but I wasn't sure I recognized the voice.

"Maybe you should have thought of that earlier."

"Well excuse me but I don't see any of *your* efforts getting you anywhere."

Dierdre let out a haughty huffing noise. "You have no idea how difficult she's been. This would have been a lot easier if we had worked things out with Eudora."

The man snorted. "If you think she would have been any less pig-headed than the girl, you clearly don't remember at all what she was like."

"Well, where does that leave us?" Dierdre asked.

"We need to get inside the house, obviously."

They were talking about *my* house, there was no mistaking it. This brought me all the way back to my first question upon arriving here: What was in the house that Dierdre wanted so badly? This man, whoever he was, was in on her plan as well.

A cold breeze flowed down the alley, picking at my too light coat and sending leaves scattering over my feet. The whistle of the wind muddled whatever the pair were talking about, but I briefly caught him saying, "Friday night."

Friday was the one night a week The Earl's Study was open late. Imogen and I would both be here until eight. Normally, I'd bring in our other part-timer, Daphne, to help Imogen on Friday nights, but for this first week I wanted to get a feel for the volume of the late-evening crowd and the much-discussed Knit and Sip crew, so I'd offered to do a split shift that would let me open and close with some time off in between.

It also meant I'd be away from the house in the evening, which I'm guessing was what these two had in mind with their plan. Whatever that plan was. They wanted to get into my house, and I had until Friday to figure out what the heck they were hoping to find in there.

Eudora owned an awful lot of things, but none of them were what I would consider to be especially valuable, with the possible exception of the Picasso painting in the bathroom that she'd mentioned. But surely they weren't going to go to such efforts just to steal a little painting?

Maybe they were. It probably *was* worth a little something.

I reversed track out of the alley, back to Main Street, and planned to just cut through the shop, in the hopes that the noise of my activity inside would spook them away from hanging around my car. As I passed the entrance to Rich's apartment, I stopped, something catching my eye.

Hanging inside the door, visible from the outside, was a khaki-colored trench coat.

Exactly like the coat I'd seen on the figure that had chased me during my run.

I froze on the spot, staring at the coat.

A lot of people owned trench coats; it wasn't weird. It was even in line with what he did for a living as a private investigator. Every good private eye would need a quality trench coat, right? Can't be Sam Spade wearing a bomber jacket.

I was so caught up in staring at the coat through the window that when I turned back toward my shop, I collided with a man walking down the street.

"Hey now, careful." He was a big man in every sense of the word, tall, broad, a little meaty. In a way he reminded me a lot of Ox, who had also commanded a big presence when he'd been alive.

This man had a vaguely familiar quality to him, but I couldn't put my finger on why he seemed like someone I ought to know. I hadn't been in town long and hadn't met very many people, and I felt pretty confident our paths hadn't crossed up until this point. Maybe I'd just seen him around. He was certainly large enough to leave a peripheral impression.

"You okay?" He placed a big hand on my shoulder, and out of instinct I flinched away. "Sorry, sorry—didn't mean to spook you." He lifted his hands apologetically and then put them in his jacket pockets, as if to appease me.

"I'm okay."

"You look like you've seen a ghost."

"I don't know. Maybe I have." I'd certainly seen something that would be haunting me for a while.

"You're Eudora's niece, right?"

Had someone sent around a photo of me along with a press release that I'd be coming? It felt like absolutely everyone in town knew who I was at first glance, and that always put me at a disadvantage. They all knew me, but everyone I met was a stranger from my point of view.

"Yeah, hi. Phoebe." I offered him my hand, and he briefly pulled his back out of his jacket pocket to give me a friendly shake.

"I'm Leo." Again, the name jangled something in me, but I couldn't put my finger on it. "Leo Lansing?" He offered his last name in the form of a question, as if he could see me struggling to place him.

Lansing. Of course!

Much like my brain had been forced to work in reverse in order to place Rich, I stared at Leo and imagined him a hundred and fifty pounds lighter and with a lot less facial hair. What I got was a round-cheeked, chubby boy who spent summer days working at his father's grocery store and summer nights riding bikes around town with Rich and me.

"Leo!" Without thinking I immediately launched myself at him, wrapping him in a big hug. He struggled to get his hands out of his pockets and hugged me back, then eased me onto the sidewalk. Sometimes people describe others as a "teddy bear," which before now had seemed like a strange description of an adult, but in Leo's presence, I suddenly understood what they meant.

"It's been a long time," he said. "Wasn't sure if you'd remember me."

"Having a lot of throwback moments this week. Ricky is apparently my tenant now. And also apparently isn't called *Ricky* anymore."

"Yeah, I heard about him and Melody. That was never going to last." He gave a little shrug. "But you can't tell that to people in love."

Didn't I know it.

"Do you guys still spend time together?" I asked, wondering if Leo might give me something to go on that would tell me one way or another if I could trust Rich. I glanced over my shoulder to where the coat was visible through the window and tried to swallow the lump in my throat.

Did I have the worst taste in men, or what?

"Sometimes. He's a bit of a hard dude to make plans with. Weird schedule."

This wasn't exactly the damning condemnation I needed, but I decided not to press Leo more, since he might tell Rich I was asking a bunch of weird questions about him. "What brings you down this way?" I asked. I hadn't seen him near the store at all this week, so I didn't think this was his regular route.

He flushed and suddenly his demeanor changed from open and friendly to closed off in the blink of an eye—it was wild. "I was just getting some air."

That didn't have the slightest ring of truth to it. For one thing, it was turning into a brisk night, where the threat of snow clung to every breath. It certainly wasn't the kind of night where you go out for a casual walk to get some air. If anything, it was a night to bundle up under a blanket, light a fire, and drink a nice cup of orange pekoe.

All things I would rather be doing right now.

Leo looked uneasy and gave me a forced smile. "It was good to see you, Phoebe. We'll have to get together. You, me, and Rich. Like old times." It was obvious he was eyeing the street behind me, either looking for someone or just wanting to escape this conversation.

"Yeah," I agreed noncommittally. "We should do that."

He gave me a final wave and then walked past me, moving down the sidewalk with impressive speed for a big dude.

As soon as he was gone, a question popped into my mind.

What were the odds of Leo just appearing on the sidewalk seconds after a mysterious man had been making plans with Dierdre? Sure, it could have been a coincidence, but there weren't many people around, with all the stores being closed, and Lansing's home was a good ten blocks in the opposite direction, so this wasn't exactly a convenient place for him to go for a stroll.

I turned, watching the form of his body get smaller and smaller.

If it *had* been Leo in the alley, what was his involvement with Dierdre, and how did he fit into this whole mystery?

Chapter Thirty-Two

B ack at Lane End House, I was greeted by an apoplectic Bob, who began to meow up a storm the moment I locked the door behind me.

"MEOW," he howled.

A quick glance at my watch told me I was almost three hours overdue for his nightly feeding, and as best I could translate from cat to human, he was screaming, *"How dare you use these starvation tactics? I will report you to the UN commission on fair treatment of prisoners."*

"Okay, okay, okay." I dropped my purse at the base of the stairs and shucked off my coat as we headed for the kitchen.

Seeing that his demands were about to be met, Bob ran ahead of me at top speed and then began howling again when he realized he had gotten to the food dish, and it was still empty.

"I can *hear* you," I said.

"MEOWOWOWOW," he replied, clearly not believing me.

I hastily filled his wet food dish and topped up his dry food—which definitely still had food in it, but since the bottom of the dish was visible, clearly starvation was moments away. "You're a drama queen."

He was too busy loudly inhaling his food to bother answering me. But I was secretly gratified to hear his loud purrs as he ate.

Because I'd had an early dinner, I wasn't hungry, which meant a night off from thinking about what the heck I was going to cook myself. A true blessing for someone whose regular recipe rotation was pretty much limited to bagged salads and Hamburger Helper.

In the meantime, with my head buzzing and a timer ticking away between now and Friday, I decided to start going through the house to see if there was a secret safe or a giant diamond, or really *anything* that might explain why so many people were interested in this house.

I also had two new mysteries lingering over me, and I couldn't figure where they slotted in, in terms of the murder and the planned house break-in. Dierdre and her mystery conspirator were obviously up to something, but I had believed Dierdre when she said she didn't know Ox, which might have been silly of me, but I just didn't think she'd killed him. Not to mention I wasn't sure a dainty, middle-aged woman like Dierdre could have killed a big guy like Ox.

Leo, on the other hand, was almost the exact build of Ox and probably would have had no problem taking him out in a one-on-one confrontation. It felt a little unfair, adding Leo to my list of suspects only minutes after being reintroduced to him, but the coincidences were just a bit *too* coincidental.

I wasn't a hundred percent sure he'd been the man talking to Dierdre in the back lane, but I also couldn't rule it out, which meant there was a chance he was connected to all of this.

And then there was Rich. Handsome, charming, wonderful Rich. I didn't want to believe he was the bad guy, but was that because I actually trusted him, or because social conditioning made me subconsciously believe attractive people were the good guys? It was hard to ignore that he'd had that coat at his back door, and while there might be no connection between him and the person who had chased me, it was still setting off all my alarm bells.

I wandered into the living room, and was immediately overwhelmed by all the bookshelves, the boxes of trinkets, the hanging art that could potentially be hiding a safe. I had two days until Friday, and this house was so burdened with *stuff*, it could take me twenty years to get through it all.

Just call the police. This voice was definitely my own because Eudora's advice rarely ever involved law enforcement.

Even if I *did* call the police, what would I tell them? "Yes, hello officer, I think Dierdre Miller and a mystery man who could be anyone are planning to break into my house to look for something. No, I don't know what. No, I don't know why."

I would be laughed right out of town. No, thank you.

I approached one of the overloaded bookshelves and started to scan the titles. Eudora had an incredible selection of books, which shouldn't have been a big surprise for someone who owned a bookstore. Books had always been an enormous part of her life, and the eclectic collection she'd developed was a testament to that.

The shelves were crammed full, stacked two rows deep, with no apparent rhyme or reason to their order.

At least at the shop things were categorized by genre, and then within the genre put in rough alphabetical order by author last name. The used books could sometimes become a bit of a disaster, especially with the bargain bin, but on Eudora's own shelves, it was nothing short of catastrophic.

Travel books sat side by side with Jane Austen novels. Nonfiction adventure stories were beside young adult romances. It was a mess, and the worst part of it, at least as I remembered from my childhood experience, was wanting to read it all immediately. Even now, with a specific goal in mind, all I wanted to do was pull books off the shelf and build myself a reading stack.

Much like choosing a title, trying to figure out where to look to find Eudora's secret was like deciding what part of the haystack might contain the needle you were hunting for.

I toyed with the necklace Eudora had left me. Glancing at the pendant, I hoped it might have a symbol or hint as to where she had kept her treasure. Honey had told me it helped with manifestation, but I suppose that didn't extend to finding objects. I briefly considered calling Honey because she'd mentioned one of her skills was in finding missing things, but I think I'd have to know *what* I was looking for in order for her to find the *where*. I didn't believe it was an actual *treasure* because if Eudora had anything of real material value, she would have made sure to leave it to me outright. So any visions of gold in the floorboards or chests filled with jewels went right out the window. She'd told me as much herself in her final letter.

Yet there was something here worth so much to people in town they were willing to buy the whole house to get it, and that meant it had *some* kind of value.

Perhaps it wasn't a thing, but rather information. Maybe Eudora knew something about Dierdre and her mystery partner, and whatever it was, it was worth the risk of a break and enter. Maybe even worth the risk of a murder.

At the bottom shelf, behind neatly stacked atlases and a few hardcover books of poetry, there was a row of leatherbound books without names. Their spines just had neat numbers written in gold ink. Dates.

I pulled out the book labelled 2000, which would have been the last summer I spent regular time out here with Eudora before my parents uprooted us and moved us to Chicago. Opening up the book, I soon realized it was a scrapbook album. There were photos of Eudora drinking wine with friends at a backyard barbecue and shots of Main Street knee deep with snow, Christmas lights strung up on each storefront. There was a photo of the front porch of Lane End House, where Leo, Rich, and myself sat hip to hip, melting popsicles in our hands and wide grins on our faces, our bikes strewn to the side.

We would have been about thirteen or fourteen in the photo, getting too old and too cool to spend summers playing with bikes and building forts in the woods, yet we'd hung onto those friendships and games for a long time. Now, over twenty years later, I had barely recognized Leo and Rich, and what was worse, I didn't know who they really *were* or if I could still trust them, no matter how badly I wanted to.

I flipped through the book but didn't find anything to give me any hints as to what Eudora was hiding. Not sure what approach to take, I stuck with the photo albums, pulling out the first one, which was labeled "1983," the year she'd opened The Earl's Study, and the most recent one, from just last year.

As I perused the 1983 volume, I smiled to see photos of Eudora with my father, both sporting short curly hair and unflattering eighties sunglasses, Eudora sporting far too much blush. The town itself looked largely unchanged in the photos, the only difference being some of the signage and a few stores that weren't still around. The old-school European vibe had been popular around here for a *very* long time.

I opened to a page that had a photo of Eudora beaming proudly, standing in front of The Earl's Study with a key in her hand, my father at her side, grinning. The window behind them had only a "For Rent" sign in it, but I could just imagine all the shelves and counters in place. It was amazing to visualize the history of something that now belonged to me.

I turned another page, and something fell into my lap, a thick envelope that looked much newer than the 1983 date on the photo album. In the top corner was a mark from Edwards and Clark, Eudora's lawyers.

Having dealt with them so recently to finalize Eudora's estate, the names were familiar, but it was still surprising somehow to see the envelope tucked into the photo album. I carefully slid it open and pulled out a dense sheaf of papers, which again looked much too new to be in a book that was nearly forty years old.

Sure enough, the first thing I noticed in looking at the stack of papers was the date in the top corner—2000—that same final summer I'd spent here. Strange that it would have gotten put into the older book, then, almost like she wanted someone to be forced to go looking for it.

Someone like me, perhaps?

As I read through the documents, I only got more and more confused. Surely, if what I was reading was accurate, the lawyers would have had to disclose it to me when we were reviewing the estate together. I glanced over at the clock on the wall, but it was well after eight now, much too late to ring up their office.

I'd have to call in the morning or go visit when my shift ended.

But one thing was certain: if these papers were legitimate, I had just found exactly what it was everyone wanted so badly.

Chapter
Thirty-Three

After laying all the papers out on the floor, I still couldn't quite grasp what it was I was reading. The letter on top was signed by Eudora and someone named George Bullock, a name that felt like it should mean something, though I couldn't figure out why.

According to all the papers that followed that signed sheet, George had been the owner and landlord of roughly two blocks of shops on Main Street, including The Earl's Study, Amy's bakery—before it had been her bakery, but I recognized the address—the plant shop, Owen's shoe store, and a dozen other business, as well as any additional spaces on the second floor of those buildings, which were either storage spaces or rental properties but increased the value of each store.

The paperwork seemed to suggest George had sold ownership of those properties to Eudora for what appeared to be the very low sum of $250,000. Even in 2000, that amount was much, much too low for over a dozen shops that comprised so much of the town's commercial real estate.

In the main cover letter, there appeared to be a caveat to the sale, that George would sell her the properties at the agreed-upon price, but only if she promised to do her part to keep Main Street and the town vital and thriving.

It did not state how she was meant to do that.

I sat cross-legged in front of the letters. Aside from the main cover letter and some legal documents outlining the title transfer, the rest of the papers consisted of the actual deeds for each store.

Having this much real estate, which amounted to control over a big chunk of the town's retail economy, was certainly the kind of thing people would break into a house for and would be desperate to find.

Perhaps it was even enough to kill for.

Swallowing down the ball of anxiety lodged in my throat, I carefully stacked the papers together again, slid them back into their envelope and clutched it to my chest. I wanted to put it back into the photo album and pretend I hadn't seen it. But I had so many questions concerning these papers that simply couldn't be ignored.

If I was now the sole owner of most of the buildings on Main Street, why hadn't anyone mentioned it to me before? The lawyers must have known about the assets since they'd been the ones to help broker the deal between Eudora and George.

It was an awfully big thing to leave out of her estate assets when we'd reviewed them only a few weeks earlier.

And if she was the landlord for so many businesses, where was all that money? By my count, there were fourteen deeds, including The Earl's Study, in the pile. That was fourteen stores' worth of rent, not counting the apartments most had on their second floor. That was an awful lot of monthly income that I certainly hadn't seen accounted for in Eudora's funds.

Forget a call—I was going to need to go visit her lawyers in person tomorrow. I had too many questions, and none of them could be answered easily over the phone.

I briefly considered just putting the envelope in my purse so I'd be ready to head out the door tomorrow, but then recalled the conversation between Dierdre and her mystery friend. If they were so motivated to have this that they were thinking about breaking into my house, then I couldn't trust the papers being out of my sight.

They'd have to spend the night with me until I was able to talk to the lawyers.

I started cleaning up the living room, putting away the albums, and remembered that I'd pulled out the one for the most recent year. Even though I'd found what I was looking for, curiosity nagged at me. I hadn't seen Eudora in the final year of her life. We'd spoken often, but the opportunities to come visit had been sparse, especially while I dealt with my divorce, so my plans for a trip kept getting put on the backburner, until suddenly she was gone.

I opened the album on my lap, immediately taken aback at the difference between the people in this one and their 2000 and 1983 versions. Eudora was noticeably older. Even though she had died a bold purple streak into her white hair, it was clear that she wasn't entirely the same person she had been in those earlier albums.

She still smiled brilliantly and was obviously invested in the town, with photos of her at a Fourth of July picnic and a Halloween dance. Every season had pictures of her posing proudly in front of the heavily decorated façade of The Earl's Study or on the lawn of Lane End House. She had taken the mission of "over-the-top" seasonal decorating to heart. I had a lot to live up to.

I flipped to a random page and stopped breathing.

There, standing in front of The Earl's Study, grinning from ear to ear like she was posing for a prom photo, was my lovely aunt.

Standing next to her was Ox, the man we'd found dead behind that same store only a few days ago.

Chapter
Thirty-Four

Things had now gone from strange to utterly inconceivable in the span of only a few minutes.

In the photo, Ox looked much like he had when I'd seen him alive: stern, unsmiling, and a little stiff. But he stood gamely with Eudora, who seemed—well, she seemed proud. It was hard to understand what I was looking at.

I slid the card out of its plastic sleeve and flipped it over to see if she had written anything on the back. In blue pen, she'd indicated *Carl, August 14, 2019. First day out!*

First day out?

Thanks to Rich, I knew Eudora sponsored ex-cons at the store, and had already considered that might be Ox's connection to my aunt, but I was surprised to see how recently they had known each other. If he *had* worked at the shop only a couple years ago, then Imogen would have known and surely would have said something about it before now. I knew Detective Martin had made the rounds, asking everyone on Main Street if they recognized him.

I stared at the picture, the incredibly different expressions on their two faces, but in spite of Ox's stiff demeanor, there was a warmth in his eyes, something I hadn't seen when I'd met him in person, possibly because he'd never made eye contact with me.

This meant he had known Eudora for sure, which made at least one part of Dierdre's story true, though I wasn't sure how much else I was willing to believe when it came to her own innocence, especially not after what I'd heard tonight.

There was something I had to do, more important than the lawyer visit. I had to go see Detective Martin.

Another glance at the clock reminded me how late it was and that she probably had a life outside of police work, but I decided rather than calling, I would take a risk and see if she was at the station.

Given what I'd heard in the back lane tonight, what I'd found in the documents, and what I'd discovered about Eudora's connection to the murder victim, I couldn't just pretend all these elements weren't related, and the police needed to know.

I put my jacket back on and slid the envelope and photo into my inner pocket, then grabbed my purse and headed for the door. All the while Bob watched me disapprovingly.

"What? I fed you."

He gave a creaky little mew, as if to say that wasn't what he needed, but I didn't have time to decipher the moods and desires of a chubby orange tabby. I would give him apology cuddles when I got home and even let him share my pillow to make up for my recent inattentiveness. Surely that would get me back in his good graces.

Before I went, I paused and rubbed him behind the ears so he'd know I still cared, then jogged back out to my car.

Raven Creek's main drag was a ghost town by this point, with the grocery store closed for the night and all the other shops darkened as well. As I drove down Main in the direction of the police station, I was amazed by how empty the streets were. It was like I was the only person alive in a zombie movie.

Driving past my own store, I noticed a light on upstairs, suggesting Rich was home. I thought again about the jacket I'd seen at his back door, and wondered if he really had been the one to chase me the other morning. If so, *why*? It didn't make sense. Though nothing about that early-morning encounter made any sense.

And neither did my unusual run-in with Leo tonight.

While finding the paperwork and discovering Ox's connection to Eudora were a step in the right direction of solving this mystery, I was slowly learning that things in this little town might be a lot weirder than I had ever expected.

Giving a second glance to The Earl's Study as I passed, I wondered if maybe later this week I could use Rich's professional skills to help figure out who had been planning to break into my house. Perhaps he'd even been home when they were out there. I decided that in spite of all my uncertainties about him, he might actually be able to help me.

I'd stop in and see him on my way home if I wasn't at the police station for too long. It was late by normal people hours, but Rich seemed to burn the midnight oil on a regular basis thanks to his job as a PI. I doubted he would mind the visit.

A few minutes later, as I parked in front of the police station, which was still brightly lit in spite of it being almost ten o'clock, I noticed there was an unmarked civilian car in the lot, as well as a marked police cruiser. Taking a deep breath, I stared up at the building and tried to decide how best to explain things to Martin without sounding either crazy or like I'd been sticking my nose into the case on my own.

There might be no helping the latter, since I had definitely been playing detective on my own without her. Like a child who had misbehaved, I was prepared to get a stern lecture about how disappointed she was, and I really wasn't looking forward to it.

I patted my chest where the envelope was, then headed into the building.

An older police officer with a round belly and thick mustache greeted me at the front desk when I came in.

"Evening, ma'am—everything all right?" I could tell he was hoping this wouldn't require his intervention. I suspected he might have been on the verge of a nap when I came in. Murder aside, I couldn't imagine there was a lot of crime that needed attending to most nights in this town.

"I was hoping Detective Martin might still be here. It's about the murder behind my bookstore."

"You're in luck, she's here late tonight. Let me just see if she's free." He got up from the desk and wandered into the back of the station, through a locked door. I waited a few minutes, feeling weirdly exposed. Even though I was inside a police station, I was continually checking over my shoulder, like someone might appear and try to snatch the deeds from me.

Finally, the officer returned, and Detective Martin held open the door, beckoning me to follow her. She looked tired, but it was after nine at this point, so I couldn't blame her.

"Gene said you wanted to talk to me about the case. Have you learned something new since the last time we talked?" Her tone was measured but had hints of both humor and disappointment in it, like she knew very well I'd been putting my nose where it didn't belong, in spite of her warnings.

"I think I have."

She led me to her desk and offered me the well-worn chair sitting next to it, where I could imagine her questioning people involved in other crimes. Just being here made me feel weirdly guilty, which was probably more on me than on her.

Martin waited patiently, not prompting me, simply sitting back in her chair and leveling me with a quiet, discerning stare. I was willing to bet she had made guilty men crack and confess just based on the weight of that stare alone. I wasn't actually responsible for any crimes, but I was about ready to confess to them anyway.

Dang she was good.

I pulled the envelope out of my inside pocket and placed the photo on her desk first. "I was looking for something in Eudora's house and came across this photo from a couple years ago." I slid it, face up, across the desk to her so she could see it better. "That's my aunt with the victim. Did you know they knew each other?"

"When we questioned Dierdre Miller about her involvement, she implied as much, saying her only encounter with Mr. Bullock was to direct him toward your store and that, aside from that, she wasn't familiar with him."

"Sorry, did you just say 'Mr. Bullock'?"

"Yes, Carl Bullock."

She had told me his full name on the phone, but I had gotten so stuck on his nickname, Ox, my brain had absolutely forgotten the rest of his real name. Carl Bullock.

"Was he any relation to a George Bullock?"

Martin's brow furrowed. I could tell she didn't love being the one forced to answer questions rather than ask them, but she turned to her computer and typed a few things in. Her frown deepened. "Yes, George was his father. Gosh, I remember George—he was a big investor in the town ages ago, but he was a major recluse. He lived in this enormous house outside town, and I don't think anyone around here ever saw him more than once or twice. I didn't even know he was married, let alone had a son. He died probably twenty years ago, and the house got torn down maybe ten years ago—no one ever claimed it. I never put those things together." Her gaze cut back to me. "What made you ask about George?"

I quickly recounted my story about overhearing Dierdre's plan the prior evening and her previous enthusiastic attempts to buy Eudora's house for unknown reasons. "Well, I think I found the reason." I handed Martin the envelope.

She carefully read through all the documents, her brows lifting higher and higher as she let their meaning sink in. "How could we have never known this? I don't claim to have known your aunt well, but did you have any idea she owned basically half the town?"

I shook my head. "She never mentioned a word of it, and neither did her lawyers."

"This stack of deeds is worth millions, Ms. Winchester. I can't say I'm surprised that people would risk death to get their hands on it. It certainly goes a long way toward explaining why George's son was trying to break into your store. He must have wanted to get back what had belonged to his father. With the old Bullock mansion being leveled while he was in prison, maybe he saw the land as being rightfully his." She was saying this more to herself than to me, but I wasn't going to interrupt her. It was incredibly interesting to watch her mind at work.

Still, I wasn't sure her assessment of Ox was right. Yes, he'd been George's son, so once upon a time the titles might have been left to him, but I wasn't sure that explained Dierdre's involvement. Had she been trying to help Ox figure out where the deeds were? And what did it matter to her? She didn't rent a store on Main Street. I honestly didn't know *what* Dierdre did for a living, besides annoying people.

On that front, she was the best in town at her business.

"You think Ox was trying to steal back the deeds?"

"The timing of it makes sense. With your aunt gone, they might have been hedging bets that you didn't know about the land ownership. I'm not sure many people did. I certainly didn't. But Carl might know because of his father. If that's the case, it was a worthwhile risk for them to take."

She flipped through the list of buildings. "It also means any number of these business owners might have been in on it."

I tried to picture Amy having anything to do with this mess and just couldn't imagine it. Still, why hadn't she mentioned being a tenant to my aunt? If I was taking over that role, I'd be the one collecting rent from all these places. Amy had gone out of her way to tell me my aunt had probably put me on the shop's *lease*, so unless she was angling for a best actress Oscar, I didn't think she had any idea about Eudora owning The Earl's Study, let alone most of the shops on Main.

So much of this still didn't make any sense to me, and I was getting frustrated because I felt like the answer was right in front of my nose and I simply couldn't focus on it.

"Thank you for bringing this to me, Phoebe. It definitely gives us a different perspective on what Carl was doing there in the first place." Martin drummed her nails on the desk, staring at the photo of Eudora and Ox, then flipping it over and reading the back. "This does match up with what we know about his time in prison. The photo would have been take the same week he got out."

"Does it make sense he would wait so long to come back, if he knew she had these papers? That was two years ago. Why not take them then, or try to?"

Martin shook her head. "Maybe he had asked her for them when this photo was taken, and she'd turned him down. Knowing your aunt, I wouldn't be surprised if she'd used some of the money from those businesses to help get him back on his feet instead. Maybe that money ran out and he came back looking for more. It's easier to take something from the dead than from the living, isn't it?"

That made me sick to my stomach, but she was right. When Eudora was alive, simply taking the deeds would have been meaningless because she'd have been able to contest ownership. I, on the other hand, had no idea about the ownership of these buildings, and if someone had gotten the deed on their own property, I'd never have known that it had really belonged to me. Detective Martin was just hypothesizing, but her theory seemed too reasonable to be ignored. Eudora *was* the kind of person who would want to help Ox, even as she declined to return the properties to him.

What an absolute mess this was. "I definitely need to clear some things up with the lawyers tomorrow. I'll let you know if they can offer any additional insight."

"Please do. Do you mind if I keep this for the time being?" She held up the photo.

"Not at all."

I stood up to leave, but she put a hand on my wrist to stop me. "You said Dierdre and her friend were planning to break into your house on Friday?"

I'd almost forgotten about that part in the midst of all the revelations we'd just been discussing. I nodded.

"And you'll be at work that day?"

"I will be."

"How would you feel about having some short-term house-guests while you're away? I'd very much like to see the look on Dierdre Miller's face when I catch her red-handed in the middle of a break and enter."

A small grin tipped up the corner of my mouth. "I think that could potentially be arranged."

Chapter Thirty-Five

It was almost eleven o'clock when I left the police station, and part of me questioned whether it would be a good idea to call Rich so late. I didn't want to seem like I was propositioning him, which I worried a late-night call might suggest. We'd just had dinner together for the first time earlier that day, and I'd been so weird about things that I wondered if we'd ever have a second one.

Maybe I could kill two birds with one stone and apologize to him for being so weird at the diner—without explaining the whole *witch* part of things—and also ask him if he'd heard anyone chatting behind my shop tonight. I worried if I left my questions until morning, he might have brushed aside any memory of hearing anything.

Sooner was always better in terms of something as fickle as memory.

Plus, Rich seemed to burn the midnight oil as a part of his job. I had a very good feeling it was typical for him to be awake at this time of night.

Pulling my phone out of my pocket I dialed his number, which he'd given me during our walk to the diner. It rang a few times, and with each subsequent ring I started to feel more and more guilty about calling, when on the fourth ring he picked up.

"Don't you have an early shift, Phoebe Winchester?"

"Keeping track of my schedule, Rich Lofting?"

"Ah, see. I knew you'd get used to calling me Rich. Though, admittedly, it was a bit of a kick to hear Ricky again after such a long time."

"I can keep calling you Ricky, if you want."

"I do not."

"Rich it is."

"Wonderful. To what do I owe this late evening call? Everything okay at the store?"

It hadn't even occurred to me that he might think I was calling for his help with the shop, but come to think of it, it was nice to know there was someone living so close in case something *did* happen that I might need help with.

"No." Then it occurred to me that *yes*, something had happened at the shop, which was why I was calling him. "Actually, yes—er, maybe? I'm not sure. Look, I'm like two minutes away, do you think you could meet me in the parking spot behind the shop?"

"Color me curious with the yes-no-maybe routine. I'll be right down." He hung up without saying goodbye, and when I pulled into the space behind the store a moment later, he was sitting on the back stoop, a shawl-neck black cardigan wrapped around his shoulders.

Before I could get out, he climbed into the passenger seat. "I should have brought my jacket—it's crisp out there." He held his hands up to the heating vent on my front dash. "All right, what's up with your maybe-sort-of issue? Store looks good to me." He gestured toward the dark, locked shop. "I'd hear if the alarm went off, you know."

"I didn't think about that, but it's good to know. Is paying attention to my alarm part of the deal Eudora cut you on your rent?"

"No, it was more of a friends and family thing we had going."

"Fair enough," I chuckled. "Have you been home all night?"

"Mostly. Ran to Lansing's after our meal to get a few things I needed, but home after that. Why?"

I gave him an abbreviated version of what had happened when I'd returned to the shop after my visit with Honey. It was hard to tell what was going on with him—I couldn't see his expression because of how dark the car was—but from the dim green glow of my dashboard light, he seemed to be deep in thought.

"I mean, I was watching TV in the living room, which is over Main, so if they were talking at normal volume, I wouldn't have heard much. I don't recall seeing or hearing anything out of the ordinary."

"Did you hear anything out of the ordinary the night Ox died?" I suddenly wished very badly I'd thought to grab a Truth Be Told scone to offer him before asking. I trusted Rich, or at least I wanted to. But a small part of me still couldn't fully let my questions go.

Rich's smile was tight. "No, because I wasn't home when it happened. Which I already told you." He let out a long sigh. "Let me tell you something about Carl Bullock, okay?"

This was a surprise statement because I didn't think Rich was going to give me anything I didn't already know, especially not after I'd essentially grilled him as a suspect. "My friends in the PD, the ones who shared his name, they also told me why he spent so much time in prison. And it was exactly what you'd imagine for a guy breaking into your shop, Phoebe. Larceny. Grand larceny. Fraud. Writing a ton of bad checks. He wasn't a great guy. And while I don't think he deserved to die, I think you're reading too much into all this. Bad people work with other bad people, and things go wrong. I know you want to be able to turn this into a grand scheme that has something to do with Eudora, but I think it's just dishonor among thieves."

I'd been considering asking him about George Bullock and what I'd learned about Eudora tonight, but after his little speech I was pretty sure he might think I was just trying to further insert myself into the investigation.

"If it was your store, you'd be thinking about it too," I said quietly.

He reached across the seat and took my hand in his, surprising me. "I'm sorry. I think that came out more harshly than I meant it to. All I'm trying to say is that guys like Carl run with a bad crowd, and chances are he just trusted the wrong person. I think this is just a robbery gone wrong."

"Then why were they talking about breaking into my house?" I asked, unable to let that part of the conversation go.

"You said one of them was Dierdre, right?"

"I'm almost totally sure."

"Well, I hate to say it, but that might not even have anything to do with the murder. In all likelihood, your aunt had something Dierdre thought belonged to her, and she's not going to let it go until she gets it back. You said you told Detective Martin?"

"Yes."

"Then you did the right thing. Phoebe, I know this isn't what you want to hear because you want to help solve this, but let Detective Martin do her job. Dierdre Miller is a pain in the butt, but she's not a killer."

At least that was something he and I agreed on at this point.

The problem was, that only eliminated one person in town from my list of suspects.

I'd thought talking to Rich would put my mind at ease about what I'd heard behind the store, but much like my earlier conversation with Honey, I was only left with more questions.

Chapter
Thirty-Six

I could barely sleep the entire night. Every time I would start to drift off, I'd dream I was in the spider's web again, only this time the spider had Dierdre's face, and as I struggled to get free of her hold, she used one of her long legs to steal the deeds from me. All the while Rich's voice was in the background, telling me not to worry about it.

After the third time I woke up, sweating and panting for breath, I decided there wasn't much point in trying to sleep anymore. It was three in the morning, and my alarm was scheduled to go off at six. I definitely had no intention of going for another early run, especially not after what had happened last time.

Not liking the lingering feeling of the dream, I turned on almost every light in the house, which of course announced to Bob that it was time for breakfast. He headbutted my legs vigorously as I entered the kitchen and turned on the coffee machine.

"No, it's too early. If I feed you now, you're going to be starving by the time I get home from work." Or at least starving in Bob's terms.

He parked his big furry butt next to his dish and blinked at me with his large yellow eyes, giving an exaggerated yawn.

"No, not yet. You need to wait a couple of hours at least."

He narrowed his eyes at me, then turned and walked out of the room, as if he had no current use for me if I wasn't going to feed him, and how dare I awaken him from his beauty sleep under false pretenses.

"Well, excuse me, then," I grumbled.

Phoebe, you're having conversations with your cat.

Sure, might not be a great sign, but better to talk to a cat than to talk to myself. Probably. Right?

I started the coffee pot brewing, and once I had a full cup, I made my way back into the living room, drawn by an unknown gravitational pull toward the shelf of photo albums. I didn't recall ever seeing them as a child, but maybe I'd had no interest then in my aunt's life before me, or what she did in the town when I wasn't there.

Eudora and I had had an incredible relationship, and she had been like a second mother to me, but I was beginning to realize there were entire chapters in the story of her life that I had no awareness of at all.

Having flipped through the most recent album, I decided to go back to earlier ones. Starting with 2001, I pulled out the book and began to flip through. It held different variations on the same annual traditions I'd seen in other albums, and nothing that seemed out of place or unusual.

Until I found a photo of Leo and Rich sitting on the porch of Lane End House. It was similar to the one taken in 2000 that featured all three of us, but this time around it was just the two of them, both young teenagers, mugging awkwardly for the camera.

Odd that they would have continued to hang out here without me.

Though maybe not. After all, they did live in town and know Eudora well. Maybe it wasn't that unusual at all. She did offer the illusion of adult supervision while allowing kids to mostly function as free-range individuals. As long as you were home before dinner and didn't do any serious damage to yourself or the property of others, Eudora considered any activity fair game.

I remembered the one summer we'd built an insane fort out in the woods behind Eudora's property. It had proper walls and a roof, and we'd spent hours there every summer, making up stories and acting out scenarios that might have been a little babyish for us, but we were still so committed to our childhoods at that point.

I wondered if the fort was still standing. It likely wasn't in great shape, but we'd put a lot of effort into it, and it had held firm for years. I would have been shocked if Eudora had torn it down. She loved hanging on to things that had emotional resonance, even years after their intended function was gone.

Part of me yearned to put on boots and go look now, but a more logical center of my brain reminded me how insane it would be to wander into the woods in the dark to look for a fort that might not be there at all.

For some reason, I felt like finding it might give me the answer to why Leo and Rich were both acting so suspiciously since I'd been back. Sure, Rich had been a perfect gentleman on the surface, but the coat and his self-directed investigation of the murder were both still raising a lot of questions for me, especially since he seemed so determined to keep me from asking more questions. Sure, he was a private investigator—and a former cop, but he had to know it looked a bit weird to poke his nose into a murder that had happened at his back door.

Not that I wasn't also sticking my nose where it didn't belong . . .

These men had been my friends once upon a time, but a lot had changed over the last twenty years. We'd lived different lives and become complicated and messy adults. These men weren't the same boys I'd known when we had been younger. *I* certainly wasn't the same.

I put the photo album back on the shelf and found another. This one had pictures of a trip Eudora had taken to Darjeeling that year, with her posed in front of beautiful mountain vistas, the fog clinging to the green hills like a smoky shawl. The mighty Himalayan mountains looked small and unimposing in the backdrop, but I knew later in the album there would be photos of her trek to Everest Base Camp.

Before that, though, were images she'd captured of women picking the early buds of the famous Darjeeling tea. She'd written a note next to a close-up of the buds that read *First flush*. I remembered that after the trip, she'd wanted to tell me how much she'd learned about the process of picking the tea buds through various seasons and how it changed the flavor of the resulting teas, but now, years later, I couldn't recall any of that wisdom.

I continued to flip, relishing the photos of Eudora bundled up against the elements. Her cheeks pink, and the hair sticking out of her beanie was touched with frost, but behind her were the most incredible mountain vistas imaginable.

People teased her about only going as far as Base Camp, and not climbing the whole mountain, but she would remind them that some dreams are smaller than others but just as valid. She had no interest in risking her life or paying tens of thousands of dollars just to say she'd done something.

For Eudora, the real trip had been to Darjeeling, to learn about the tea and its cultivation. Everest just happened to be nearby, so she thought she'd check out one of the world wonders while she was there.

It was a very Eudora way to experience the world: tea first, always.

Just flipping through the book brought me an unexpected amount of peace. For the time being, however short, it felt like Eudora was still here, and none of the mess I was going through now was really happening. She'd walk in any minute, give me a big hug, and tell me she would take care of it, because that's what Eudora did.

She took care of things.

I was almost disappointed that Honey had told me that the things I felt were just memories, not Eudora's actual ghost. If anyone was going to haunt this house, I had hoped it might be my aunt.

The album passed into the summer months, and once again, to my surprise, there was a photo of Leo and Rich on the porch. They were starting to fill out more, and this time they weren't sitting on the steps. Leo leaned awkwardly against one of the porch pillars, and Rich's long limbs were draped over the porch railing. They both tried to project a too-cool-for-this air, but weren't quite settled enough in their teen bodies to be able to pull it off without looking a bit silly.

I pulled the photo out and looked at the back, wondering if there might be a clue as to why the portraits kept appearing and why the boys kept hanging out here without me.

The only thing written on the back was *Leo and Ricky, Summer 2002*.

I closed the album and put it back on the shelf. I was sure if I went through them, the pictures would continue for who knew how long. I supposed, at the very least, it made sense why Rich would turn to Eudora for a place to stay when things went south with his wife. growing up, he'd obviously been closer to her than I'd ever known.

And if that was the case, then could he really have been involved in the murder of someone else she'd known?

Chapter
Thirty-Seven

There was no way I'd be able to stop at the lawyer's office before opening the store, so I would need to wait until Imogen arrived before begging off on a quick break. Likewise, the grocery store was closed when I drove by, meaning I couldn't go in and grill Leo about why there were so many photos of him in my aunt's albums, and why he'd been acting so strangely last night.

Perhaps it was for the best, because I could take time to formulate a better line of questioning than just *"Hey, why are you being such a weirdo?"*

Taking that approach would probably get me shipped out of town pretty quickly, and in spite of everything, I did really want to fit in here.

I also wanted answers, though.

Amy immediately noticed the change in my mood when I went in to get the morning pastry. "That's a mighty dark cloud hanging over you." She started to make me a latte without even being asked. I probably looked even worse than I felt, considering my limited and uneasy sleep last night.

"Amy, who do you pay your rent to?" The question tumbled out of my mouth without my being able to stop it. I should have kept my cards close to my vest, but I truly did trust Amy, and I didn't think she had anything to do with the plot to take the deeds away.

"Well, it's an automatic withdrawal from my business account on the first of every month to a company that manages most of the businesses on the block. I'm sure Eudora's lease is set up the same way. It's probably all been automated to come from her business finances."

So, Amy clearly didn't know it was Eudora who owned *her* building. Interesting.

"What's the name of the management company?"

"Mountain View Management."

"And you said they own most of the places nearby?"

Amy gave me a strange look, but said, "Mm-hmm. You're not thinking of leaving, are you?"

I shook my head quickly, suddenly seeing how my line of thought could be misconstrued. "No, nothing like that, I was just curious how everyone else around here does it. First time owning a business and all."

"Yeah, well just thank your lucky stars. I think Eudora told me once she had been under rent control since leasing the building, but she wouldn't explain how she managed to get such a sweet deal. So in your case no one can jack up prices. Though, to be fair, our management company is almost *too* fair with rents. Don't you dare tell them I said that. Haven't raised the rent even once since—well, since my mom and dad still owned this place. So, twenty years?"

Right about the time Eudora would have taken ownership. "And how do you contact them if you need anything?"

"Well, they have an office in town, but I've never had to go in. Usually, you just call up a toll-free number and leave a message with them, and by the next day whatever problem you had is fixed. Pretty nice, all things considered."

"Have you ever heard of George Bullock?" I figured if Amy's parents had owned the bakery before her, then she'd likely been around town a good long time. If anyone might know something about George, and by extension Carl, then it would be Amy.

"Oh, gosh, there's a name I haven't heard in a dog's age. Wow." She leaned against the counter, wiping her hands on her apron. "Sure, I know *of* George, though I wouldn't say that anyone really *knew* him, if you know what I mean. George Bullock was an eccentric old coot, though maybe that's a bit mean of me. I hear he put a ton of his own money into various projects around here that really helped turn Raven Creek into the town it is now, but he was mostly about signing a check when it was needed, rather than participating in any town events."

"Do you know if he had any family? A wife, kids maybe?"

Amy shrugged. "I heard so many rumors about him growing up, it's hard to know what was true and what was just fanciful gossip, you know? Some people said he was here because his whole family had died, and that's why he just wanted to be left alone. Other people said it was only his wife who died, leaving him to raise their son alone, and he was so worried about what might happen to his son that he wouldn't let the poor kid go out and socialize or attend school, and it was all private tutors

215

and expensive nannies up there. But I never met anyone who worked directly for him, and then, about twenty years ago, he just up and left town. I heard he died not long after that, and then they tore that old mansion down. I would imagine if he had any family, they would have done what they could to save that place. The property is still there, maybe five minutes outside town if you're curious. No one ever bought it, and after they tore the house down, a private donor shelled out the fees to turn it into a bird sanctuary. It's actually really pretty."

Well, that might explain a lot about how Carl Bullock had been able to come back into town after his release from prison, and again this week, without anyone recognizing him. It seemed like the Bullocks had been incredibly insular, and if Amy's account was correct, no one knew one way or the other if George even had a son, let alone one they might remember.

George had obviously thought pretty highly of my aunt, though, if he'd been willing to sell her all the Main Street properties for a song. I wondered if perhaps an unwritten agreement in the sale was that she would also look out for Carl, along with the well-being of the town.

It might help explain why Eudora had a photo with him and seemed to know him, when the rest of the town did not.

What kind of life must that have been for Carl, to be cooped up in a big old house with an overprotective father and no real exposure to the world outside? My heart hurt for him a little, even if he had possibly been breaking into my store.

"Thanks, Amy." I took my pastry order and my coffee and tried to give her what I felt was a genuine smile so she wouldn't worry too much.

Aside from this insight into Carl, there was another new clue I had to explore: Mountain View Management. There would be some googling in my near future, because I'd never heard of the company before, and it certainly wasn't mentioned to me during the reading of Eudora's will. Perhaps there was a mix-up and the deeds weren't accurate? Maybe there was a different group in charge.

That said, knowing Mountain View had taken over right about the same time as George had signed the properties over to Eudora, and that the rent hadn't gone up a single time since then, was telling me my aunt most likely had something to do with this after all.

I felt like the pieces of the puzzle had almost all been assembled, but I was being asked to put the last three or four into place while wearing a blindfold. I knew the answers were all in front of me. I just needed a little help to figure it all out.

Since there was nothing I could do about it right that second, I put all the pastries into the glass case and set about making the cookies for the day. It had absolutely escaped my mind to go get avocados last night after leaving, so if I was going to do fancy avocado toast for lunch, I would need to go to the grocery store after all.

A perfect excuse to grill Leo for a little information.

The sourdough I'd prepped the day before had risen perfectly and was ready for the oven, but since the cookies would be done faster, I figured there was no harm in letting the dough sit just a little longer.

By the time the cookies were out and cooling, the oven was ready, and I slid the first two loaves of sourdough in to bake. I'd made four in total, and if all went well, I'd sell through them all by the end of the day. Otherwise, I'd be taking some home to freeze or make into croutons. Sourdough was a resilient bread, and unsliced it would be good for days, but once I cut into it to make toast, it would need to be used up pretty quickly.

It could get rock hard with surprising haste once the moist, crumby interior was exposed.

Soon enough the kitchen smelled amazing, and with the timer clipped to my apron, I went to open the store. Owen walked by on his way to the shoe store, and I waved.

He curled his lip at me first, then lifted one hand in the most half-hearted greeting imaginable.

I still needed to get some new work shoes, and unfortunately his was the only shop in town. In the past, I'd had no luck buying shoes online to fit my wide feet; otherwise, I wouldn't bother going to Owen's shop. Maybe tomorrow, during my split shift, I would pop over to see if he had anything suitable and try to mend whatever slight he seemed to think I'd committed.

Ever since he'd come in to scold me about Dierdre, I got the sense he hoped I wasn't going to stick around town long. I couldn't have that kind of animosity brewing between myself and someone who worked practically next door. It would only make coming into work an anxious ordeal if I needed to worry about seeing him every day.

I reflected on my conversation with Amy, and before Owen could disappear inside his shop, I stepped out onto the sidewalk and called out to him.

He paused, and I felt certain he was trying to decide if he could pretend he hadn't heard me. Given that he was only two doors down, however, he couldn't fake it. He turned toward me again, his best forced smile plastered on his lips.

"Good morning, Ms. Winchester."

I did a double check down the block so it was clear that there was no one immediately heading for either one of our shops, and stepped a little closer. The Green Thumb was still closed, though a light was on inside, so it seemed likely they might be opening any minute. If I was going to ask Owen a few questions privately, I'd need to hurry.

"Good morning, Owen. How are you?" Politeness, above all else, would pave the way for me with him, I felt certain.

"I'm very well. Is there something I can help you with?" He gestured toward the storefront, and while I did indeed need new shoes, this wasn't the time.

"I actually just had a really quick question for you. I'm assuming the police stopped by and showed you a photo of the victim, right? I heard they were making the rounds."

"They did indeed—a mugshot, no less. Seems the man was an unsavory sort of character, so I can't say I'm surprised he met his demise in such a grisly fashion."

His cold attitude aside, it was hard to blame him for jumping to that kind of conclusion. Carl *had* been a criminal, and although I hadn't asked Detective Martin what his criminal history was, Rich had given me a solid overview, and it hadn't been flattering. Still, I didn't love how dismissive Owen could be about a man's life. Even one who had been an *"unsavory sort of character."*

"I assume that means you didn't recognize him, then?"

"No, he was a stranger to me. As I told the police. Why do you ask?" He gave me a quizzical look, and the weight of his question made me feel guilty, even though I was only asking a few harmless questions.

"How long have you had a shop on Main?" I asked.

"Almost thirty years now."

"So you've been in Raven Creek a long time."

"My whole life." In this, he sounded exceptionally proud.

"Do you remember a George Bullock?"

Owen's expression changed almost immediately, his beaming smile becoming a tight frown. "What does that have to do with anything?"

I wasn't sure if Detective Martin would want me to share what I'd learned from her last night, so I tried to find a more reasonable excuse to be asking. "I found his name in some of Eudora's papers yesterday evening and was curious if maybe they'd been an item, or old friends. I thought you might know him."

"What kind of papers?" he asked.

I shrugged. "Just some old photo albums." This, at least, was the truth.

"I *do* remember George Bullock, but not well. He was not a very social man and spent very little time in town with the *common* people, you see. Thought that he could buy his way into our good graces. I can't say that anyone missed him when he left."

"You don't know how he and Eudora knew each other, then?"

"No. Though, if you don't mind my saying, your aunt was a bit of an odd duck, you know? Perhaps there was something going on between them. Like tends to attract like."

I did mind him saying it and didn't like his implication about my aunt, but I left it alone.

"Thank you, Owen. I appreciate it. And I'll stop by some-time this week for some professional help." I gestured down to my boots.

"Oh, thank heavens. I didn't want to *say* anything, but those are simply dreadful." When he realized how rude he sounded, he gave a soft smile. "For your posture, that is."

"Sure."

He ducked into his shop, and as I turned back toward The Earl's Study, I noticed a small Japanese woman sweeping the front step of The Green Thumb.

"Good morning," I greeted politely.

"Oh, *hello.*" She sounded much too cheerful for this early in the morning. "You must be Phoebe, Eudora's niece. I meant to stop in yesterday but didn't get the chance." She propped her broom up against the front of the shop and came down the sin-gle step to meet me. She was only about five foot three, maybe a bit taller than Dierdre, and her dark hair was going gray.

At this point I'd stopped wondering how people knew me on sight, and just assumed there had been a blast in the town bulletin.

I offered her my hand. "Phoebe Winchester, pleasure to meet you."

She gave me a firm handshake. "I'm Sumiko Tanaka, my husband, Hideo, and I run The Green Thumb. When you're settled in town, we hope you'll let us invite you over for dinner."

Sumiko didn't wait for me to reply, but instead held up one finger, as if she had forgotten something, and quickly ducked into the shop. When she returned, she was holding a potted plant with dark green leaves that had mixed tones of yellow and orange on them, which made it look as if the plant was on fire.

"A croton," she explained, handing the pot to me. "A gift."

"Oh, Sumiko, I couldn't. This is so generous."

She waved a hand at me dismissively and clucked her tongue. "Please. We were your aunt's friends for a long time, and now we are your friends. If you need anything, just come ask. Promise?"

I nodded. Since I had her attention, I quickly grilled her about the Bullocks, but Sumiko and Hideo had only lived in town for about fifteen years—so after George had left. Sumiko had never even heard of him, let alone of all the rumors lifelong locals had brewed up.

I took my new plant back into the shop and set it on the window ledge in the bookstore so it would get plenty of light, and more importantly, I wouldn't forget to water it.

Imogen had left the shop spotless the night before, but there were still a few books on the trolly that needed to be re-homed, so it was an easy way to kill a little morning time while I mulled over my conversations with Amy, Owen, and Sumiko. I also had to submit an order for more books. While Eudora's orders were so far ahead we'd be getting new releases for weeks to come, I still needed to look through the publisher catalogs to assess what we would want to stock, especially with Christmas coming. We'd also received some special order requests from customers, and I wanted to make sure those were submitted so they would arrive as soon as possible.

I got lost in the work, only taking breaks to pull one batch of bread out and replace it with the other. I left the loaves to cool in the back, filling the shop with the unmistakably mouth-watering smell of fresh sourdough bread. Wonderful stuff.

Before I knew it, the front bell chimed and Imogen came in, announcing that I'd quickly passed the first three hours of my day without noticing.

I wanted to run to the lawyer's office immediately, but with the lunch rush looming, I knew the most important thing to do first was to head to the grocery store. My pulse thudded nervously at the idea of bumping into Leo again, mostly because I hadn't come up with a plan of attack to ask him what his connection to Eudora had been all those years I was away.

I also wanted to causally ask if he'd talked to Dierdre recently, not that I thought he'd outright admit to meeting her surreptitiously behind my shop last night, but all the same, he might trip up. Too late to thaw out one of the truth-telling scones now.

"I need to go get some avocados. I'm thinking of a lunch-time snack special of sourdough avocado toast." I grabbed my purse from the office.

"Ohh, that sounds delicious—count me in." Imogen hung her coat up on the same hook I'd just taken my purse from and dropped her own bag on the floor, closing the office door behind us.

"I should only be a couple of minutes."

"Not sure how I'll handle this bustling crowd without you." She winked and looked over at old Mr. Loughery, who was half dozing in the chair by the fire, a cup of tea next to him and an old Sue Grafton paperback in his hand.

He'd actually bought the book a few days earlier but had come back every day this week to read it by the fire, with a cup of tea or two. Imogen explained this was his daily routine, and once he was finished with the book, he would sell it back to us for half-price store credit and buy another one, repeating the cycle.

Apparently, Eudora had told him once he could just come in and read without buying anything at all, but he insisted on paying for whatever it was he was reading, and so every five days or so, like clockwork, we'd make about three dollars in book sales off him. The amount of tea he paid for in that time was likely worth five or six times what the books were.

I suspected he just liked getting out of the house and feeling involved in the community. Imogen had told me he was over eighty years old, and his wife had died ten years earlier, which was when this daily tradition had begun.

At first, I'd found it a bit strange, but now I liked the rhythm of it when he opened the door at nine and doffed his cap in silent greeting. He drank strictly Irish Breakfast tea and would wait patiently at the counter for me to steep it.

Mr. Loughery was one of the reasons I suspected I was really going to like staying here. Because of him and perhaps the gossipy old ladies of the Knit and Sip crew. Imogen made it sound like they were a hoot. There were definitely good reasons for me to remain in Raven Creek. Once I sorted out a few mysteries, that is.

Chapter
Thirty-Eight

I got to the grocery store about ten minutes later, somewhat regretting my choice to walk instead of drive, as the wind had kicked up considerably, leaving my hair a mess and my cheeks bright red from the unexpected chill. Fall was definitely here, no doubt about it.

Making a beeline for the produce section, I was delighted to see that they had stacks of ripe avocados in stock, the perfect softness to be turned into a flavorful mash to top the bread. I grabbed a few dozen, hoping I wasn't overshooting. If I'd bought too many, I'd be living off homemade guacamole for the rest of the weekend.

I couldn't remember what we had in the cupboards at the shop, so I also grabbed some shallots and two dozen eggs, thinking some folks might want the extra protein on their toast. I was in the spice aisle, looking for red pepper flakes, when I spotted Leo stocking up the cans of pie filling.

Again, I was struck suddenly shy, as if I couldn't go up and talk to him. Years had passed, certainly, but we had still been friends once. And as long as he wasn't part of a conspiracy to steal the deeds that belonged to my aunt, I imagined we could be friends again.

Quickly grabbing the jar of chilies, I approached him slowly, hoping not to spook him since he was holding so many cans that might tumble to the floor.

"Hey, Leo."

He was on a ladder, which meant in addition to being much taller than me to begin with, he was also an extra eighteen inches or so in the air. "Well, hey there, Phoebe." His gaze drifted to my basket. "You buyin' me out of all my avocados?"

"Doing an avocado toast special for lunch. Come down later if you have a chance. You won't regret it." I'd been so worried about talking to him again after our run-in the other night, I was surprised by how easily the conversation began to flow.

His cheeks reddened at my invitation. "We'll see. Gets busy here over lunch." His focus quickly shifted back to the shelves.

I couldn't help but notice how much Leo had grown. He'd been fairly chubby as a kid, and still carried some extra weight, but he had aged really well. He was incredibly tall and broad across the chest, and had the kind of protective, inviting presence to him that set people at ease, or at least that's what it was doing to me. He was actually very handsome, now that I could see him in better lighting, what with the full beard and his dark green eyes, not to mention the immediate urge I had to hug him every time I saw his bearlike frame.

I bet he gave great hugs when he was ready for them. I'd sort of surprised him with mine the night before.

"Hey, you haven't seen Dierdre around lately, have you?" I blurted, forgetting all about my intention to take a cool, patient approach to questioning him.

"Dierdre Miller?" As if there was another Dierdre in town.

"Yeah."

He shrugged. "She was in a couple days ago, talking Chandra's ear off about the murder and being questioned about it by the police." He glanced at me again. "If I'm being honest, I don't make a habit of sticking around long when Dierdre's involved." He smiled softly.

Guess I wasn't the only person in town not particularly enamored of the pint-size redhead. The slight softening in Leo's demeanor gave me what felt like an opening. "Do you mind if I ask you something?"

He went slightly rigid, and for a moment it seemed as if he was looking for any excuse to get off the ladder and hightail it away from me. Not seeing an obvious escape route, apparently, he said, "Sure."

"I was going through some of Eudora's things." I paused, wondering if he might show some type of response that indicated an interest in the deeds or any kind of awareness of what was coming next. The deed for the grocery store wasn't among those in my files. His family had owned the building and property outright for decades, but that didn't necessarily mean he had no interest in getting his hands on a block or two in the middle of town.

"Yeah?" He didn't show any eagerness or guilt. Good to know.

"There were a lot of photos of you and Ricky . . . Rich, that is. Pictures of you guys hanging out at Lane End House in the summers after I left. Were you and Eudora close?"

This did get a response. He smiled again, his big cheeks aglow, warming his entire face. "Your aunt was a tremendous lady, Phoebe. You know Rich . . . well, his business isn't mine to tell, but I think you know his home life wasn't the greatest growing up. So, your aunt would ask us to do all sorts of menial chores around the house and yard, stuff she absolutely could have done herself, tough old bird that she was. But it kept Rich out of his house, and I was at a stage where the last thing I wanted to do in the whole world was learn about taking over this store. But your aunt was sneaky: she taught us both a lot about responsibility and what it was like to have ownership over things. I don't know that I would have ever been the right kind of person to take this place over from mom and dad if not for her." He was speaking as if I wasn't even there, a faraway, sad look on his face, even though he was still smiling. "Heck of a lady, Eudora."

My eyes had started to water as he spoke, bringing forth tears I had convinced myself I had long since stopped crying. It had now been over a month since she'd passed, and I was sure it had gotten easier, but hearing Leo talk about her brought her presence so close to the surface that it felt like losing her all over again.

"Sorry, didn't mean to get all sentimental. I know how much you must miss her." He got down off the ladder and came over to me, placing one big hand on my shoulder, his eyes watching my face carefully, I think to see if I gave any indication of not welcoming his touch.

More than ever, I wanted to give him a big hug, but Leo and I hadn't been close in decades, so I wiped my eyes with the heel of my hand and smiled at him to show I was okay. "I'm glad to know she had you guys when I wasn't here. I'm sure it could have been lonely, being in that big house all by herself. It's good to know she wasn't always alone."

Leo let out a big, booming laugh. "Oh, your aunt was never alone. I've known people in their twenties with less of a social life than Eudora Black. She was on every committee you could think of in this town. If there was a bridge to be restored or a charity drive to be run, she was there, front and center, making sure that Raven Creek was always the idyllic, beautiful place where she'd grown up. I can't tell you how many evenings my mom and the other ladies in town spent at Eudora's place plotting out their next big improvement project. No, Eudora was too busy to be lonely, I think."

For some reason I thought of a line from the letter in which George sold the properties to Eudora. He'd said something about the requirement of the sale being tied to the town's well-being. I would need to check it again when I wasn't out in public. Leo's words brought that right to the front of mind. It also made me wonder, since Leo's parents had been on all those committees with Eudora, if they knew anything about her secrets.

"Hey, your family has been here forever. Do you remember anything about George Bullock?"

Leo frowned, his face twisting as I could see him actively trying to put a memory to the name. "Man, that's a name I haven't heard in a long time. Ole George was one of our first ever delivery clients. Never wanted to make his way into town, so dad had weekly drop-offs out at the old mansion. Don't think I ever saw his face, if I'm being honest."

"Do you know if he had any kids?"

Leo shrugged. "Heard he had a son, but I also heard he was a vampire, so it's not like I put much stock in any of the rumors. Though as a kid, I can tell you I didn't want to go anywhere near that old house if I could help it."

If Leo was even the slightest bit curious as to why I was asking, he didn't let it show, asking no follow-up questions and returning to the work of shelving.

From what little I'd learned of George Bullock today, it seemed like Eudora might have been his only friend—if she'd even been that. And he'd made her quite a deal on those properties, whose rental income alone must have been worth thousands of dollars a month.

But Eudora had only a small inheritance to leave me.

Between that, and the promise written into the sale of the deeds, I was beginning to have a lot of questions.

If the money for rent hadn't been going into Eudora's bank account, and she had set up a corporation to manage the day-to-day operations of those leases, then what *was* she doing with all that money? I was starting to suspect some of it must have been sent to Carl to support him, but what about all the rest?

I suddenly wanted to know very, very badly.

Chapter
Thirty-Nine

B y the time I left the grocery store, I knew there was no chance I'd be able to get to the lawyer's office before lunch rush started. The Earl's Study wasn't a restaurant, but it seemed there were a fair number of people in town who wanted nothing more than a hot tea and a pastry or a small nosh on their lunch break.

It was already eleven, and if I wanted to start prepping the avocado toast, I'd need to hustle back to the shop immediately.

I would work through lunch, but usually things slowed down around one thirty, so perhaps I'd be able to find some time when I took my break. My head was swirling with the information Leo had given me. I thought he'd just been gushing about Eudora, but I found it especially interesting to learn how many committees she was on and how much she was doing for the town.

Had she just been helping by giving her time, or was there more to it than that?

I got back to the shop and saw that a handful of customers were inside, and Imogen was busy helping someone at the tea counter while another patron waited to buy books. The mystery table at the front had been picked almost bare again, I realized, and we'd need to restock today, if we had enough books left to do it. I didn't want it empty for our evening crew on Friday.

Smiling at the waiting customer, someone I didn't recognize, I quickly abandoned my bag of groceries and purse in the kitchen. I was hesitant to leave my purse in an unlocked room, but the kitchen was so close that there was no way someone could sneak in there without Imogen or me noticing. I'd lock up the papers in the office as soon as I was done here.

One customer turned into a half dozen, and before I knew it, the lunch rush had hit. I'd had my worries about the popularity of the avocado toast offering, thinking maybe it was too simple or too "big city" to be popular out here, but by the time we hit one o'clock, I was onto my fourth loaf and had only three avocados and two eggs left.

To call it a success would be the understatement of the year.

We had nonstop customers from the moment I got back to the shop all the way through until almost two, which was when I was supposed to take my break. When the last of our whirlwind of lunch guests had torn through, I brought out a plate of toast for myself and one for Imogen, setting it in front of her on the tea counter. The glass display case was nearly empty, with only a dozen or so pastries left to last us through the evening.

"You think I should go see if Amy can part with a few more goodies, or do we just call it luck of the draw for today?" I asked.

Imogen mumbled around a mouthful of avocado and egg, "Don bovver." Once she swallowed, she tried again. "Don't bother. If it was tomorrow, I'd maybe consider it, but even then the evening crowd doesn't go through as many snacks as you would think. They're usually here to stock up on loose leaf tea and get books to read for the weekend, but they don't hang around, with the exception of the older ladies. On a Thursday? Not much point—we close in a few hours."

That made sense. I hadn't even thought about ordering extra pastries for tomorrow, so it was good to know the Friday crew would be the Knit and Sip ladies, people heading home after a busy workweek, or those who were looking to spend some money before seeing a movie at the theater a few blocks down. The movies it played were a few weeks past being considered *new* releases, and the theater was only open Thursday through Sunday, but evidently that was enough to keep the place open all these years.

Guess no one in town minded being a few weeks behind on the hot new movies if it meant they didn't need to drive several hours to the next biggest city to see them. I certainly never made a point to see new releases the night of, even when I'd lived in Seattle, so I liked the idea of getting them eventually, but not being in a rush.

"You think you can hold down the fort for a bit while I run a quick errand?" I asked, picking up her empty plate and mine.

"I get the feeling you're not used to taking breaks." Imogen laughed. "You're going to learn pretty quickly that this is the kind of place where people actually close up shop for fifteen minutes or an hour if they need to go somewhere. The world doesn't stop running if you decide to take a well-earned break, Phoebe."

This was an entirely foreign concept to me. My whole adult life I'd worked in high-pressure jobs where the burden of the daily workload or schedule of my meetings did not allow for even a quick break, let alone the lunch hour I was supposed to receive every day. I'd gotten so accustomed to that lifestyle, I felt guilty about taking a break here, even though I was my own boss.

It was definitely going to take some getting used to.

"You're the best, you know that?" I said, grabbing my purse from the kitchen. I triple-checked, and the paperwork was still there. It had been foolish of me to leave such important documents just sitting around, but thankfully nothing bad had happened to them.

"I am well aware, but it's nice to know how quickly you've learned." She grinned at me and pulled up a stool at the cash register, opening a well-worn paperback whose cover I couldn't see.

That was another thing I was going to need to adjust to, letting life go slowly. Imogen wasn't skipping out on doing any work: the dishwasher was running; the shelves were clean and stocked; and right now there was nothing that needed her immediate attention.

She *could* read. So could I. This was all entirely up to me to decide, and clearly it had been Eudora's policy that staff could read on the job if there was nothing else to do.

I had been accustomed to the "there's always something you can be working on" mentality, but we were a small, well-run store, and the busiest part of our day was over. There should be time in that to enjoy the quieter moments.

I smiled and headed for the door, imagining quiet winter evenings spent at the counter with a cup of tea and a good book, ready and willing if a customer came in, but not needing to be *on* the whole time. It sounded fairly dreamy, if I was being honest.

"Where are you off to?" she asked casually, turning her book facedown and giving me her attention.

"I just need to talk to Eudora's lawyers about something. Nothing serious," I assured her. "I just had some questions."

Imogen made a face that made me pause in putting my coat on. "Not on a Thursday, you're not."

"Why?"

"I guess in addition to taking breaks, you're going to need to learn business hours aren't, shall we say, 'business as usual' over here? Tuesday and Thursday the lawyers only work half days. They're done at noon. I wish you'd said something earlier. I would have told you to run out before lunch. Sorry." She looked genuinely repentant she hadn't psychically known what my plans were.

She had no reason to apologize. I wouldn't have had any other opportunity to get away earlier, not with how busy we'd been.

"Well, darn it." My shoulder slumped, and suddenly the packet of papers in my purse felt a thousand times heavier. "I was really hoping to clear that up tonight."

She gave me a curious look. "Clear *what* up?"

I chewed the inside of my cheek, debating how much I wanted to share with Imogen before speaking with Eudora's lawyers. Since I didn't know what was going on with the deeds, I wasn't sure what I *could* say about that, and didn't want to speculate too much. But maybe talking to Imogen would help me work through some details.

"Did Eudora talk to you much about the business end of things here? Rent, lease-related stuff?"

Imogen turned to look at me, her attention now lasered in on me and her curiosity evident on her face. "She shared most of the daily operations with me. I think she assumed if you didn't decide to take things over after she passed, I might take on the business."

"Would you have?"

"I told her so a few times. I'm glad you're sticking around—don't get me wrong—but I would have also been willing to buy you out of the business in order to keep it going. I think this town needs The Earl's Study, and I would have been just fine being the one to run it. So, yeah, she showed me just about everything."

"Did she ever talk to you about the rent?"

Imogen shrugged. "She told me it was all automated, and if there were ever any issues to just call Mountain View. They're the property manager for most places on Main."

They certainly were.

"She also told me how cheap rent was up and down the block, and I've got to admit that it was the big reason I was so willing to take this on if you weren't. I'm not sure it's polite to call a business *foolish*, but Mountain View does not seem to be aware of what lease rates are like in most places in Washington."

Or, perhaps, there was someone else, behind the scene, making decisions about those rental rates.

"How long have you lived here?" I asked.

"Six years. Came for Christmas one year, fell in love. I'm basically a Hallmark heroine, except my true love is the town instead of a Christmas tree farmer or a cute handyman. Though, if you bump into any single ones, let me know." She winked.

Six years. Definitely not long enough that she'd know about the Bullocks, so I didn't bother bringing up George, but she *had* been around in 2019, when Carl took that photo with Eudora.

"The police showed you a picture of the victim, right?" I asked.

"Yeah, pretty gnarly mugshot."

"And you didn't recognize him?"

Imogen shook her head. "No. I mean he has the kind of face you probably wouldn't spend a ton of time memorizing, though."

"You'd never seen him in the store before? Rich mentioned that Eudora often let ex-cons work in the shop to get some job experience after release."

"Oh yeah. She's had two or three different guys in here since I started. They were all really shy, honestly. Soft spoken, kept to themselves. I know she didn't hire anyone with a history of violent crime, but she believed people deserved a chance to land on their feet again, which I really liked. Did you think the victim might have been one of those guys?"

I *knew* who the victim was, but Imogen clearly didn't, meaning whatever time Carl had spent here, it hadn't been long.

"I'm not sure."

"Might be worth mentioning to Detective Martin. I'm sure Eudora has records of all former employees on her computer."

That was a good point. I'd do a quick search on Carl's name in the computer, but based on what Imogen was telling me, I didn't think it was very likely I was going to find anything.

I yawned, the very idea of more sleuthing making me want to lie down and have a nap. How did real detectives do this every single day? It was just so many clues and threads to keep straight.

Imogen chuckled. "Look, why don't you head home a bit early? I've got things taken care of here. Maybe you and Rich could get a bite to eat later." She waggled her brows at me in an all-too-knowing way, like she was either aware that I'd stopped here last night, or knew I had developed a pretty school-girl crush on my upstairs tenant. Busted.

"He works weird hours" was all I could think to reply. Another thought sprang to mind then, completely unrelated to Rich and whatever was happening between us.

"Hey, Imogen?"

She had picked up her book again but hadn't gotten lost in the pages just yet. "Mm-hmm?"

"Would it be weird if I brought Bob to work tomorrow?"

"Bob?" She put the book down, briefly mystified. Then she understood what I was asking. "Eudora's cat?"

I nodded. With Detective Martin planning to have officers in my house tomorrow, I didn't want to worry about Bob's safety and well-being. Having him in the shop with us for the long day would give me peace of mind. I also suspected the customers would get a real kick out of having the tubby tabby around.

"Oh gosh, yes. How fun. You know, Eudora was playing with the idea of bringing in a cage or two and working with the shelter over in Barneswood to see if we could host a rotating bunch of adoptable cats. I don't know if she ever mentioned that to you?"

I shook my head. "No, but what a lovely idea. Do you think that would be a problem with the café?"

"I think she looked into that, and because we're not an actual restaurant and technically there's a divide between the shops, it wasn't going to be an issue. I think it would be a lot of fun, plus maybe we can help some kitties find homes." Her eyes lit up, and I was starting to think perhaps Imogen wanted to help a cat find a home with *her*.

"Let me think about the logistics. We'll start out with just Bob for now. I'll bring him in with me tomorrow." Now that I'd settled on this plan, I figured I'd make a quick run to the pet shop on Harper, one block north of Main, back in the direction of Lane End House. It was *not* one of the buildings I might now own, but I'd noticed it driving around on my way back from getting gas a few days earlier. "You know what, Imogen? I think you're right. I'm going to go early, do a bit of exploring. You sure you've got everything under control here?"

She raised a brow at me and gestured to the almost-empty store. Only old Mr. Loughery was here, and he was completely asleep beside the fire, his Sue Grafton novel almost finished.

"Point taken."

I figured since I was only going a block and a bit, I would walk, but I didn't want to bring the valuable paperwork with me, so I stopped in the office and locked it up in the small safe under Eudora's desk. It wasn't the *perfect* place, and obviously some people were willing to break into the store to look for it, but with Imogen in the shop, I had to assume it would be okay for a couple hours. I'd stop by on my way home and grab them.

The air was crisp when I stepped out, but it was a beautiful fall afternoon, with a clear, bright sky and loose orange and yellow leaves skittering across the sidewalk. For the time being, I pushed aside all the stress and worry that had been pressing down on my shoulders and headed in the direction of Harper Street.

The shops down here were similar to the ones on Lark, where Honey's new age store and the diner were. These stores were built primarily on the main floor of charming, brightly colored Victorian mansions, with wooden signs on their lawns announcing the shop names.

One was an antique store, which I'd definitely have to explore on a day off. I could get completely lost looking through a good antique store, and this place had a warm, welcoming vibe that suggested it would keep me busy a long time. Next door was Perky Pets, with a cat and a dog engraved on the wooden sign out front.

The store was on the ground floor of a house that was painted a soft lilac, with a pretty deep plum trim. The front interior door was open in spite of the fall chill. I stepped through the screen door, and a man behind the counter looked up from the magazine he was reading.

See? I really did need to learn to relax and do nothing sometimes.

"Hello!" he said brightly.

"Hi there. I'm looking for your cat stuff." Boy, I sure sounded like a seasoned pet owner.

"Anything in particular? New addition to the family?" He was probably in his early forties and was Native American, his dark hair pulled back into a long braid. He wore a button-down flannel shirt and nice indigo jeans.

"No," I said, then quickly back-pedaled. "Well, new to me, I suppose. But he's firmly established in the house. I'm the new one." I sighed, realizing how bonkers I must sound. "I'm Phoebe Winchester, Eudora Black's niece?"

"Oh, of course." He nodded. "I'm Charlie Bravebird. I was really sorry to hear about your aunt—lovely lady. That means you've taken over her shop?"

"Yes. And her cat."

"Ahh, it all makes sense now. So you probably have most of the basics? I'm assuming Eudora had things like dishes, a litter box, all that good stuff?"

"Yes, we're all set at home, but what I actually need is a few bonus things so I can bring him to work with me sometimes. I'm thinking a cat bed, a few new dishes, some toys?"

Charlie clapped his hands together excitedly. "Yes, let's get you what you need. I assume you have food at home and won't need extra?"

"Yeah, he's got plenty of that for the time being."

With his mission locked in, Charlie came around the counter and started collecting items. He asked a few more questions, and by the time he was done, there was an impressive mound of items next to the till. A fluffy cat bed, new metal dishes for food and water, a pet carrier (I hadn't even considered needing one of those), and a few toys that might help make Bob feel more welcome at the shop, including an adorable, catnip-stuffed pink pterodactyl.

When it was all said and done, I'd spent well over a hundred dollars just to bring Bob to work for one day, but if he liked the experience, I'd probably make it a regular occurrence. At least now I had a proper carrier for future vet visits.

I mentally added *where is the vet?* to my never-ending list of things to figure out in my new hometown. Come to think of it, Charlie would probably know.

"Hey, is there a vet in town?" I asked, then quickly added, "He's perfectly fine, but just in case."

Charlie grabbed a business card from in front of the cash register. "Not in Raven Creek, but over in Barneswood. The vet comes out every spring to do a vaccination clinic, though, so keep an eye on the town bulletin board, and you can plan to get your cat's annual shots without having to make a special trip."

I took the card and slipped it into my bag, grateful I'd asked.

Once I had paid, Charlie leaned over the counter, as if he had something important to tell me. "I know this might sound like an overstep, so forgive me, but I just want you to know I hope you don't sell the business. That shop is such a fixture in this town."

I blinked at him. "Who told you I was going to sell the business?"

"Well, she didn't say it like it was a done deal, but Dierdre—"

"Dierdre Miller. Of course. What is her *deal*? Like what does she even *do* in this town?"

"Oh, you don't know?" Leon chuckled. "She's a real estate agent. I think she was hoping you'd hate small-town life and cut and run. She probably has some ideas for a space that big."

"I bet."

Too bad for Dierdre I wasn't planning on going anywhere.

Chapter Forty

D ierdre Miller, real estate agent.

Well, at least that made a lot of sense for her. She *was* always wandering around town, and she did seem aggressively dedicated to trying to get property from me.

I wasn't sure which rumor of hers made me more annoyed: that I had accused her of murder or that I was planning to sell the business. If I ever *did* sell, which I had no plans to do, I wouldn't let her anywhere near that deal.

I didn't care if she was the *only* agent in Raven Creek, I'd pay extra for someone to come from another town.

As I lugged my new goodies for Bob back to The Earl's Study, now feeling like a true cat mom, I noticed that Owen's shop was still open. My throbbing feet were a good reminder that I still needed to pop in and get him to help me with new work shoes.

Ugh. I wasn't a huge fan of Owen, given our brief encounters, and he certainly hadn't been that inviting this morning, but now would be as good a time as any to pay him a visit and save my soles all in one shopping trip. I made a quick stop at my own store first, Imogen letting out an appreciative whistle when she saw me come through the door, my arms loaded with parcels.

"Maybe I *shouldn't* encourage you to take time off. It looks like it could be dangerous for your credit card balance."

I let out a quick laugh. "I want to make sure Bob has what he needs. I might have gone a bit overboard."

"A *bit*? Your cat is never going to want to go home."

"And miss out on being the only cat in an entire mansion? I think not." I dumped all Bob's goodies in the office and headed back out again. "Off to do a bit more damage to ye olde MasterCard," I announced on my way out.

Imogen's laughter followed me through the door.

I bypassed The Green Thumb next door, not daring to look in the window and be tempted by a new houseplant I didn't need and would probably kill, even though Sumiko's gift from that morning had only succeeded in making me want some new plants for home. Instead, I made a beeline for Owen's store, Talbot and Son. I wondered briefly if he was the "Talbot" or the "Son."

As soon as I stepped inside, an electronic chime announced my presence. Owen appeared from a back room immediately, a fake smile plastered on his face that faltered immediately as soon as he realized who I was.

"Ah. Ms. Winchester. We meet again."

"Owen, you can just call me Phoebe. And I don't know if it's intentional, but I get the sense you don't really like me very much." Maybe it was too bold of me to come right out and say it, but I also couldn't stand the idea of tiptoeing around him for years to come. Better to get things worked out now.

"Now, Ms. Winchester—Phoebe—I wouldn't say that."

He clearly had no idea how obvious his looks of disdain were. "I know things between us started off on the wrong, uh, foot." I chuckled at my own joke, gesturing around the store.

Owen did not laugh.

"Anyway," I continued, "I really appreciated your sharing your insights with me this morning, and I also just wanted to clarify that I didn't actually *accuse* Dierdre of murder. So, I was hoping you and I could maybe start over? Our shops are so close together, and I want to have a good relationship with my neighbors." Not to mention, they might also all be my tenants.

His mouth formed a thin line, and I briefly thought he might dismiss me outright, but after an agonizingly long silence, his shoulders eased slightly, and his smile became warmer. "You're right, Phoebe. If we're going to be neighbors, we should give it a proper try, shouldn't we? And I'm sure Dierdre may have, shall we say, *embellished* her encounter with you. I'm sorry I didn't give you the opportunity to share your version of events. I should learn to be more open."

A tension I hadn't realized I was carrying lifted from my shoulders, and I let out a tiny sigh of relief. I had really been very nervous about having to either avoid Owen or deal with *years* of him giving me the evil eye whenever he walked by.

"Thank you. Honestly, that really means the world to me. And as we talked about this morning, I'm hoping you can help me."

"Oh?" He raised a brow. He really was very handsome for a man his age. His silver hair was perfectly styled, and his clothes looked freshly ironed, even though he'd been working all day.

I pointed down to my boots. "These aren't going to cut it anymore. I need something to work in every day."

Owen let out a quick, genuine laugh and came around from behind the cash desk. "Yes, of course. I'm so relieved you're coming to your senses and getting something more . . . appropriate. I have just what you need."

He led me over to an area with cute low heels and ballet flats, where he immediately took a pair of black loafers off the display stand and held them out to me. "Size eight?"

"How . . .?"

"Side effect of being in the business my whole life. Trust me, after wearing those boots all week, these are going to feel like you're wearing slippers."

I sat down and undid my boots, and as I slipped the loafers on, Owen asked, "Say, I've been curious about something. After we spoke this morning, you really got me thinking. Have the police officers indicated they know why that man tried to break into your store? He was such an unsavory-looking man, and clearly a criminal if that mugshot is an indication. I'm simply wondering if I might need to increase my own security here."

I paused with the loafer halfway onto my foot. This was the risky side effect of asking too many questions. People started getting curious themselves. I obviously knew a lot more about the case than I wanted to share with anyone other than the police, but I didn't want Owen to think anyone was going to break into his place next.

"I don't think you need to worry about anyone coming for your stuff."

"Do you think they have a lead on who killed him, then?"

With the shoes completely on, I stood up and took a few test steps. He was right—these were absolute heaven. I'd thought the loafer style might look a bit old ladyish for me, but they were actually really cute.

"These are perfect," I declared. "Do you have any other colors?"

"They come in a nice brown as well."

"I'll take both." I slipped them off and handed them back to him since I didn't have the box. "And I don't know if the detective has any suspects, to be honest. I'm sure they're working hard on it, though. Why? Do you have an idea who it might be?"

Owen's cheeks flushed. "Oh goodness, no. I guess it just isn't all that often something so . . . exciting happens at your own back door, you know?"

I nodded and followed him to the counter. Now that we were on friendly terms, it was interesting to have him open up. But was he really just curious, or was he doing a little investigating of his own?

Now that I had Owen all to myself and we weren't standing in the middle of the street, I figured it might be a good idea to ask him something else that had been bothering me.

"Owen, I hope this isn't too forward, but I heard that after Auntie Eudora passed you had expressed some interest in taking over the space where my shop is."

He paused in ringing up my shoes and gave me a long, assessing look. "Who told you that?"

I didn't want to throw Amy under the bus, so I just said, "A few people told me there'd been some interest in the space."

"Are you thinking of leaving?"

I shook my head, not wanting to give him false expectations. "No, I'm here for the long haul. But I was just curious if it was true. The way I heard it, I was told you were pretty upset the space wasn't going to be for lease."

Owen laughed, but it rang hollow. "You know how small-town gossip is, Phoebe. Or I'm sure you're learning very quickly. Yes, I did inquire about the plans for that space after your aunt died. I've long wanted to expand my shop so I can bring in a cobbler and offer on-site repairs, but this suite is much too small to allow for that. I have a small workroom upstairs, but your aunt's unit would be really ideal. When I learned the shop was being kept in the family, I let the matter drop. There was nothing dramatic about it. A little disappointment at the time, perhaps, but I'm just as thrilled as everyone else that The Earl's Study will stay open."

I wasn't sure if I believed the last part, but his explanation rang true. Talbot and Son was a small space, definitely not big enough to expand his business.

I left the shoe shop with new insights and two new pairs of loafers. And, at least for the time being, a peaceful new friendship with Owen Talbot.

Chapter
Forty-One

After leaving Owen's shop with my hefty bag of new shoes, I headed back toward The Earl's Study. Before I could get to the door, however, a familiar and not unwelcome figure appeared on the sidewalk in front of me.

"Doing a little shopping?" Rich asked, smiling at the bag in my hand.

"You should see the packages I already dropped off at the store." I jerked my chin toward the front of my shop. "I guess I'm single-handedly trying to endear myself to the other business owners in town by putting myself in debt."

This wasn't true at all—at least the debt part. I wouldn't consider myself *wealthy* by any means, but if I'd learned anything in my divorce, it was the importance of spending within your means and having a little emergency fund set aside.

In coming to Raven Creek, I'd known there would be some initial expenses associated with moving to an entirely new city, things like stocking the pantry, making the space comfortable to my expectations, and gathering cleaning supplies, linens, and the like. I hadn't counted on pet supplies and shoes, but I definitely had a budget put away for just this kind of rainy day.

Rich took the bag from my hand without asking, and I relented. After hauling all the cat supplies earlier, I was frankly ready for a break, not that he had very far to carry them. "You're off a bit early today. Or is this just a quick shopping break before you go back?"

"No, Imogen is getting sick of seeing me. She kicked me out."

Rich laughed at that. "She's not exactly the kind of employee who likes being micromanaged."

"I was *not* micromanaging. I just don't have much else to do if I'm not working. I think between the whole moving-to-a-new-town thing and the murder, I've only seen about three blocks of Raven Creek in the past week."

"Oh, that won't do. We need to correct that. Look, if you're free, why don't we drop these off, and I'll show you around a little? I want to apologize again for being a bit of a jerk last night. And you need to see more than just the business district. This town actually has a lot to offer."

"You're telling me this like I've never been here before," I teased. "And you weren't a jerk." He'd been a little terse, but I think it had been with good intentions.

I hoped.

He blushed a little as he ducked in the front door of the shop and said hello to Imogen before sneaking past her and putting my bag in the kitchen, since the office remained closed and locked.

"Excuse me, Rich Lofting, but unless you're planning to do the dishes while you're back there, I'd direct your attention to the sign." Imogen teasingly pointed to the "Employees Only" sign over the hallway that led to the kitchen and office.

"I have permission," he replied, winking at her before returning to me.

"I'll allow it." Imogen's eyes were sparkling mischievously in a way that clearly indicated she wanted to say something about seeing Rich and me together, but was doing her best to bite her tongue. I was grateful because if she made one crack, I might blush myself to death on the spot.

"I'm going to give Phoebe the unofficial Raven Creek walking tour," he announced proudly.

Imogen's gaze drifted back down to her book. "How riveting. Here's a covered bridge. Here's a gazebo. If you look to your left here's Town Hall."

"*Historic* Town Hall," Rich countered.

"Mm-hmm, well you two crazy kids have fun. I'll stay in here with Mr. Loughery like a sensible person."

I didn't want to admit that staying inside *did* sound like a nicer option given how chilly it was outside, but I also didn't want to turn down a little time with Rich.

We had been getting closer, and after our dinner and then the brief chat in my car the previous night, I was getting the vibe that he might actually like me, and not just in a nostalgic way.

I was pretty bad at reading signals after more than ten years off the market, but yeah, Rich Lofting was definitely flirting with me.

Maybe I could use the walk with him to try flirting back. I was rusty, but I thought I might still be able to manage a good eyelash flutter or hair toss with the best of them.

We headed outside, and while it was certainly chilly, I was warmed just being shoulder to shoulder with him. His dark hair looked a little curly today, and the way it tousled in the wind reminded me of what a mess it had always been when he was a kid. Rogue, tangled curls had been the Ricky Lofting style of choice.

I followed him a few blocks away from the areas I was most accustomed to, with the homes and businesses of downtown Raven Creek disappearing behind us. He *did* point me in the direction of Town Hall as we moseyed down Hummingbird Avenue. It was a big red brick building, three stories tall, and with a clear view down Hummingbird, you could see the rolling hills that would crest into actual mountains a few miles away.

Raven Creek wasn't smack dab in the middle of the mountains like other nearby small towns were. We were more in the foothills, though either direction you chose to leave town, you'd eventually find yourself in the mountains proper.

Still, because of how much greenery surrounded the town, with fir, cedar, and pine everywhere you looked, it was often difficult to see the mountains for the trees, and it was neat to see the lifting terrain.

Living in Seattle, I'd been a bit spoiled by mountain views, but I also missed being around so much *green*. I knew there were plenty of nearby hikes that gained enough elevation so that on a good, clear day you could see an ocean of greenery, along with the nearest peaks of Mount Stuart and Dragontail Peak.

Here, though, we were insulated by evergreen, and it absolutely smelled like it. Outside town proper, everything smelled vaguely of Christmas and pine-scented candles. It was a crisp, invigorating smell, with the cold air and damp ground underfoot adding to the magic.

Rich guided me to a short hiking trail that did, as Imogen predicted, take us across a covered bridge with peeling red paint that safely transported us over *the* Raven Creek, a bubbling tributary that idled on the outskirts of town and was presently filled with orange and yellow leaves. It was so idyllic that it looked like an image you might find on desktop wallpaper.

Rich stopped on the far side of the bridge, resting his arms on the wooden railing and looking out at the slow-moving water.

"I can see why people make the effort to stop here," I said, taking in the stunning view. You'd never know we were only a few minutes north of town, or that there was civilization anywhere close by, with the exception of the old bridge. Several black-capped chickadees flitted between nearby trees, chattering at each other with their distinct *chika-dee-dee-dee* trill.

I pulled my jacket more tightly around me, but away from the open streets of town, it wasn't too cold out here.

"I think you're going to find there's a lot to like about this place. If you stick around." He glanced over at me, smiling softly, and he held my gaze for a long moment until I flushed and looked down at my hands. "Are you planning on staying?"

I nodded. "I don't want you to take this the wrong way, because I do love it here, and I think I'm going to be very happy. But the truth is, I don't really have any other options. It's this or going back to Chicago and moving into my parents' guest bedroom, and I don't miss Chicago-style hot dogs badly enough to make *that* seem worthwhile."

"I don't know, Phoebe. Those hot dogs are pretty good."

I smiled at him, braving another look in his direction. He was back to watching the creek, giving me ample opportunity to take in his chiseled jaw and slightly crooked nose.

Swoon.

"What about you?" I asked.

"You think I should move in with your parents?"

I snorted and slugged him in the shoulder, feeling more like a teenager now than I had at the diner. My flirting skills were definitely about as good now as they'd been when I was fourteen.

"You mean why do I stay here?" he asked.

"Yeah."

He shrugged and our eyes met, a little thrill going through me. "It's home. I'm sure I could have gone elsewhere, made more money, gotten away from the parts of my past that make me sad, but I think there are things that make you sad no matter where you go, so you might as well choose somewhere that makes you happier more often than it makes you sad." He gestured broadly toward the creek and the birds. "This makes me happy. Town makes me happy." He smiled at me, his gaze briefly dropping from my eyes to my mouth and then back. "People here make me happy."

My heart could have skipped all the way home to Lane End House on its own given how frantically it was fluttering in my chest.

"I think being here will make me happy too."

"I hope so."

He must have noticed me trembling and mistaken it for cold, even though I could barely feel the temperature anymore, because he nodded at the creek one last time and then said, "Okay, let's get you back to the shop. I can show you more another day."

I wanted to tell him I wasn't cold and I would stay out here all afternoon if he wanted, but he put his hand on the small of my back and gestured me toward town before I could protest.

Maybe there really were things in this town that could make me happy.

I just needed to find a killer before I could let myself get too distracted by a pair of pretty eyes and a smile that could turn me into a puddle.

One thing at a time, Phoebe.

Chapter
Forty-Two

F riday dawned cold and cloudy, the ideal weather to heap on sweaters and hide indoors all day.

Too bad Bob and I had a date with the bookstore, and I had at least one mystery I was hoping to solve with a trip to the lawyer's office later. My internal resolution was to keep my mind busy until lunch; otherwise, I'd just dwell on the paperwork I was bringing to the lawyer's. I quickly fed Bob his breakfast, then loaded him in the new cat carrier.

He was *not* a fan.

As soon as I had him on the passenger seat of my car, he began to howl in a most melancholy fashion, reaching his chubby orange arms through the metal bar, trying to get a hold of me.

You would think I was trying to murder him.

Blessedly, it was only a five-minute drive to the store, and as soon as we were inside The Earl's Study, I let him out to explore the space. Imogen, apparently excited for the special guest, had set out all his new supplies last night. The cat bed was next to the fireplace, and near it were his new food and water dishes, the one for water already full. She'd even assembled the new hidden litterbox Charlie had talked me into. It looked like a bench, but inside was a place where Bob could do his business, and no one in the shop would be able to tell.

Or smell, hopefully.

While Bob made himself at home in the shop, I headed next door to Amy's to grab the Friday order. In spite of Imogen insisting that the Friday crowd weren't big eaters, as soon as I got into the Sugarplum Fairy, I breathlessly asked, "Do you think I could get some extra croissants and muffins today?"

"Worried about the Knit and Sip ladies eating you out of house and home?"

I chuckled but nodded all the same. "Can you tell it's my first Friday?"

Amy smiled and began to fill an extra white box with goodies from her own cases. "Don't worry—I've got you covered."

Back at The Earl's Study, balancing three boxes and my morning latte, it was an extra-challenging morning routine while I unlocked the door *and* made sure Bob wasn't waiting to make a break for it.

Much to my delight and amusement, though, he wasn't sitting by the door, but had actually made himself perfectly comfortable in one of the chairs next to the fireplace.

"Too good for a cat bed?" I asked him, putting the pastry boxes on the counter.

"Mrr," he replied, not bothering to lift his head.

Since it meant he wasn't going to be underfoot all morning, I left him to sleep and set about doing my preopening routine.

Routine—funny how something can become second nature so quickly.

I set about my usual work, prepping the Earl Grey short-bread, starting another batch of sourdough that I could bake on the weekend, and making some basic sourdough drop biscuits with the discard. For those, I bypassed using tea and decided to go for cracked black pepper and parmesan. Delish.

As the items baked, I made sure everything out front was good to go, but of course Imogen had done an impeccable job cleaning up before she'd left last night. She had restocked the mystery table, but it was definitely sparser than it had been earlier in the week. We were probably almost out, so we'd need to come up with something else to feature on that table, starting Monday.

Perhaps a horror theme for Halloween? That could be fun. That reminded me that I was going to need to start planning decor for the shop. The Halloween displays around town went up precisely two weeks before the big night, which gave me barely any time at all to come up with a theme and see what existing ornaments and decorations Eudora had. I knew perfectly well how seriously this town took its holiday decorating, and I wasn't about to drop the ball on an event as big as Halloween.

Mr. Loughery came in shortly after nine, right on time, and ordered his usual Irish Breakfast, which I had already started steeping for him a bit before the turn of the hour.

"You're going to need to get a new book today," I told him.

"Mm-hmm." His eyes crinkled warmly, and he took his tea over to the fireplace, pausing to look at the chair across from his usual station. "Whosis?" He glanced over at me, then jutted his chin toward my cat.

"That's Bob." I tensed, worried he might complain about the new furry mascot for the store.

"'Ello, Bob," said Mr. Loughery, and settled into his normal spot.

"Mrow," Bob greeted politely, then rolled onto his side and settled back in to dozing. The two gents clearly had hard work to attend to.

An hour later Imogen came in, shaking off her raincoat. A chilly wind chased her through the door. I peered through the window behind her and realized I'd been so wrapped up in my work that I hadn't noticed the darkening sky and looming bad weather. It was practically nighttime dark outside, and heavy rain was beating down on the sidewalk.

"Whoa, when did that start?" I asked.

"About five minutes before I could have avoided getting soaked. It's *freezing*—would you mind making me a cup of Pumpkin Earl Grey?"

"Not at all." I set about prepping a cup for her.

She left her coat in the office then came back out front, rubbing her sweater-clad arms and gladly accepting the piping hot mug of tea. "Mmm, thank you."

We didn't have much time to catch up before the weekday lunch rush kicked up. It was too bad, too, because I would have loved a bit of girl talk about my encounter with Rich yesterday. Maybe I was reading too much into it, but I really had thought he was flirting with me. I was a bit out of practice with dating, but I wasn't immune to a good flirtation from a handsome man.

Bob was an enormous hit with the patrons, who went out of their way to pet him and coo at him, which he ate right up. I imagine some cats would have hated all the attention, but Bob purred and butted his head into people's hands. He even relented and gave up the chair when someone wanted to sit down, settling into the warm cat bed next to the fireplace.

Things started to calm down around one thirty, and it seemed like the weather might let up long enough that I could make a quick dash for the lawyer's office. I was about to ask . . . no, *tell* Imogen that I was taking my break, but got distracted when Bob let out a loud yowl.

Hustling over to see if he'd hurt himself, I saw him standing with his paws pressed up to the big picture window, and he was letting out a low, constant growl. When he saw me come in, he hissed and pawed at the window.

"Dude, what the heck?" I looked out the window to see if a stray cat or passing dog had put him on edge, but only a figured wearing a dark hooded coat disappeared past the shop and heading by the Sugarplum Fairy before I could see who it was.

"Bob, it's okay. Chill."

He panted for a second, then trotted over to me, weaving between my legs and softly meowing. I bent over and gave him a firm pat on his side and scratched behind his ears until he was purring.

"Is he okay?" Imogen asked as I came back into the tea shop.

"Yeah, I think he got spooked by someone walking by, but he might just not understand hoods and umbrellas." I shrugged, unable to read my cat's mind. "He seems okay now. I'm going to quickly run to the lawyer's office. Can you hold down the fort? Keep an eye on the boss for me?"

Imogen chuckled. "I'm sure he'll tell me if I'm slacking. Take a break—we'll have a fun Friday tonight."

"Maybe we should order a pizza, and you can help me plan our Halloween display, and pick what books to order for Christmas."

Imogen's eyes shone. "You don't need to ask me twice. Now go relax. Not that you can really *relax* at a lawyer's office . . ."

I headed for the back door, but Bob raced after me, standing in front of the door and blocking my path, pawing at the leg of my pants.

"Hey, pal, it's okay—I'll be back before you know it. Go hang out by the fire."

He yowled again, ramming his head into my shin. Maybe it had been a mistake to think he could manage at a busy store all day. I shooed him out of the way and snuck out the door before he could come after me, but his sad meows followed me through the door, breaking my heart a little.

But I had business to attend to, and I didn't think the lawyers would appreciate Bob tagging along.

Chapter Forty-Three

Outside, I briefly considered driving, but the lawyer's office was only a few streets south on Beagle, and it felt overindulgent to take the car such a short distance. It wasn't raining right now, and I was hoping I'd only need to fill the car's tank every two or three weeks. In the summer I might even get one of the old bicycles in Eudora's basement tuned up and leave the car at home most weekdays.

For now, it was worth it to drive to and from the shop, especially when I had things to bring in or had to get groceries on the way home. But for a quick trip to the lawyer's office, I suspected I could survive a few blocks, even in such a frigid breeze. I tightened my coat around me and hugged my purse to my chest, imagining a sharp breeze catching hold of the envelope and taking it off down the block. Talk about a nightmare.

Out of the corner of my eye, I thought I spotted a figure in a familiar trench coat, but when I turned my head, there was nothing. Bob's antics earlier had me on high alert looking for unsavory characters in rain gear.

Squeezing the deeds, wondering if I was starting to get paranoid, I picked up my pace. Maybe I should invest in a safe deposit box or something. These papers felt much too important and valuable to keep lying around Eudora's house. Just having them with me right now felt dangerous. It was too much anxiety, thank you very much.

I got to the lawyer's office a few chilly minutes later but almost immediately realized the door was locked.

"No, no, no," I muttered under my breath, pulling the door handle a few times as if it might change its mind and suddenly decide to be open for me.

I stepped back, my hair whipping around my face, and spotted a sign with the hours. The sign said five o'clock, but there was a sheet of paper taped inside the glass door that read, *Internet down, closed for the day. Back Monday. Sorry for the inconvenience.*

Of course.

Imogen had warned me they were closed early on Tuesdays and Thursdays, but obviously she hadn't known they'd have a mid-Friday internet outage. This was truly just my luck.

Then, as I quietly cursed the note, I spotted something else. Since I'd never been to their office in person before, it made sense I would never have seen it, but all the same it felt like something I should have known.

Underneath the firm's name on the door was a second logo, this one reading "Mountain View Management" and indicating the upper floor office of the same building. They didn't have hours listed or a buzz code.

Everything I could see indicated they were part of the same office as the law firm.

Curiouser and curiouser.

Now I had something *else* to ask the lawyers about, because they couldn't claim to be ignorant of what was going on with Eudora's business dealings if they happened to be in the very same office as those dealings.

Logically, it seemed most likely that the lawyers were also responsible for the property management business, or were at least overseeing it, which was unusual to say the very least.

There wasn't much I could do about it now. I'd make an appointment for Monday and come back then. Hopefully, nothing too disastrous would happen between now and Monday. That might be asking for a lot, though.

I decided to take a shortcut back to the store, hoping to cut down on my wind exposure. The sky had gotten incredibly dark, again with heavy black clouds looming overhead and the earthy smell of rain lingering in the air. Tiny droplets spit down, and I had no doubt I was going to get poured on any moment.

In spite of it only being midafternoon, it was dark enough the streetlights came on automatically.

I tucked my purse inside my coat and headed down a narrow lane between the streets. Soon I was back in the alley that led to the shop, surprised by how dark and empty it was. There was absolutely no activity here, and I immediately regretted not sticking to the main streets.

As I crossed the vacant lot behind the store, all the hairs on the back of my neck stood on end. Despite the howling wind, I heard the distinct sound of footsteps hammering behind me.

I was being chased.

At first I wondered if it was my paranoia acting up again, or if the dark atmosphere and low lights had reminded me of that terrible dream I'd had about being on the streets with the sound of footfalls, but not being able to see who was coming for me.

As the sound grew closer, I decided I didn't care if it was paranoia or my overactive imagination—I just wanted to get back inside. Immediately.

The lot was big, but the shop was so close I could see the back light and the distinct shape of my car. I didn't need to get far—I was almost there.

Run, I thought.

It didn't matter if I was imagining it, I just needed to get moving.

But whoever was chasing me was very real, and much faster than I was. One moment I was running, and the next I was hitting the ground hard. Because I was holding onto my purse inside my coat, I didn't have an opportunity to brace my fall. I landed on my elbows first, then slumped onto my face, the rough pavement scraping my skin.

As I rolled over to see who had knocked me down, the sky let loose and began to pour.

Chapter
Forty-Four

Fierce drops of rain assaulted me, blocking out my vision and stinging the fresh scrapes on my skin. A dark figure loomed over me, black hood obscuring their face, and while I didn't see any sign of a weapon, that didn't mean there wasn't one.

"I don't have any money," I squeaked. Under normal circumstances I'd just hand over my purse, but with the deeds inside, I was pretty willing to put up at least some kind of fight against a mugger.

"That certainly isn't true," the masculine voice scoffed. I immediately recognized it as belonging to the man who'd been speaking to Dierdre last night, and also knew for certain it couldn't possibly be Leo. Not only was the figure much too lean to be him, but the voice was also too high and didn't have his rumbly tenor.

Even as I was scared to my bones, I was relieved to know it hadn't been Leo conspiring with Dierdre. Likewise, the voice was all wrong to be Rich's.

The man didn't leave me guessing for long. He pulled the hood back and revealed his face, a bright flash of lightning illuminating the whole lot briefly before plunging us back into darkness.

Owen.

I had thought of a lot of people as potential suspects, but even though Owen and I hadn't exactly gotten along swimmingly, I had never even once thought he might be the one who had been talking to Dierdre about breaking into my home—or the one who had killed Ox.

When we'd first met, he'd been less than friendly, but now he looked downright mean, his face twisted into a snarl, his fists balled at his sides. "Why did you have to make this so difficult for us, Phoebe? If you'd just sold Dierdre the house and left town with the buyout, you wouldn't have been any the wiser, and all this risk would have been unnecessary. Now it's too late."

I pushed myself backward across the sidewalk, hoping to put some distance between us. He had one hand in his pocket, leading me to believe there was something in there, and I didn't want to find out what it was.

"I don't know what you're talking about," I lied. While the shape of the whole story wasn't exactly clear, I knew enough at this point. He and Dierdre wanted the deeds, and they'd been willing to do almost anything to get them from me, including breaking into my home tonight to steal them.

Now, it appeared, Owen might be willing to kill for them.

"Don't play dumb with me."

I managed to get into a sitting position, where I tried to avoid the rain getting in my eyes. I could see how angry he was. The rage was pulsing off him so visibly it looked like he was shaking. Fine, he didn't want me to play dumb—then I wanted some answers too.

"You can't just kill me, Owen. People will figure it out."

"Will they? The cops here haven't even been able to figure out that I killed Carl, and that was nearly a week ago. If they can't figure *that* out, do you think they're going to put two and two together for you?"

And there it was, his confession. It had seemed obvious as soon as he knocked me down that he might be willing to resort to violence, but I hadn't been convinced he was capable of murder until he outright admitted it.

Owen seemed like the kind of person who would write a bad Yelp review for a parking lot, but he had never struck me as someone remotely capable of committing murder. Maybe I needed to reassess my willingness to trust people. I obviously had bad judgment.

For now, I just needed to find a way to avoid becoming his next victim. "I'm sure they'll start asking questions when you suddenly have the deeds for a whole block of real estate. Not to mention, if you kill me now, you'll never know where they are." I hoped this might buy me a little time. I tried to wipe the rain off my face but only succeeded in pushing hair into my eyes. He continued to edge closer to me. The back of my store was so tantalizingly close, I wondered if I could make a break for it, or if he'd catch me again and I'd just end up as another chalk outline behind my own shop.

Then I remembered the back door was locked. Even if I could get there, I wasn't sure I'd be able to get it open before he did whatever it was he planned to do.

"Your aunt went *decades* without anyone knowing what she owned. You think I can't keep a secret? And I just followed you to the lawyer's office, I saw how you were holding your bag the whole time, precious as a little baby. I'm no fool, Phoebe."

So much for that idea.

"Why did you kill Ox? What did he have to do with all this?" If I could keep him talking long enough, I might be able to figure out how to get myself out of this. But I had to admit, part of me was just curious to know why he'd done it.

"He was the one who came to me. He'd known all along that Eudora had bought the properties from his father, and I guess after his old man died, she was sending Carl money in the slammer. She even helped him get on his feet when he was released." He shook his head, either to get the rain out of his eyes or because he couldn't believe that Eudora would help an ex-con. "He said he waited until after she died because she'd been good to him, but he wanted his dad's property back. Said it should have gone to him. I disagreed."

So did I, but I also didn't think it should go to Owen, who I suspected didn't have the most altruistic purposes for wanting all that rental income.

"But why kill him?"

"He wasn't being patient. We were sure the paperwork was at Eudora's house—no way she'd keep it in the shop—but he insisted, said if we weren't going to help him, he'd go look on his own. I decided he put us at too much risk, and if he was going to act like that, we couldn't trust him to share when we got the documents."

"We." He kept saying we, and logically I knew he meant Diedre, but I wanted to hear him say it, to confirm everything I'd believed this whole time.

"Dierdre doesn't know what I did to Carl. I don't think she's even convinced it's connected. She didn't know George had a son, but my family knew the Bullocks. I knew George had a son, so I wasn't surprised when Carl showed up this week, sniffing around. Dierdre just thought he was some stranger who knew Eudora, and I let her think that. If I didn't need her connections to the real estate market, I wouldn't have bothered to include her in the first place, but she already knew about the deeds and wanted her cut. She's not a smart woman, but she's persistent. A lot like you."

For one thing, I was insulted to be compared to Dierdre Miller in any capacity. For another, everything he was telling me helped fit in the remaining puzzle pieces of the mystery. It explained how, after eating my scone, Dierdre could be telling the truth, but not the *whole* truth, because she didn't actually know the whole truth.

"People are going to notice when I don't come back, Owen."

"It's a shame there's a killer on the loose in Raven Creek, isn't it? Poor Phoebe Winchester, gone before we ever had a chance to know her. In a week you'll just be a cautionary tale, and when I close that stupid bookstore, no one will remember you or your family at all."

Of all the things he'd said in the last minute, that one was the turning point. It was the thing that took me from being scared to angry.

"No one will forget my aunt." I pushed myself up to my feet, every inch of my body protesting, my elbows and knees screaming from their fresh scrapes.

"I guess we'll find out. Too bad you won't be around to see what happens." He pulled his hand from his pocket, and as lightning streaked across the sky, I could see that he was holding a gun, and it was aimed right at me.

Chapter Forty-Five

I panicked.

I'd never had a gun pointed at me before, and while I'd generally like to consider myself a smart person who avoided danger, I did just about the stupidest thing imaginable in that moment: I lunged for Owen.

He must have assumed I would shrink back, huddle in fear, cry, and beg for mercy. He probably assumed a lot of things about how people would react to seeing a gun, but there was no way to account for my brain's harrowing misjudgment of fight versus flight.

It chose flail.

I slammed myself into Owen with the precision of a football linebacker, sending him staggering backward a few steps and knocking the gun from his hand.

For a long moment, blinking through sheets of rain, he and I stared at each other stupidly, as if neither of us knew precisely what to do next, since this wasn't exactly going according to his plan.

We both scrambled for the gun.

I was at a disadvantage since I was still clinging tightly to my purse. The only thing he wanted was the deeds, and if I dropped those, I would lose everything. I had no idea what the official sale had looked like between George Bullock and Eudora, or if there was any other documentation besides the deeds that would keep Owen from getting what he wanted. I knew alarmingly little about any of this, which was why I'd been on my way to talk to the lawyers. But I knew he wanted what I had *very* badly. Once he got his hands on it, he'd have no reason to keep me alive, and I'd lose the one thing Eudora had left me that was so valuable she'd needed to keep it a complete secret.

Not to mention, I'd lose my life.

Owen and I reached the gun at the same time, and as he scrabbled across the ground to pick it up, I kicked it. I hit his fingers with the toe of my brand new shiny black loafers, and he yowled in unexpected pain. The gun skittered across the asphalt, stopping near a big green dumpster.

As he raced after it, I realized this might be my only chance to get away from him and get to the bookstore, where I could call for help. While Owen dropped to his knees on the ground, I bolted. There were only a few hundred yards between me and safety. If I could just get to that narrow alley between my building and The Green Thumb, I would be okay.

The rain pelted down on me blinding me as I sprinted, turning all the scenery around me into a smeared blur of gray and black. I could barely tell what direction I was running, but I had to believe I was going the right way.

"*Stop!*" he screamed.

Run! I told myself.

If this was what had been waiting for me in the dark recesses of my dream, I was glad I'd woken up before seeing how it would end.

A crack echoed over the parking lot, and at first I thought it was thunder, but then a searing pain fanned out over my left shoulder. I stumbled, dropping to one knee, only a hundred yards to go from the shop. I touched my arm and my fingers came away bloody.

He had *shot* me.

I looked back over my shoulder to see Owen running toward me, and this time when he raised the gun, there was no hint of hesitation in his eyes. He pulled the trigger just as lightning darted over the pitch-black sky.

Probability.

That's what Honey had called my power. She'd said I had the ability to control probability, and that while it was unlikely I could summon the power at will, it would come to me when I needed it most.

The sky was lit up bright white, such a blinding amount of light it obliterated the flash from the gun's nozzle.

All around me, the rain had stopped, droplets hanging in midair. Reflections from the gun and the lightning illuminated Owen's eyes, and his face locked in a twisted snarl. The bullet was frozen in place, halfway between him and where I was kneeling on the ground.

I sucked in a deep breath, my heart hammering, my shoulder screaming in agony, and staggered to my feet, stepping out of the line of fire. I wasn't sure how long I could control this, or if I had *any* control over it. The only time it had happened, I'd been able to catch a falling glass, and then everything had snapped back to reality when I put the glass back on the table. If I only had a few seconds of frozen time, at least I'd be able to dodge a moving bullet.

I had already been shot once, and that was more than enough for me, thanks.

There was a very high *probability* that when Owen fired his gun at me for the second time, I would die. I was standing right in the path of the bullet, at a close range, and no normal human being could just dodge a bullet. That isn't how science works.

Except in this case, science couldn't surmount or account for magic.

I approached the bullet from the side, staring at it carefully. The rain, where it was touching the small metal object, sizzled. The bullet was hot. I don't know why it had never occurred to me before that a bullet would be hot. I guess I'd never been in a position to wonder. The first time I'd done this, I hadn't known what I was capable of. Now I at least understood that this was magic, and it was *my* magic, which had to mean I was able to work my will, to some extent. I tapped the bullet with my finger, remembering Honey's words to me about intention.

Fall, I thought, and as if it had understood my instruction, the bullet fell to the ground, like it had been struck dead on the spot.

My head pounded and my shoulder throbbed, the pain stealing away much of my focus. I suspected I didn't have much time left. When I'd caught the glass at the diner, things had returned to normal speed very shortly after I put the glass back on the table, and while I had a slightly better understanding of what was happening now, I doubted I'd get a long time to change the present. I made my way over to Owen. It wasn't easy to move great distances in frozen time, something I hadn't noticed when I'd been in the diner and had only really been moving my arm. Maybe because I was only catching a glass and not moving my whole body several feet, but it felt like I was wading through molasses. The more I moved, the more a sharp pain presented in my temples as well. By the time I reached Owen's side, it was a full-blown migraine.

I took the gun from his hand and threw it as far as I could, which wasn't far, but at least he wouldn't know where to start looking.

Time started to speed up then, the drops of rain being the first thing to escape my power. The lightning flash ended abruptly, making me blind in the sudden absence of all that light. And last, Owen began to move, a triumphant cackle dying on his lips as he slowly comprehended, first, that I wasn't where I should be, and second, he was holding an empty hand out in front of him.

An instant later he realized I was standing beside him.

"You messed with the wrong witch," I said, and hit him with my best right hook.

It wasn't a *hard* punch, but it took him so much by surprise, he crumpled to the ground. Unfortunately, the intense pressure of manipulating space and time, not to mention getting shot in the arm, had taken its toll on me as well.

Owen hit the concrete, and I swayed, pinpoints of light dotting my vision.

The last thing I remembered before collapsing was the figure of a man in a khaki trench coat running across the parking lot toward us.

*   *   *

I wasn't sure if hours had passed or minutes, but the next thing I remembered was being warm. Warm and dry, though my clothes were still soaked, it was no longer raining on me.

There was also something very warm vibrating on my lap.

Bob.

I blinked several times before realizing where I was. I was wrapped in a rough wool blanket, sitting in one of the huge armchairs in front of the fire in The Earl's Study. Blue and red lights bounced off the walls, but all I kept thinking was *We don't have any blankets.*

The next thing I registered was Imogen hovering behind the chair across from me, a look of obvious concern straining her features. Kneeling in front of me was a pretty young woman in a navy-blue paramedic uniform, her blonde hair pulled back in a tight bun.

"Hey, there she is," the woman said. "Phoebe, my name is Megan, can you follow this light for me?" She shone a flashlight in my eyes, and I blinked several times, recoiling from it like it had punched me. "I know—sorry—but just try to follow the light."

I did as I was asked, my gaze trailing the glowing orb back and forth as directed. Bob lifted his head like he might hiss at her, but I put a hand on his back to let him know it was okay.

"That's great, thank you."

There were fresh bandages on my hands, and while I couldn't see my face, something slightly scratchy was on my forehead, which I anticipated to be another bandage. I tried to lift my arm, but it hurt too much.

"Owen," I croaked, my voice unexpectedly raspy. "It's Owen. He killed Ox."

"We know," a familiar voice said behind me.

I tried to look over my shoulder, but turning my head was more movement than I could handle. Whoever it was came around me to stand behind Megan, obviously trying to stay out of the way.

"Rich."

I remembered the flash of khaki trench coat running toward me. The coat he was currently wearing, still dripping water onto the floor.

"I heard the gunshot and came out to see what was happening. But by the time I got there, you'd already knocked him on his butt."

"He shot me." This, I realized, sounded incredibly stupid since Rich had just said he'd heard the gunshot.

"Lucky for you he had terrible aim," Megan chirped. "The first shot grazed your left arm—didn't even need stitches, though you're likely going to have a pretty gnarly scar there, I'm sorry to say. I bandaged it up, and you'll want to go to a doctor in a day or two just to make sure it's not infected, but you got *really* lucky, Ms. Winchester. Two shots at such a close distance, and he somehow missed you with both. You'll be sore tomorrow, but if you take it easy, you'll heal up in no time. I want you to go to the hospital immediately, though, if you start feeling dizzy or nauseous, you understand? I'm expecting your friends to keep an eye on you for the next few days too." She gave warning looks to Imogen and Rich, who both nodded.

"Friends," I mumbled stupidly, sinking into the chair with a soft smile. "I have friends." The fire felt incredibly nice on my face, but the scratchy blanket and wet clothes underneath were not going to make it easy for me to drift off peacefully.

Wet clothes.

I sat bolt upright, and Bob dug his claws into my leg to hold on. "Where's my purse?"

Imogen disappeared and came back with it a moment later, handing it to me. It was damp but still intact. I peeked inside, and all the papers were exactly where I'd left them, untouched by the rain. I let out an audible sigh of relief.

"He's being pretty tight-lipped." Detective Martin was on her phone as she entered the room, but then her attention pivoted to me. "I have a feeling someone here can tell me a bit more, though."

I hugged my purse to me inside the blanket.

"I think I'm going to need a cup of tea first."

Chapter
Forty-Six

Two days later

"You have to understand," Eric Garland said, his voice calm but with the slightest edge of worry. "We had very specific instructions from your aunt not to disclose anything about the real estate until you came to us. You see, she specifically structured her estate so that Mountain View was its own entity, and she wanted you to learn about it on your own."

"Did she say *why*?" I could tell he was being ever so careful because he was a lawyer and wanted to absolve himself and his firm of any wrongdoing. Since Owen had tried to kill me only a few days earlier, in order to get his hands on some documents, I knew Eric and the firm were on pins and needles to absolve themselves of any liability in my near-death.

"She actually left you another letter." He slid a thin envelope across the desk to me, Eudora's familiar writing on the front, spelling out my name.

I opened it up, and Eric pretended to busy himself with other documents as I read.

Phoebe,

Darling, I hope you can forgive me for a little secrecy, but I promise I had your best interests in mind. You see, I've seen money do some incredibly foolish things to even the best of people, and in not telling you about the properties right away, I had hoped you would have enough time to settle in town and learn to love Raven Creek the way I did. The way you did as a child.

Buying the property was never about the money for me, I hope you can understand. George was dying when he sold it to me, and we both knew that when he passed, the properties would be sold to the highest bidder. He loved his son, but he knew the best way to care for Carl would be to keep the properties away from him so he couldn't sell them off at the drop of a hat. For a long time, developers had been circling, hoping to put box stores and fancy chain retailers on Main. George and I knew that if that happened, it would be the end of everything that made our town special. One small business after another would be forced to close.

George was many things: a romantic, a dreamer, but he wasn't a crude businessman. He could have sold those properties for at least ten times what I paid for them, but he didn't. Instead, he made it a caveat of the sale that the revenue continue to help the town.

That's why I established Mountain View, with the help of Eric. I do hope you won't be angry with me for keeping this from you, but I needed you to know the town first, needed you to understand why it was so important we do things this way.

Mountain View is funded by the rent on the properties, which we haven't raised since I bought them. We use some of the money to pay for repairs and upkeep on the properties, but the rest goes into a high interest account, and we use it for the town. There aren't many who know where the funds come from: Eric, the mayor, and now you. I hope you'll continue to do with it what I have all these years, but it's your account now, and I know you'll do what's right for you.

Much love,
Eudora

I stared at the letter, stunned at the reality of what it told me. On paper, I was a millionaire. I was the sole owner, through an investment account, of a substantial swath of property in a prime location. In theory, I could sell it all and never work another day.

Then I thought about Leo, the things he had told me about Eudora's committees and all the work she had done to improve the town year after year.

I folded up the letter and slid it back into the envelope, then put Eudora's letter inside the thicker envelope with all the paperwork on the sale.

"If you don't mind, Mr. Garland, I would like you to keep these in a safe place for me." I pushed the chair back and got to my feet, my joints still aching, and a small bandage on my forehead hiding the most visible of my wounds. "And if it's all right with you, I'd like to keep it business as usual."

Perhaps he'd been expecting me to say something else, because he looked momentarily surprised before breaking into a broad smile. "She'd be really proud of you, you know?"

I smiled back. "I sure hope so."

* * *

Outside, the air was unexpectedly warm for mid-October. Businesses were busy decorating their storefronts for the upcoming Trick-or-Treating event that was hosted by the Chamber of Commerce. To make things safer for kids and easier for parents, businesses along the major streets all got into the Halloween spirit and got candy to give away to the kids.

Of course, I had some decorating to do at Lane End House too. There were so many seasonal items in Eudora's basement, I couldn't use them all at The Earl's Study. A giant spider, in particular, had a place of honor over the front door of the house. Having spotted it in the basement recently, it occurred to me that my spider-themed dreams might have had more to do with decor than with any actual murderers. Now I was hoping the spider could remain a decoration rather than a star player in my slumber.

I hoped I could live up to the expectations Eudora had set for decorating. Now that she was gone, it was up to me to maintain the image of having the witchiest house in town.

Despite knowing that Owen was locked up, I still stuck to the main sidewalks to get back to the shop. I had taken the weekend off and gone to Barnesville to a walk-in clinic to get a doctor's stamp of approval on my healing arm. It was my first day back at work since Friday's scuffle, but if it had been up to Imogen, she would have preferred I take more than two days to rest. Too bad for her I couldn't stand being at home—I needed to keep myself busy.

I'd opted to park in front on the street, though, as I was not entirely comfortable spending time in the alley alone just yet.

Much to my general disappointment, and Detective Martin's as well, Owen had been arrested before anyone had a chance to attempt a break-in on my house, so if Dierdre had been planning to sneak her way in that evening, we didn't have the opportunity to catch her red-handed. She'd also firmly denied knowing anything about Owen's plot, or that he'd killed Ox.

I believed part of her story but knew she was more willingly involved than she was letting on.

Unfortunately, since Owen wasn't saying anything to police to implicate her, Dierdre Miller was free to annoy the general public of Raven Creek for another day.

I approached the front of The Earl's Study to see a familiar form draped against my car, arms crossed over his chest.

"How long have you been waiting there?" I asked. "Because the pose looks really cool, but if you've been standing there for an hour waiting for me, way less cool."

Rich smirked. "I was just inside asking for you, figured if your car was still here you couldn't have gone far. Looks like I was right."

He was wearing the same khaki trench coat, and it made my heart skip a beat in an unpleasant way. I knew he had nothing to do with the murder, and everything Owen had told me about the plan suggested Rich was completely innocent of any involvement.

But the coat still bothered me.

"I'm going to ask you a weird question," I said.

"I like weird questions."

"Last week, early in the morning, did you chase after me when I was on a run? Wearing that coat?" I jutted my chin toward him.

His expression went from jovial to serious so quickly I had my answer before he even opened his mouth. "I wouldn't say *chase*, but yes, it was me."

When he didn't offer any initial excuses, I just kept staring at him, hoping my face was impassive. I refused to be the first one to bend, even though there were a thousand follow-up questions I wanted answered. Primarily: *Why?*

He pushed himself off the side of the car and came to stand close to me. It was nice outside, but still autumn, so the proximity of his body immediately made me feel warmer.

I took a step back.

"I was on a job," he said finally.

"A job to chase me?"

He shook his head. "No, but a job to keep an eye on you. When you spotted me that morning, I was sure you knew it was me, and I ran after you to explain, but you were too quick. My job was to make sure you were safe. At least until you figured everything out."

I stared up at him, my mouth suddenly hanging open in a very unladylike way. "What did you say?"

"The job. Maybe not a job so much as a favor, but it was something I took very seriously. Your aunt came to me a few weeks before she died and said when you got here, you wouldn't understand what you were, and she wanted me to make sure you were safe. She asked me to look out for you because she couldn't."

My brow furrowed. "And what am I, exactly?"

Rich pushed a lock of hair behind my ears and smiled. "Well, that's easy, Phoebe Winchester. You're the new resident witch of Main Street, aren't you?"

Recipes

Amy's Chocolate Hazelnut Latte

2 T chocolate hazelnut spread (such as Nutella)
2 shots hot espresso
1 cup steamed milk (or milk substitute of choice)
1–2 pumps hazelnut syrup (optional)

Put hazelnut spread in cup of choice, and pour hot espresso over the spread. The hotter, the better for your espresso, as it will be used to melt the spread. Use a small whisk or spoon to mix the espresso and spread together, then add 1–2 shots of hazelnut syrup, if using. Amy likes to add the syrup to maintain the hazelnut essence so it's not too chocolate-forward. Then pour in your hot milk and serve!

Makes 1 latte

Eudora's Famous
Earl Grey Tea Shortbread

2 cups all-purpose flour
2 T loose tea leaves, ground*
½ tsp salt
¾ cup confectioner sugar
1 tsp vanilla extract (Eudora would recommend measuring
    vanilla with your heart rather than a spoon)
1 cup room-temperature butter, cut into cubes

First, grind your tea leaves. This will keep you from getting big chunks of tea in your cookies, but you still want to *see* the tea. Use a coffee or spice grinder, or a mortar and pestle if you have one. It should still be chunky, not a powder, but nothing so big it will get stuck in your teeth.

To a food processor, add flour, tea, and salt. Pulse ingredients together until blended. Add sugar, vanilla, and chunks of butter, then blend until the dough is combined enough to stick together. Put dough onto plastic wrap and roll into the shape of a log about 2½" in diameter. This should sit in the fridge for at least 30 minutes, but as long as overnight.

While you wait, preheat oven to 375ºF, and put parchment paper on baking sheets. Enjoy a nice cup of tea.

After 30 minutes, remove dough log from fridge, and take off the plastic wrap. Use a sharp knife to slice dough into rounds that are roughly 1/3" (thinner cookies are crisper).

Bake for 10–12 minutes, but remove before edges become too golden.

Makes about 2 dozen cookies

*A note on tea: Although you can use any bagged Earl Grey tea for this and just cut open the bag, Eudora would recommend something a bit fancier. Ask your local tea shop if they have any special seasonal Earl Grey tea blends. The Earl's Study favors one with freeze-dried strawberry in it.

Parmesan and Black Pepper Sourdough Biscuits

1 cup all-purpose flour
2 tsp baking powder
½ tsp salt (use 1 tsp if omitting parmesan)
½ cup, or 1 stick, unsalted butter, cold and cut into small cubes
1 cup sourdough discard (best when unfed)
¼ cup grated parmesan cheese
Cracked black pepper to taste

This is arguably the easiest and most delicious way to make use of your discard.

Put your oven rack in the slot above center and preheat to 425ºF. Line a baking sheet with parchment paper and set aside.

In a large bowl, combine flour, baking powder, salt, and pepper. Mix until crumbly (if you don't have a pastry blender, a food processor works great for this step). The ideal amount of pepper will have black flakes speckled evenly through the pastry dough.

Add your sourdough discard and parmesan, and continue to mix until evenly combined.

Flour your counter, and empty dough onto floured surface. Form into a small disc roughly 1" thick. Depending on the number of biscuits you want, use either a 2" or 3" cutter.* 3" will yield about 6 biscuits; 2" will get about 8.

*Don't have any biscuit cutters? No problem, just use a glass in your cupboard—beer glasses work great.

Put biscuits on lined tray, leaving about 2" of space between each.

Bake for 20–22 minutes, until golden brown, then remove and let cool slightly. They're best served warm with butter but will stay fresh for at least 4 days in a sealed container.

Makes 6–8 biscuits

The Earl's Study Avocado Toast

2 slices fresh sourdough bread
1 ripe avocado
1 small shallot
1 clove garlic
¼ tsp red pepper flakes
Salt and pepper to taste
1 egg (optional)

While this recipe is best with homemade sourdough, not everyone has time to make it fresh, so feel free to cheat with a store-bought loaf.

Cut open and empty avocado into a small bowl, discarding the seed and peel. Finely dice the shallot and garlic clove and mix into avocado along with salt and pepper to taste.

Toast two pieces of sourdough bread to preferred doneness.

Smear half of avocado mash on each slice of bread. Sprinkle with red pepper flakes if you want a spicy kick. If adding the egg, fry on medium-high heat in butter or oil until white has set, then flip, frying for another minute on opposite side, to allow yolk to set. On toast, the egg is best when a little runny, but cook longer if you prefer it firm.

If you're feeling adventurous, a poached egg is also a great addition.

Serve immediately.

Makes 2 slices of avocado toast

Acknowledgments

First and foremost, there's only one reason I was able to finish this book and get it to where it is now, and that was making the very difficult decision to quit my full-time day job after seven years. I was truly amazed by the understanding and enthusiasm I received when I made that decision, and for that reason, I have to give my thanks to Ellen and Saeed for being so encouraging and lovely as bosses, and to Felisha, Hazel, and Lola, my ever-lovely team.

I also owe an enormous debt of gratitude to my community of friends and baseball enthusiasts on Twitter, my SBN colleagues, and my family and friends for your support this past year, it has come in all forms and truly meant the world to me. To Brandon, Danny, and Al especially, you are a huge reason I'm able to write for a living and I cannot thank you enough.

To my mother, always and forever, for being my biggest fan and supporter.

Acknowledgments

And last but certainly not least, my eternal gratitude to my editor, Melissa Rechter, who saw something in this book almost immediately. Phoebe and Bob could not have found a better champion, and I'm so thrilled to be working with you and the incredible team at Crooked Lane.